"I wouldn't say that at all," Ciar responded. He grasped her shoulders, admiring the way Emma's bottom lip was fuller than the top, pouting and begging for a kiss. "Any time you have a yen for a late-night snack I do hope you'll end up at my door."

She curtseyed, and with her movement, long, thick tresses swung forward. "Thank you for being so kind, m'laird."

"I must bid you good night," he said, his voice suddenly husky.

He dipped his chin to kiss her cheek, but she turned, and her lips skimmed his. That full bottom lip swept across his and along with it came a wee gasp that made his heart melt like sweet cream butter in the afternoon sun.

Within the blink of an eye, he captured that alluring mouth, closed his eyes, and kissed her. Emma's delicate fingers slipped to his waist. Unable to stop, Ciar moved one hand around her back while the other cradled her head. Ever so gently, he swept his tongue inside her silky warmth, asking permission to take more. Her sigh whooshed through him as she returned his kiss...

THE HIGHLAND CHIEFTAIN

"*The Highland Chieftain* was a smoking romance that was both endearing and sexy!"
—The Genre Minx

THE HIGHLAND GUARDIAN

"A true gem when it comes to compelling, dynamic characters... With clever, enchanting writing, elements of life-or-death danger and a romance that takes both Reid and Audrey completely by surprise, *The Highland Guardian* is an historical romance so on point it'll leave readers awestruck."
—*BookPage*

THE HIGHLAND COMMANDER

"Readers craving history entwined with their romance (à la *Outlander*) will find everything they desire in Jarecki's latest. Scottish romance fans rejoice."
—*RT Book Reviews*

THE HIGHLAND DUKE

"Readers will admire plucky Akira, who, despite her poverty, is fiercely independent and is determined to be no man's mistress. The romance is scintillating and moving, enhanced by fast-paced suspense."
—*Publishers Weekly*

THE HIGHLAND LAIRD

ALSO BY AMY JARECKI

Lords of the Highlands series

THE HIGHLAND LAIRD

A Lords of the Highlands Novel

AMY JARECKI

FOREVER
New York Boston

Copyright © 2020 by Amy Jarecki
Cover design by Daniela Medina
Cover photography and illustration by Craig White
Cover copyright © 2020 by Hachette Book Group, Inc.

Forever
Hachette Book Group
1290 Avenue of the Americas, New York, NY 10104
read-forever.com
twitter.com/readforeverpub

First Edition: October 2020

Forever is an imprint of Grand Central Publishing. The Forever name and logo are trademarks of Hachette Book Group, Inc.

The publisher is not responsible for websites (or their content) that are not owned by the publisher.

The Hachette Speakers Bureau provides a wide range of authors for speaking events. To find out more, go to www.hachettespeakersbureau.com or call (866) 376-6591.

ISBNs: 978-1-5387-5097-1 (mass market), 978-1-5387-5098-8 (ebook)

Printed in the United States of America

OPM

10 9 8 7 6 5 4 3 2 1

To all lovers of Scottish historical romance.
You are the champions who make my Highland heroes
come alive.
Thank you from the bottom of my heart!

Acknowledgments

I am deeply grateful to all the wonderful people behind the scenes who have helped to bring the Lords of the Highlands series to print. Thank you.

THE HIGHLAND LAIRD

Chapter One

July 29, 1714
Achnacarry Castle
The Scottish Highlands

*E*mma Grant gripped the silk ribbon tied around her sister-in-law's waist while she hastened forward. "You're walking too fast!"

A plethora of guests crammed the passageway, the boisterousness from their conversations almost deafening.

She tightened her fist. "Janet! Did you hear me?"

No reply came as someone shouldered Emma aside, making her lose her grasp on the ribbon. A chill pulsed through her blood.

No!

"Janet?" she called, the crowd forcing her against a wall.

"Robert!" She shouted her brother's name while people brushed past as if she didn't exist.

"Help," Emma whispered, almost too terrified to raise her

voice. Was she safe here? Robert had insisted she would be, but after a lifetime of being hidden away from society, years of pent-up fear crept across her skin.

Unable to utter another sound, she clutched her trembling fists around her medal of Saint Lucia and squeezed her eyes shut. Robert would find her just as soon as he realized they'd been separated.

Please!

"Miss Emma?" a voice murmured beside her.

The deep tenor made her heart beat faster. A different type of chill raced up her spine. But this was a much more pleasant sort of racing. "Ciar? Is it you, sir?"

Warm hands wrapped around her fingers, which were still clutching the medal of her patron saint. "Aye, lass. Whatever are you doing standing in the passageway? With this many people milling about you could be trampled."

"I-I was with Janet and Robert, but we were pushed apart."

"Not the best place to lose your guide," he said, his tone teasing a bit while he moved her palm to the crook of his elbow. "Allow me to escort you the rest of the way."

With Emma's next breath, her fear vanished. Thank heavens for Ciar MacDougall, chieftain of Dunollie.

My knight in shining armor.

"Thank you," she said, letting him take the lead. Dunollie was her brother's greatest ally, and Emma trusted him implicitly.

With her next step, the floor changed from stone to hardwood. The scent of roasted lamb and fresh bread enveloped her. "Have we entered the hall?" she asked, her mouth watering.

Ciar gave her arm a reassuring pat. "Indeed, we have."

"Do you see Robert and Janet? By the rumble of the crowd, I fear there are so many people in attendance I'll never find our table."

"Not to worry. I see them already." Ciar tugged her a few steps to the right. "It must be difficult to travel away from Moriston Hall."

"Och, is that not the truth? Wedding feasts would be so much more enjoyable in Glenmoriston, where everything is familiar."

"Agreed." Ciar slowed the pace. "Good Lord, your brother looks as worried as a mama goose who's lost her gaggle of goslings."

Emma chuckled at the notion. Robert might be a laird, but he never ceased to worry about her. "Good. In their haste to reach the hall, he and Janet left me in their wake."

"Hardly likely, knowing Robert. I'll wager he came close to losing his mind when he realized you were no longer behind him."

"He most likely did. He's so overly protective, 'tis very like him to do so." Emma gave her escort a nudge. "Does he see us now?"

"Aye."

"Is he smiling?"

"Not exactly."

She waved and grinned as wide as her cheeks allowed. "I do not want him to think I was afraid."

"You? Afraid?" Ciar's deep chuckle rumbled through her. "Och, Miss Emma, you're the bravest lass I ken."

"Hardly," she said, though a bubble inside her chest swelled. Dunollie thought her brave? Did he truly, or was he simply trying to make her feel more at ease? She certainly hadn't felt brave standing in the passageway gripping her medal of Saint Lucia and praying she wouldn't be trampled.

"We're approaching the stairs." Ciar slowed the pace. "Take hold of the railing at your right. There are three steps. Are you ready?"

"Yes." Holding her head high, she collected her skirts, shifted them to the side, and ascended. One. Two. Three. Thank heavens for Ciar. Even though he was an important man, he'd always been ever so thoughtful.

"Emma," Robert barked, his footsteps pounding the dais. "What happened? One moment you were right behind us and the next you'd completely disappeared. Are you hurt? Are you ill? Did you fall?"

Ciar's arm dropped away and was replaced by her brother's firm grasp, nowhere near as pleasant or alluring or enticing, and in no way did her heart palpitate.

Wanting to thank Dunollie, Emma reached for him but only managed to pass her hand through thin air while her brother pulled her forward. "I lost my grip on Janet's ribbon, and when I called out, the pair of you were nowhere to be found."

"She's safe now," said Ciar, following, thank goodness. "No harm done."

"No harm?" asked Robert. He made it sound as if Emma had been traumatized in the town square. He urged her into a chair. "Do you have any idea how difficult it is for my sister to be anywhere outside of her home?"

"I do." Dunollie slid into a chair to her right. "In fact, we were discussing how well she's adapting given you left her alone in the midst of a mob."

Robert said nothing, which meant he was rather irritated. Though there was an air of fun in Ciar's tone, his words most likely struck a dissonant chord. In truth, if Robert had still been a bachelor, he would have left Emma at home— as he'd always done. At home she never fell behind. In fact, everything was so familiar, she never needed assistance moving about the estate.

"I'm so sorry we lost you. How are you handling the crowd, my dear?" asked Janet from the left.

Emma chewed her lip. If only she could babble excitedly about Dunollie's rescue and how thrilling the ordeal had been because it was he who'd found her. But admitting her delight would not only be improper, the laird might realize how deeply she cared for him, which would be unconscionably mortifying. Moreover, aside from her own embarrassment, Robert would suffer heart failure.

Emma clasped her hands beneath the table. "Quite well. Aside from the wee mishap, 'twas as if we rehearsed the procession from the chapel to the dining hall."

"Wonderful." Janet's silverware tinked. "'Tisn't as if you've never been to Achnacarry before."

"Aye, but there weren't as many people last time."

"Why should it matter? You're with your family, and no one loves you more than we do."

Emma brushed her sister-in-law's arm and whispered, "Did you have anything to do with the seating arrangements?"

"I believe that undertaking was done by Lady Lochiel herself." Her Ladyship was the hostess, stepmother to both Janet and the groom.

"Do you not wish to sit beside me?" asked Ciar, giving her arm a wee poke.

"Are you jesting? I'm glad of it." Emma tapped her fingers over her place setting, identifying her plate, silverware, and wineglass on the right. "Being seated beside you, sir, is far better than sitting next to some old laird who is too filled with self-importance to speak with the likes of me."

"Och, I reckon anyone who believes themselves above your riveting conversation is undeniably daft—or in their cups."

No matter the situation, Ciar always managed to say something kind or funny, or kind and funny. And Emma had no doubt Robert's wife had arranged for Dunollie to be placed beside her. Janet just didn't own to it.

He leaned in, his breath skimming her cheek. "Yellow suits you, miss. You'd best be careful how broadly you smile, else you'll outshine the bride."

Emma covered her mouth before she laughed aloud yet again. Should she believe him? *Nay. He's just being nice.*

"All rise!" boomed a man.

"The bridal party," whispered Ciar as he helped Emma to her feet.

"Behold Lochiel the Younger and his bride!"

Emma applauded with the crowd. "Is she bonny?"

"Radiant as a bride ought to be," Ciar said as they resumed their seats. "She's almost as lovely as you are this eve."

"You're teasing me."

"Not at all."

"And what of the groom?" she asked, trying to ignore the flittering of her heart. "Is he as fearsome as they say?"

Ciar snorted. "Kennan? He'd like to think he's fearsome."

"I beg your pardon, that is my brother to whom you're referring," said Janet. "And I daresay he looks dapper in the weave of Cameron plaid."

Delicious smells of roasted lamb, baked fowl, and warm bread grew more potent. Emma licked her lips. "They're wasting no time bringing the food."

"I'm glad of it," said Ciar. "After the vicar's monotonously un-invigorating sermon, I'm starved."

"Is that your way of saying you had difficulty paying attention?" Emma asked.

"Perhaps, though I'd best not own to it."

She inhaled as the dishes were placed on the table. "I can pick out the musk of lamb straightaway, but what is the fowl?"

"Partridge, and it looks like French beans as well."

"Wine, my lady?" asked a footman.

She held in her urge to snicker. Everyone at the table was either a laird or a lady except her. But correcting the servant would only draw attention to her station, and she certainly didn't want to do that. "Please."

"And you, m'laird?"

"I'm never one to turn down a Lochiel vintage." Ciar tapped her elbow. "Would you like me to dish your plate?"

"Janet can—" Emma patted her chest. *Why not let him?* "Pardon me. If it would not be too much trouble, I'd be grateful, thank you."

"One slice of lamb or two?"

"Two."

"Brown sauce?"

"Please. And a wee bit of partridge and beans as well."

"Your wish is my command."

She flicked open her fan and hid her chuckle behind it. "Tell me, how are things at Dunollie?"

"I suppose they would be better if the queen saw fit to fairly tax her constituents in Scotland. Aside from that, I'm grateful to say the high demand for wool and beef is keeping clan and kin afloat." He placed a few more items on her plate. "And how fare things with you? If I recall, the last time we met was right here when your brother wed Her Ladyship."

"My, how quickly a year passes." Emma cut a piece of roast and savored it. "I'm sure it comes as no surprise to hear Lady Janet has been a lovely addition to Moriston Hall. Thanks to her, I have a new lady's maid. On top of that, I've given two small recitals and am becoming proficient at knitting."

"Recitals? I did not know you were musical."

Janet nudged Emma's shoulder. "Until I arrived in Glenmoriston, Robert had hidden her talent from all of society. But she is astounding. And mind you, I am not exaggerating in the slightest."

"Are you a vocalist?" Ciar asked.

Emma cut her lamb and raised the fork to her lips. "Harpist."

"Aye?" Ciar's voice filled with admiration. "All these years I've been visiting Moriston Hall, and I never knew you had such a talent. I hope you will be sharing your gift with the guests during the wedding celebrations."

"What a wonderful idea," Janet agreed.

Batting her hand through the air, Emma shook her head. "No, no. I'm certain Her Ladyship has quite a schedule planned for the gathering. I most certainly would not want to put a kink in her preparations." Besides, Robert mightn't approve when in the company of so many strangers. And all these guests might not approve of her. "Unfortunately, I'm afraid I left my harp at home."

"Not to worry." Janet patted her arm. "There's a harp in Achnacarry's music chamber. I'll speak to Lady Lochiel at my first opportunity."

"Oh, no, please. I do not want to be a bother."

"Bother?" Ciar's plate clanged with the tapping of his knife. "If you are proficient, I'm certain Her Ladyship will be delighted, as will I."

Pushing her food around her plate, Emma bit her bottom lip. Since their parents had passed away, her brother had assumed guardianship, and he was rather protective. Most likely he'd forbid it. "I suppose if Robert agrees."

Janet squeezed Emma's fingers. "Leave His Lairdship to me."

Prickly heat spread across her nape. Indeed, she could

play the harp in her sleep. But what about the other guests, the ones who didn't know her? What might they think? For years her brother had hidden Emma from all but close kin. And for good reason. It wasn't easy for Emma to expose herself in public. Many Highland folk were superstitious. They feared the blind and thought them demons. Drawing attention to herself so far away from Clan Grant didn't sit well. What if someone jeered? What if they didn't like her music?

But then Ciar had mentioned that he wanted to hear her play. Had he meant what he said? Emma would gladly pluck the strings all night if he asked. On the other hand, the laird was most likely being nice. He was always incredibly kind, almost the antithesis of Robert, who was affectionate but severe. Dunollie was not only affectionate but polite, thoughtful, warm, and...

Emma sighed for what seemed like the hundredth time.

If only Dunollie might look upon her as a woman and not the sister of his friend and ally.

Perhaps if they didn't discuss it again, Janet would forget to mention the recital to her stepmother. Besides, the feast had only just begun. With Janet on Emma's left and Ciar on her right, she fully intended to enjoy herself, starting with the delicious fare. Through the first and second courses, she listened to the friendly banter, savoring the food and wine while trying not to laugh too boisterously at Ciar's wit.

After a dessert of trifle served with macaroons, a Highland folk tune rose over the hum in the hall. Emma counted three fiddles, a bass violin, a drum, and a flute. Clapping, she sat taller. "I daresay there will be dancing."

"I cannot imagine a wedding feast without dancing." Ciar's knee lightly brushed hers as he shifted toward her.

The inadvertent touch made Emma gasp as gooseflesh

rose across her skin. Rubbing her thigh, she pretended to be unruffled. "Tell me about the musicians."

"The orchestra is up on the balcony, and the ceiling of the hall is vaulted, which makes the music resonate."

She ran her spoon around her bowl just to ensure she hadn't missed any sweet. "Ah, that's why they're so clear."

"The musicians look to be a band of tinkers. There's a scrawny fiddler and another who appears to be the cook's trifle sampler."

Licking her spoon, Emma grinned. "And the third?"

"Och, your ear is impressive. He's a wee lad of no more than thirteen, but I daresay his bow work is effortless—though you'd be a better judge." The footman removed their bowls. "I had to blink twice when I saw the bass fiddler."

"Why?"

"'Cause the enormous rosewood contraption is being wielded by a wee lassie. The thing dwarfs her. I can't be completely certain from here, but she must be standing on a box."

"She's keeping tempo."

"Aye, and who wouldn't with a drummer who looks like a stray dog."

"Truly?"

"He's the most ragged of the lot, from his moth-eaten kilt to whiskers that haven't been groomed in a half year or more."

"I wonder if he has a bird's nest in all that hair," said Robert.

Laughing, Emma rubbed her fingers along her jaw imagining the man's beard tangling with his drumsticks. "And the flutist?"

Ciar's shoulder bumped hers as he leaned nearer. "That fella's almost as large as I am. 'Tis a miracle his fingers aren't too thick. I think mine would end up covering multiple holes at once."

"But his do not?"

"Mayhap he's not quite as large as I."

Tapping her lip with her tongue, Emma shifted her shoulder just to brush his once again. Her heart gave a wee flutter. "I do not hear a piper."

"Because there isn't one. At least not yet. But if I ken Lochiel, he'll be saving the pipes for later."

Something heavy screeched across the floorboards—several somethings. Emma clasped her hands beneath her chin. "They're moving the tables!"

"Lassies and laddies," boomed the steward. "The wedding party will now join Sir Kennan and Lady Divana in the first dance."

As rustling filled the hall, a country tune with a three-beat rhythm began. "Is the wedding couple very bonny together?" Emma asked.

"They are stunning." Ciar brushed Emma's arm, making tingles tickle all the way up to her neck. "Have you met the bride?"

Emma tapped the place he'd touched, wishing he'd do it again. "Briefly. Janet and I visited her chamber before the ceremony."

"Ah, then I suppose you already ken she has hair the color of fire."

"Aye, my lady's maid mentioned the radiance of Divana's tresses. D-do men like fire-red?"

"Some do. Though there are fools who fear it."

Emma wrung her hands beneath the table. She oughtn't have asked Ciar if he liked red hair. It wasn't polite and, by his tone, she already knew he did. Emma's hair wasn't exactly fire-red. Mrs. Tweedie, the housekeeper at

Glenmoriston, said it was auburn. And Janet insisted it was the color of cinnamon. Emma had a strong sense of fire. It was warm and could burn if one drew too close to the flame. Fire was useful, necessary, and desirable. Conversely, cinnamon was a spice. True, it was pleasant-smelling and she loved the taste, but it was nowhere as dramatic as fire.

If only I were astonishingly dramatic, perhaps I might be more appealing to Ciar.

"Is something amiss?" Janet whispered in her ear.

"Not at all. Just enjoying the music." Emma raised her chin, affecting the serene expression she'd practiced with her lady's maid. Had her smile fallen? She mustn't allow herself to appear fearful, aloof, or disinterested—according to her sister-in-law's tutelage. It didn't take a seer to realize Janet was eager for Emma to marry, though Robert seemed none too keen to boot her out of Moriston Hall.

"Is not the tempo of a country dance a bit fast for the bride and groom?" she asked.

"Not for them," said Janet, lowering her voice and whispering again. "I only learned when we arrived that Kennan's bride hasn't enjoyed the benefit of dancing lessons as we have. In fact, she is fortunate to be alive."

"Oh?"

"She was left for dead on a deserted isle. As it turns out, Clan Cameron is much in her debt. The lass saved Kennan's life after his ship was attacked by pirates."

"Gracious. Bless her soul."

"Amen to that." Janet flicked one of Emma's curls. "They do make a lovely couple. Perhaps I'll see you dancing with your groom one day soon."

"Sh—do not speak of such things in mixed company."

"Hmm."

Emma wasn't thrilled with Janet's tone. She'd heard it before, and a "hmm" could be ever so meddlesome. Did Emma want to marry? Aye, more than anything in the world. She wanted a husband and children—lots of children. But she cared not to ever spend another day away from Glenmoriston, which posed quite a conundrum. Wives, especially daughters of esteemed lairds, generally moved to their husband's lands. The mere idea was utterly terrifying. It was difficult enough to visit a new place for a fortnight, but to leave Moriston Hall and venture somewhere completely foreign frightened Emma to her toes.

As the music ended, she joined in the applause.

"Will you do me the honor of granting me the next dance, miss?" Ciar asked, lightly brushing her elbow.

"Me?"

"Aye, you, lassie. We've danced before. In this very hall, mind you."

How could she forget? Dancing with the Dunollie laird might have been the most exhilarating moment in her otherwise unvaried life. Though Ciar looked upon her as a sister, deep in her heart Emma burned for him. In all these years he'd never feared her. Whenever he visited, it was as if the sun shone into every room and bathed her face in its warmth.

She tried very hard to not sigh like a lovesick waif. "I shall never forget."

He took her hand ever so gently, making a tingle shiver up her arm. "Then let us not delay."

"Thank you." Emma wrapped her fingers around his. She absolutely mustn't ever mistake his kindness for anything more. Regardless of how much she *desired* more. He was the chieftain of Clan MacDougall of Dunollie and, though she was the daughter of a great clan chief, any woman afflicted with blindness, no matter how wellborn, had nary a chance to win the affections of a great Highlander the likes of Ciar MacDougall.

Nonetheless, she felt utterly secure as he led her to the dance floor.

Not only secure but filled with a sense of purpose. Filled with desire. Filled with a grand sense of belonging, even though dozens of strangers surrounded her.

"Are you ready?" he asked, squeezing her hands.

"Aye," she chirped. If only she could wrap her arms around his neck and tell him how much it meant to dance with him—the most wonderful man in the hall.

When he left her in the ladies' line, the orchestra played the introduction to a reel. Emma's heart soared with the tempo, and she joined in with the clapping. The floor rumbled from the beat of the dancers' shoes and the alternating tapping of their toes.

She skipped toward Ciar and joined hands, sashaying in a circle. But her chest tightened with unease when he passed her to the corner for a turn. Confusion from twirling caught her off guard as the caller said back to home.

"Not here, lass," grumbled a gruff voice.

Gasping, Emma drew her fists beneath her chin. "Ciar!"

His confident hand took hold of her elbow. "Here we are."

"I'm sorry."

"Not to worry," he said, his voice filled with amusement as he twirled her around. "You're doing remarkably well."

Indeed? She felt as if she were bumbling with everyone staring at her. "That is kind of you to say."

"Now we'll sashay along the outside of the lines and I'll grasp your hands at the end. All right?"

"If we must," she replied, skipping along and tripping over her skirts. About to fall, she flung out her hands, only to have them caught by a pair of meaty palms. As soon as she inhaled she knew who'd saved her.

"This way," whispered Robert, sashaying with her to the end of the row. "Dunollie is waiting now."

Though she appreciated her brother's help, Emma hated to be so reliant on others. She drew a hiss of air in through her teeth, vowing not to make another mistake.

As Robert guided her hands to the left, Ciar caught them—his scent, his gentle touch made her recognize him at once.

"There you are," he said, his voice low and gentle.

"Saved by my brother."

"Grant's a good man."

"As are you," she agreed as they skipped through the tunnel of dancers.

The music ended, and Emma curtsied. "Thank you, m'laird." She turned away, hoping Robert would escort her back to her table, but it was Ciar's sure grasp that caught her elbow.

"I haven't thanked *you*, miss."

She smirked. "No need. I ken I was awful. Now you are free to partner with whomever you please."

He urged her to walk beside him. "Perhaps you mis-stepped a time or two, but you danced as well as everyone else if not better. And the tempo of a reel is fast."

"But not unfamiliar. There were too many dancers and the floor uneven."

"Which makes me all the more impressed."

"Please. There is no need to fill me with false praise."

"I assure you, lass. There is nothing false in a word I utter."

Chapter Two

Ciar stood in the shadows beneath the hall's balcony and sipped a frothing ale as he watched Emma Grant interact with the people on the dais. The bonny lass never ceased to amaze him, and tonight was no different. In fact, every time he set eyes on her she grew more radiant.

And he had no business noticing.

Presently, peril gripped the kingdom. Queen Anne had taken to her bed and wasn't expected to rise. With no heir, the monarchy was in crisis. Or was soon to be. Every Jacobite loyalist stood ready to march into battle, including Ciar's army.

He hoped and prayed this political unease would not erupt in war. When the time came to appoint a successor, surely people on both sides of the dispute would see reason. There was only one rightful king, regardless of his religion, and it was nigh time to own to it.

At any moment the MacDougall clan might be called upon to take up arms. Men would die, and Ciar certainly had no illusions of invincibility. His kin had lost their lives fighting for the *cause*. Until this matter was settled, his life as well as the lives of his men were in peril, and he could do no more than appreciate the courage of his greatest ally's sister and admire her from afar.

Braemar Livingstone, Dunollie's top man and closest friend, sidled beside him. "Are you enjoying the festivities, m'laird?"

Nodding, Ciar raised his cup. "Lochiel always entertains with a grand gathering, I'll say."

"No argument there." Livingstone took a tankard of ale from a passing footman. "Any rumblings about...*er*...the state of the kingdom?"

"'Tis neither the time nor place. Lochiel's heir was married but a few hours ago, though I reckon in the coming days I'll be summoned to the chieftain's solar."

"I'd think no less."

Ciar swilled his ale. Over the rim of his tankard he watched as Grant escorted his sister to the floor for a strathspey—a slower, more civilized dance than a reel. Moving like a swan, Emma wore a primrose-colored gown that accented her rich auburn tresses. In truth, he'd adored that mane of hair since the first time he had set eyes upon the lass.

She'd been no more than seven years of age when they'd been introduced, and even as a child, she was a sight to behold. At thirteen Ciar had considered himself far older, and in no way smitten. He had, however, instantly felt a need to protect the lass, though at Glenmoriston her malady never seemed to pose much of a problem. Blind since birth, Emma went about as if all of her senses were engaged. She brushed things with her fingertips to find her way. Her hearing was as acute as a doe's. Indeed, she'd discerned the various dishes at tonight's meal, demonstrating her keen sense of smell.

This eve she wore her coiffure pinned up in a chignon with soft ringlets framing her face and slender neck. Her curls bounced as Grant led her through the dance.

Pity those lovely eyes had failed her.

"I'm looking forward to the games," said Livingstone, interrupting Ciar's thoughts.

"I am as well."

"You seem reserved, m'laird. Is something amiss?"

Ciar emptied his tankard. "Not at all."

"You wouldn't have eyes for the Grant lass, would ye?"

He arched an eyebrow. "What makes you say that?"

"Well, you were sitting beside her at the high table. You danced with her. And I clearly remember you danced with her last time we attended a wedding at Achnacarry as well."

"Observant of you to remember, but Miss Emma is the sister of my closest ally. The host saw fit to seat me beside her, and it was the right thing to do to ask the maid to dance."

"She's bonny, except—"

A spark of fiery heat flashed up the back of Ciar's neck. "Except nothing. You'll do well to leave your observations at 'bonny.'"

"Aye, m'laird." Livingstone saluted with his tankard. "I believe there's a lass across the hall who hasn't taken a turn. Perhaps I'll find someone to introduce me."

Ciar nodded toward the crowd. "Do not let me stand in your way."

Placing his cup on a tray, he wove his way through the bystanders toward the door while the dancers applauded at the end of the piece.

"Dunollie, where are you off to?" asked Grant, his sister on his arm.

Ciar couldn't help but notice how a lock of long, auburn hair had escaped from the lass's chignon. He rubbed his fingers together, longing to feel if it was as soft as it looked. "I was about to step out for some air."

Emma pulled a fan from her sleeve and cooled her face. "'Tis rather warm, is it not?"

"Would you care to join me?" Ciar asked, arching an eyebrow at her brother, who appeared agreeable.

The lass smiled brightly enough to match the glow from the chandeliers above. "That would be lovely."

"I must rejoin my wife," Grant said, beckoning a maid from her perch along the wall. "Have you met Betty? She's my sister's lady's maid and an excellent chaperone."

Ciar's jaw twitched as he bowed. "My pleasure, madam." Odd. The invitation had been extended to them both. Grant was so overly protective, it wasn't like him to let Emma take a turn around the courtyard with a man, even a fast ally. What was he up to? Perhaps his friend's priorities had changed since he'd married Janet.

Betty had a square but affable face and wore a linen coif atop her head that bobbled when she curtsied. "M'laird."

He gave Grant a pointed look over his shoulder before he took Emma's hand and placed it in the crook of his elbow. "Shall we?"

The lass's skirts swayed as she walked with her face turned to the skies. "I love this time of year."

"The long daylight hours?" he asked.

"Ahem." She coughed a bit. "I wouldn't notice if it were day or night, but the weather is fine. Even in the evenings I scarcely need a cloak."

He could have kicked himself. She was bloody blind. Of course she didn't notice the fact sunset hadn't occurred until after ten. "Are you chilled?"

Her bottom lip quivered with her next inhalation. "Not terribly."

Even in July, Scotland's night air most likely cut through the silky fabric of her gown. Fortunately, several braziers dotted the courtyard, their fires providing not only light but warmth. He led Emma toward one not surrounded by people. "This ought to help. But we must stand far enough away to ensure your gown isn't ruined by a spark."

Inclining her ear toward the fire, she stretched out her hand. "'Tis nice."

"Aye," he mumbled, not paying a lick of attention to the flames. That blasted lock of hair glistened like copper with the dancing of the fire. Ciar slid a finger beneath the curl and let it slide across his palm.

Softer than silk.

She smoothed her hand over her head. "Is there a breeze?"

His gaze flickered to the curl. The night was oddly still. "Aye," he fibbed. Ciar spotted Betty sitting on a bench a good fifteen paces away.

"Lochiel's gathering is planned for a sennight. Ye ken everyone must travel so far for a wedding. We certainly did," the lass continued. "And Robert intends to stay for a fortnight on Janet's behalf. She misses her kin ever so."

"That's understandable. Do you enjoy visiting the Cameron lands?"

The corners of Emma's eyes crinkled as she scraped her teeth over her full bottom lip. "May I be forthright?"

"Please."

As she released a long sigh, her shoulders relaxed. "Visiting anywhere is quite an ordeal."

"Oh?" he asked. "You always seem to be enjoying yourself."

"I try to make the best of circumstances, though in truth

I'm forever bumping into things. And I cannot go anywhere without clinging to someone's arm. It is annoying."

He reached out to give her shoulder a squeeze, his hand stopping halfway. He was a single man, standing in a court-yard late at night with a marriageable woman. Embracing her, no matter how well-intentioned, might be misunder-stood. "I can only imagine. But you do manage quite well at home."

"As long as Mrs. Tweedie doesn't move the furniture, I'm able to move about as I wish."

Ciar busied himself with checking his pocket watch while he envisioned the lass walking straight into the rear of a settee, tumbling over it, and landing on the seat, sprawled on her back. "How inconsiderate of her." As he returned the watch to his waistcoat pocket, a sparkle of silver caught his eye. "Och, you're still wearing the medal of Saint Lucia."

Smiling, she grasped the medallion around her neck. "Al-ways. It was a gift from my mother, God rest her soul."

"I remember how precious it was to you. I also remember the time you were up a tree howling as if Satan himself was holding a torch to your toes because you'd lost it."

She hid her face in her palms. "Do not remind me."

"Why ever not?" Cair grasped her elbow and urged her hands away. "I always enjoy a laugh when your brother is wrong. Or acting like a sore-headed bull."

"You do have a way with words, m'laird." Her curls bounced. "Ye ken I didn't want him to pull me out of the tree. The medal was one of the few things I had to remind me of Ma. I wanted him to find it."

"Yet he didn't listen."

Biting her bottom lip, Emma shook her head. "He never listens. But..."

"But?" Ciar asked, waving his palm above the brazier's fire, letting it warm his fingers.

"You do," she whispered, moving a wee bit closer and making Ciar's heart skip a beat. Perhaps more than one. "You found it sometime after Robert had thrown me over his shoulder and hauled me into the house like a bushel of grain."

He swallowed, making the rhythm of his heart return to normal. "Quite a sight that—he was red-faced and determined whilst you kicked and shouted all the way."

"I was so embarrassed."

"You shouldn't have been. You were angry and fought valiantly."

"I do not ken about that, but I'll never forget what happened next." A delightful giggle made her shoulders waggle. "That's when I decided you were my knight in shining armor."

Ciar grinned at the memory of her ardent affection—the glee of a seven-year-old lass. "When I returned it?"

"Aye." Emma coyly twirled her errant lock around her finger. Lovely. Womanly. Most certainly no longer seven years of age. "You came up to the nursery."

"Ah, yes." How could he forget? That's when she first twisted his heart around her finger just as she was now doing to her hair. "You were curled up in a tiny chair clinging to a floppy doll and crying as if the world had ended."

"Mm hmm. And then you opened my palm and said—"

"I would have searched all night to make you smile again."

"See? That's why you're so dear to me, Dunollie. You've always been ever so thoughtful."

And you've always been ever so precious. Ever so vulnerable yet immeasurably courageous.

He blinked. "Perhaps we ought to be heading back to—"

"M'laird?" Emma asked.

"Aye?"

"We've been friends for a very long time."

"We have, indeed," he said, drawing out the words. The twist of his gut warned him to tread carefully.

"And yet, I've never seen you."

His throat closed. Poor lass, how difficult it must be. "No," he whispered.

She raised her hands. "May I?"

"Pardon?"

"Och..." She pinched the tips of her fingers together. "I see through touch."

"Uh...right. Yes, of course." Ciar glanced aside. Still on the bench, the lady's maid leaned forward as if she were about to intercede. "That is if your chaperone does not object."

"Betty will not mind." Emma turned her head, though not quite in the maid's direction. "Will you, Betty?"

The woman sat back and folded her arms while Emma stepped improperly near. Two hands' width separated them at most. The whisper of her breath caressed him, the scent of fresh lavender filled his senses as if she'd bathed in the blooms only moments ago. The lass placed her hands square in the middle of Ciar's chest and slowly slid them upward. Though his heart thundered loudly enough to be heard above the music in the hall, her face remained unaffected by the intimate contact. Her expression was serene, and the moonlight made her skin luminous like that of an angel. Slowly, her fingers explored his cravat and, when they moved to the exposed skin beneath his chin, he shuddered with a twinge of awareness sparking through his body.

Emma's lips parted, making her look too tempting. Indeed, she had developed into a stunning woman.

He pulled away a bit. "I...ah...doubt you'll like what you find, lass."

Her hands stilled. "Why?"

"Because I'm a bit…" Some said he was a beast, others an oaf. His features had always been severe. But then he was a man. A Highlander as rugged as the mountains surrounding his home. "Gruff."

"Then I'll reckon you are far more interesting that most." She stepped even nearer, a bit of puzzlement crossing her features. "You're shivering. Are ye cold as well?" she asked, her fingers inching upward. "Your skin does not feel cold."

His Adam's apple bobbed. "Ah…I-I am simply not accustomed to such familiarity."

She snapped her hands away. "Forgive me."

"There is nothing to forgive." He grasped her wrists and drew her fingertips to his cheeks. "Carry on."

Steeling his mind, Ciar made himself impervious to her gentle but overly familiar touch as she carefully explored the landscape of his face, spending an inordinate amount of time examining his crooked nose, broken more than once.

Surely she will recoil in shock soon.

He let out a long breath when she moved on to his eyes. Though his relief was short-lived when she examined the skin beneath. It was as if the pads of her fingers could detect the dark circles from spending two restless nights on the trail as he and his men had ridden to Achnacarry. With delicate brushes, she examined his thick eyebrows. Did she like what felt, or did she find him a troll with brutal features? After all, most would agree *troll* was an apt descriptor.

When Emma slid her fingers into his hair, she gasped. "Oh, my, your locks are thicker than mine."

Before she went further and brought him to his knees with her beguiling touch, he again grasped her wrists. "I'm a wee bit of a hairy oaf, I suppose."

"Not at all." She wrenched a hand away and fingered a lock at the edge of his cheek. "'Tis fabulous."

"Emma," Betty warned, "you'd best take a step back now. You mustn't be too familiar."

The corners of her mouth tightened. "Very well."

As the lass lowered her hands, Ciar caught her palm. "So now that you've *seen* me, are you disappointed?"

"Not in the slightest. Your face is quite…quite *interesting*. Masculine."

Ciar hadn't been gifted with an attractive mien. He looked more like the black Irish side of his kin, with hair the color of obsidian and a beard that needed to be shaved twice daily to keep it in check.

The lass started to draw her hand away, but he held it firm. "You, lassie, are far bonnier than I."

"'Tis kind of you to say, but—"

"No arguments." He bowed and politely brushed his lips across her knuckles. "I am Dunollie, and my word must be taken as gospel."

* * *

Wrapped in her robe, Emma tapped her cane across the floor of the chamber she'd been appointed to share with Betty. She had to do something to keep her mind off Ciar MacDougall. Goodness, the back of her hand still tingled where he'd kissed it. Not that she'd never been kissed on the back of the hand before, but there was something about His Lairdship that stirred her blood every time he was in the same room—or courtyard.

She'd learned something new about him under the night sky—something that had made her mouth grow dry and her knees wobble. The laird was a deeply passionate man even if he did not care to own to it. She'd felt the powerful beat of his heart beneath her fingertips, the tightness of the skin around his mouth. Most of all, she'd sensed the strength of his passion in the way his breath caught when he feared she would not like what she "saw."

But she liked it too much. Her dilemma? She must never admit to a soul how much what she'd uncovered had intrigued her, enticed her, made her want to know more.

"Betty, do you find Dunollie attractive?" she asked, trying to sound indifferent. Everyone commented on Emma's expressions. Even Janet said she was as readable as a placard. But mayhap if she pretended to be preoccupied with learning the lay of the chamber, Betty wouldn't notice exactly how curious Emma was about the man.

"Hmm." The maid's voice came from across the room where she was stowing her gown in the portmanteau. "I'll say His Lairdship is robust and perhaps a bit rough-hewn."

"Rugged but attractive?" she asked, nearly squeaking as she pondered such a delicious prospect.

"Well, I wouldn't want to meet him alone in a dark wynd, mind you. Though by the girth of his shoulders, I imagine your brother was wise to make Dunollie a fast ally."

A smile stretched the corners of Emma's mouth as her cane tapped a piece of wooden furniture and, by the rattle of ewer and bowl, she knew exactly where she was standing. Though her discovery was not what made her grin. Ciar's hands had been coarse and powerful, and so much larger than hers. However, she'd never admit such a thing to Betty.

Emma rapped again. "'Tis eight paces from the end of the bed to the washstand."

"Very good, and how many from the bed to the door?"

Without using the cane, Emma walked back to the bed, then resumed her tapping until she hit the wall. "Ugh."

"You're nearly there. Just two steps to the right and you'll find the latch."

"I loathe change."

"You must change eventually."

"And why is that?"

"To begin with, Robert will arrange your marriage."

Emma chuckled and thumped her way to the settee—six paces from the door and seven from the bed. "I think Robert is perfectly happy to have me reside in Glenmoriston for the rest of my days."

"I don't know. He wants you to be happy."

Sitting, Emma found her knitting where she'd left it. "And why can I not be content to remain in the home where I've resided all my life?"

"One day a fine gentleman will come round, and you'll steal his heart with that bonny smile of yours, not to mention your delightful conversation. I'll wager you'll fall so much in love, the idea of moving to a new home will not be frightening in the least. You might even find yourself living in a castle."

"I believe you have read too many fairy tales." Snorting, Emma picked up the needles. It was no use talking to her lady's maid about marriage or where she might live when and *if* she married. First of all, she did not want to leave Glenmoriston, and secondly, Robert hadn't ever spoken to her about finding a husband.

If someone who might want me actually exists.

She ran her fingertips along the wool, counting the loops, then started a new row of the scarf she was knitting. She and Janet made scarves, hats, and mittens for the unfortunate. "What color are his eyes?"

"Whose eyes?" asked Betty as her footsteps creaked over the floorboards.

"His Lairdship's, of course."

"Which one?"

The maid was baiting Emma for certain. "Och, the same one of whom we've been speaking. Ye ken."

"They're blue."

Emma had a strong sense of color by association. Warm sunlight was bright yellow, just as fire was red. Autumn leaves were auburn, and the sky on a fine day with a gentle breeze was blue silk. "What sort of blue?"

"Stormy, I'd say. Like the sea in the midst of a tempest." Betty placed a hand upon Emma's shoulder. "'Tis time to brush out your locks, then off to bed with us. I ken you've had an exciting day, but it is very late."

The last thing Emma wanted to do was sleep. Ciar MacDougall had eyes like a tempest and a face that struck fear in the hearts of men. How utterly romantic!

Not that she should dwell upon the idea. She must never do such a thing.

Betty attacked Emma's tresses with the boar's-hair brush, hitting a knot and making her wince. "Ow."

"Sorry. The curls are wound tighter than I thought. I'll start at the ends."

Sighing, Emma folded her hands. She must remind herself that she'd encountered Dunollie many times before. He had always been affable and polite. But things had never gone beyond pleasantries. He'd oft danced with her, and tonight he'd strolled in the courtyard with her, but it did not escape her notice that the invitation had been extended to Robert as well. Aye, Ciar was an able dancing partner, but a man such as he was far too important to entertain affection for the likes of her. After all, he was one of the most powerful men in the Highlands. And she?

I'm a fond childhood friend is all.

By the way her brother dragged his feet, she doubted Robert would ever find a suitor for her. Besides, if she remained a spinster for the rest of her days, her wish would be granted and she'd never be forced to move way from Moriston Hall.

I would be content with such a life. After all, I'm happy there. She bit her fingernail. *And safe.*

Sighing, she smoothed the back of her hand across her cheek—the hand Ciar had kissed. Emma could still dream. And in her dreams the great and powerful laird would always remain her knight in shining armor.

Chapter Three

Ciar patted his horse's shoulder and handed the reins to a stable boy. "Give him an extra ration of oats. This fella's earned it."

"Had a good run, did ye, m'laird?" asked the lad.

"I did, and 'twas a fine morning for it."

Taking a deep breath, Ciar headed for the keep. There was nothing like enjoying a brisk run across a lea with his steed, and the flat land leading to the River Arkaig had given him a wonderful opportunity to push his horse to a full-on gallop. Not often could he afford the time to ride for the pure joy of it. At home he was forever busy with the running of his own estate, which included Dunollie Castle. He boasted two thousand head of cattle and fifteen hundred head of sheep. Shearing alone had kept him and his men busy for the past month. Fences were always in need of repairs, and wool had to be kept dry and taken to market. It was a good life but one filled with never-ending duty.

As Ciar strode past a hedgerow bordering the Achnacarry gardens, conversation of the feminine variety resounded over the foliage.

"I cannot believe my brother has taken his new bride to a rustic old hunting cottage in the mountains," came a familiar voice, that of Janet Cameron, now Lady Grant since her marriage. Ciar had known the woman since before he could remember, the lilt of her voice making him stop.

"I fail to see why you're all aflutter. They're in love and together."

He recognized Emma Grant's voice straightaway as well. Peering around the hedge, he found the two ladies sitting on an iron bench in the shade of a circular garden arbor.

"It is not exactly romantic, if you ask me," Janet said. Of course she would know what her brother was up to.

Smiling, Emma clapped her hands over her heart and feigned a swoon. "I think it is romantic."

"Oh, please. There are no modern comforts. One must cook on a griddle that hangs above a fire pit and sleep on a lumpy pallet."

"But they are alone—removed from the overbearing festivities."

"They have a responsibility to their wedding guests. Mind you, I did not write all those invitations on their behalf for naught. Besides, I'll say there are a hundred places in the Highlands where I'd rather spend my honeymoon than a dusty old cottage."

Emma laughed. It was an infectious laugh, unfettered and utterly genuine. It made Ciar want to chuckle along with her.

"Whatever do you find so amusing?" Janet asked.

"As I recall, you and Robert spent some time in a rustic bothy of all places."

"That's because we were trapped in the midst of a snowstorm and there was no other place to go."

"Och, aye?" Emma pressed her fingers to her lips, her shoulders shaking with that delightful giggle. "But not long afterward, you were married."

"Obviously your memory is addled. It was quite a while after—"

"Good morn, ladies." Ciar stepped out from behind the hedge and beneath the arbor's shade. "Enjoying Lochiel's fine garden, I see."

"Dunollie!"

As soon as Lady Janet spoke his name, Emma smiled as if he were Christmas morn. "Ciar, wherever did you come from?"

"I took a ride to the river."

"Was it wonderful?" Emma asked. "One of my favorite places in all the world is Moriston Falls. Have you been?"

"The falls are on our lands in Glenmoriston," Janet clarified.

"I cannot say I have."

Emma sat taller, her gaze focused well above him. A stranger would have thought the wisteria hanging from the arbor had caught her attention and not Ciar's comment. "After all the times you've visited, Robert hasn't taken you?"

He strode nearer. "The next time I visit Glenmoriston, you'll have to show me, Miss Emma, since your brother hasn't done so."

Janet cupped a spray of flowers in her palm. "Whilst we are here, you must admit the Achnacarry gardens are something to behold. Dunollie, have you seen the plot of summer blooms?"

"Aside from a cursory glance, I cannot say I have."

Emma reached out, managing to brush Ciar's forearm.

"Och, you must see the roses. There are countless fragrant varieties."

"Careful not to appear too familiar, my pet," said Janet. "I'm sure the laird has far more important business."

The poor lassie's face fell. "Apologies."

"Not at all." Ciar tapped his thigh with his riding crop. "Where are these roses? Would you ladies care to show me?"

Emma clasped her hands, looking as if she intended to give the tour herself. "Of course."

Lady Janet patted her belly. "If you don't mind, Emma will take you. I will, however, remain right here in plain view."

Ciar gave Her Ladyship a sideways glance—the situation would be less awkward if Janet were to accompany them. Was she with child? She didn't look to be, but what did he know about these things?

"I would be delighted to have Miss Emma show me these brilliant blooms." What else ought he say? After all, they were attending a gathering where one was expected to enjoy things like flowers and gardens.

The lass started to rise, and Ciar immediately took her hand. He'd been around Grant's sister enough to know she wasn't one to ask for help, whether she needed it or not. "Allow me."

"Thank you," she said, reaching back. "My cane."

Janet grasped the walking stick and shifted it away from Emma's fingers. "You oughtn't need it if you're on the arm of His Lairdship."

Ciar eased Emma's hand to his elbow as he arched a brow at the lady. What was she up to? Playing matchmaker? These parties were all the same. There was always someone trying to convince him to take a wife, and if Janet continued along this line, she'd end up sorely disappointed.

"Agreed," he said. Hell, why not enjoy Miss Emma while he was there? She was amusing, and as long as she was on his arm, no other lass would vie for his attention, which was fine by him. "I'll be your guide."

"And if you should need assistance," Janet added, "remember I will be within earshot."

"Yes, m'lady." Ciar craned his neck, searching the vast garden. "Now where are these roses?"

"Down the path to your right," said Emma.

Again, he slapped his thigh with his crop as he led the way. "How do you ken?"

"I can smell them from here."

He sniffed; the air was pleasant but not heady with the fragrance of roses. "Are they your favorite flowers?"

"Must I have a favorite?"

"Absolutely not."

Twenty paces or so on, they came to the rows of blooms. "Here they are."

She stopped at a vine, its branches bowed with the weight of a multitude of brilliant pink roses. Closing her eyes, she leaned forward, inhaled deeply, then cradled a flower as if she'd known exactly where it was. "This is exquisite."

Suddenly more relaxed than he'd been in ages, he agreed, "It is."

What was it about Miss Emma that always seemed to put him at ease? That she couldn't see him? Or was it her unabashed enthusiasm for everything around her? She seemed to harbor none of the false pretenses of so many young ladies who attended parties and gatherings only to whisper behind their fans and pretend to be aloof. In fact, there was never anything false about this young woman.

"The petals are softer than lamb's fleece." She breathed

in again, her face rapturous as if she were capturing the essence of the rose. "And its bouquet is pure."

Straightening, Emma almost looked him in the eye. Hers were a haunting shade of pale blue and grew lighter in the sun. At the moment her eyes looked to be flecked with silver. "Do you know what I think?"

"I have no idea."

A brilliant smile spread across her delicate pink lips. "Heaven smells of roses."

He couldn't help but grin along with her. Only Emma would make such a comment with such unquestioned conviction. "So, you do favor them?"

"Aye, but there is lavender in heaven as well."

"Just roses and lavender?"

"Oh, no." She tugged his hand and started off. "Come this way!"

"Are you leading *me* now?"

"I am. But please ensure I do not step off the path and fall into a patch of brambles."

"I think Lochiel's garden is too well maintained to worry about those."

She pursed her lips, giving a wee snort. "Thorns, then. The roses have already managed to prick my finger as well as snag my hem."

Ciar shifted her hand to his elbow. "Never to worry, lass. I'll nay allow you to tread where you oughtn't."

"Thank you."

As they crossed beneath a trellis, Emma abruptly stopped. "Here."

"What—"

"Close your eyes and breathe!" she demanded with utmost urgency.

As Ciar obeyed, a sweet, heady fragrance enveloped him

while a dreamy sense of calm pulsed through his blood. "Astonishing," he whispered.

"The bees are at work."

"Hmm?"

"Shhh. Just listen."

The buzz of a bee came from above and then another from the right. A slight breeze rustled the vine's leaves.

Emma stood very still for a time while all the worries of the world faded. "Are your eyes still closed?"

"Aye."

"Promise to keep them shut."

"Why? So the fairy folk can come and play tricks?" he jested.

"Nay," she whispered as the softest brush of a petal caressed his cheek and slowly traced a circular pattern, gradually moving over the bridge of his nose and then down to just above his lips.

He grinned at the tickle.

"Tell me what you sense."

Women and whisky, he nearly growled, but doing so would be utterly inappropriate. "Ah...the sweetness of honey, a feather mattress with new linens, aaaand..."

As he opened his mouth, sweetness spread across his tongue. "Mm." The sound came out lazily as if he'd been abed all day.

"Name a person who is not drawn to the alluring nectar of the honeysuckle and I'll show you a person who hasn't lived." Good Lord, she was confident for a lass who'd been cloistered in Glenmoriston all her life. "Now tip up your chin and open your eyes."

Ciar slowly opened his eyes and saw only the yellow trumpet-shaped flowers framed by green. "But they're so small."

"Does a flower's size matter?" Throwing her arms wide, Emma turned her face to the trellis, her smile radiating with sunshine. "See why I cannot decide which I love better?"

"You are remarkable."

Suddenly serious, her brow furrowed. "Why is that?"

"Because you have such a unique perspective. No tutor of mine ever led me beneath a trellis and asked me to close my eyes."

"'Tis a pity. There is so much to be experienced with senses other than sight. At least, for me."

"I reckon you're right." Ciar again placed her hand in the crook of his elbow. "Where to now? Is there lilac in bloom?"

"Nay, silly, 'tis too late in the season."

A yap came from the other side of the hedge, then another. Emma gasped. "What—?"

"Haste," Ciar said, spotting Janet under the arbor, now deep in conversation with her stepmother, Lady Lochiel. The two women were completely ignoring him. *Thank God.* Deciding there was no harm in slipping out of sight for a moment, he led Emma around the hedge.

They found a lad rolling in the grass with two black dogs, one a pup at an awkward, nearly grown stage.

"Do you like dogs?" Ciar asked.

"Like them? I absolutely adore them."

"Come," he said as he led Emma toward the boy. "Are your hounds friendly?"

The lad looked up, shading his eyes from the sun. "Aye, sir. If ye are friendly to them."

Uninvited, Emma promptly sat, tucking her legs and skirts to the side. "What is your name?"

"Sam. Me da's the coachman."

The younger dog climbed onto Emma's lap, planted two white-socked paws on her chest, and licked her face. Giggling, she wrapped him in an embrace. "This one is awfully familiar."

Ciar kneeled beside her, ready to take charge if need be. The dog's exuberance was a bit overbearing, but the chime of Emma's laughter made him hesitate. Had he ever heard her make such a happy sound?

Sam slung his arm over the larger of the pair. "The pup's name is Albert. And this is his ma."

"Like Albert the Great?" Emma asked, hugging the over-grown, squirming ball of fur, stretching to keep her face away from his overactive tongue.

"Not exactly." The lad scratched the bitch behind the ears. "He was the runt of the litter. I've sold them all except this fella."

Emma raked her fingers through the dog's thick coat. "How many were there?"

"Six."

Albert circled and made himself comfortable amongst the volumes of the lass's skirts and rested his head on her knee. "Och, he's precious. I care not if he's different from his littermates. He has mettle in his bones. I can sense it."

Ciar scratched the little fella behind the ears. "It looks as if you've found a friend."

"Emma!" Janet called.

Hopping to his feet, Ciar strode to the hedge's end. "We're here, m'lady."

As Janet stepped around the foliage, her lips formed an O. "Leave it to my sister-in-law to find a dog, or a lamb, or a baby goat, for that matter."

"The pup's for sale, m'lady," said Sam. "They're water

dogs. None smarter. Ken how to paw the water to attract fish, they do."

Emma's face brightened. "Truly?"

Janet sniffed. "I can only imagine riding back to Glenmoriston with a young dog in tow. He'll run after every rabbit he sees. And you can tell by his feet he's not yet fully grown."

"How old is Albert?" asked Emma.

Sam stood. "Nine months, near enough."

Emma smoothed her fingers down Albert's coat. "Well, I think he's perfect."

"He's quite sweet, I'm sure. However, now is not the time." Janet grasped Emma's hands and pulled her up. "My dear, I've just had a word with Lady Lochiel, and she is ecstatic to have you give a recital tomorrow evening."

"So soon?" Emma cringed.

"Aye, and you'll be marvelous as always."

"But there are so many people here. They might not..."

"Not what?" Ciar asked, a bit of heat flaring up the back of his neck.

The lass huffed. "They might not *approve* of me."

Every muscle in his body clenched. He hated superstitious dimwits. "If anyone says an untoward word, I will personally invite them outside and readjust their priorities."

"This is your extended family," Janet added. "My kin love you just as yours do in Glenmoriston. I promise, there is nothing to fear. This is your chance to shine."

With the word "shine" Emma's face brightened as she turned toward Ciar. Then she smiled as if the sun had broken through the clouds.

He patted Emma's shoulder. "I'd truly love to hear you play."

"Y-you would?" she whispered, sounding utterly hopeful.

"My word is gospel, remember?"

"Very well." There was quite a bounce in the lass's curtsey. "My apologies, Dunollie. I must practice on the keep's harp at once."

Albert rubbed against his leg as he bowed. "Not to worry. I was on my way to meet with Lochiel. I suppose I cannot put it off all day."

Chapter Four

As they sat on the field's sidelines the following day, Emma turned the leather-clad ball over in her hands while the game progressed just beyond. "I don't believe I've ever held a shinty ball before. 'Tis lighter than I imagined."

"The inside is hewn of cork," said Betty right before she shouted, "Stop them! They're on yer flank!"

"Are we losing?" Emma asked, leaning forward with the sound of the players' grunts and thundering footsteps coming nearer.

Janet's knitting needles clicked. The only person who knitted more than Emma was her sister-in-law. "No one has scored yet, dearest." How could she knit at a time like this? Clan Grant had joined with Clan MacDougall and were facing the Camerons.

"Do you not care who wins?" Emma asked.

"I cannot possibly." The needles stopped. "If I pick the visiting team, I'd incite my father's ire for certain. And with Robert out there I simply cannot comprehend cheering for the home."

"But you're a Grant now. 'Twould be *mutiny* if you chose the Camerons." Betty's voice rose with her every word.

Nudging her maid, Emma squeezed the ball. It molded perfectly into her palm. "You appear to be rather fanatical about shinty."

"Scotland's only true game, it is." Betty rapidly clapped. "Bash him over the head with your caman, Dunollie!"

"No!" The ball fell from Emma's grasp. "Ciar MacDougall would never do a thing like that."

Emma had attended enough shinty games at home to gain a general sense of the play. Only men were allowed on the field. They smacked a little ball around the grass with mallet-like sticks, and the only rule was there were no rules. Needless to say, it tended to be a bit rough. At Glenmoriston one of the men had suffered a broken ankle only two years past.

"Well, he gave the lout a good shove, all the same," Betty replied.

Janet patted Emma's arm. "Did you enjoy your stroll with Ciar yesterday?"

"Very much. And I think I may have taught him a thing or two about flowers."

"How so?"

"He's right behind you!" shouted Betty, not following the conversation at all.

Emma fished for the ball with her toes. "Of course he has an appreciation for blooms. He just hasn't ever seen them as I have."

"Then I wish you could take half of the folk in the Highlands on garden tours. 'Twould enrich them ever so."

"Stop him!" Betty shrieked. "Now. The good Lord didna make ye a colossal brute for naught!"

Emma trapped the ball between her arches. "Och, Betty, I do believe you're taking this match far too seriously."

"Aye? 'Tis the laird of Dunollie who is leading this mob of ruffians." Betty's excitement grew infectious. "Score!"

"Well done, Robert," cried Janet.

Bending forward, Emma collected the ball. "Robert scored?"

"Indeed he did," said Betty. "But only after an assist from the MacDougall laird."

"I think the two men work well together. After all, they've been friends since they were lads."

Janet's needles resumed their clicking. "Indeed."

Betty gasped. "Oh, dear."

Emma's fingers tightened. "What happened?"

"We need the spare," shouted Robert, sounding as if he was running.

"Some Cameron lad smacked the shinty ball halfway to the river," said Betty.

Footsteps padded the grass, and a masculine scent approached. It was laced with the overtones of musk and wool. "Miss Emma," said Ciar, making a swarm of butterflies take flight in her tummy. "I believe you're the keeper of the standby."

"I am, sir." Her hand trembled as she held it up. "You are playing quite well."

"Your brother scored the only goal."

Rough fingers brushed hers as Dunollie took the ball, making a delightful gooseflesh trail up her arms. "Robert only scored because of your finesse."

"It does take a team," he said, his voice husky.

"Resume play!" bellowed a man.

Emma sighed. "Has someone gone to fetch the other ball?"

"A lad," said Janet. "The same one with the dogs."

The memory of a sloppy tongue licking her face made Emma warm inside. "I adored Albert. If only we didn't have a long journey to Glenmoriston, I would have insisted we take him home."

Janet gave her shoulder a pat. "Perhaps we can convince Robert to buy you a dog when we return."

"I'd like that."

"In the meantime, you are performing tonight. You had best go inside and prepare."

"Now?" Betty balked. "What about the game?"

"She must be a vision of beauty as well," Janet insisted.

Emma nudged her sister-in-law. "Why do you say that?"

"Because you are as bonny as your music, and I want all of Achnacarry to see it."

* * *

After the evening meal, servants began moving the furniture to make way for Emma's harp performance.

"Come, sit beside me, Dunollie," said Lochiel, beckoning him to the front row of chairs arranged in front of the dais. "We've a great many things to discuss."

Ciar took a seat right in the center. "It seems the kingdom has been in a state of unrest for the past year."

"'Tis more like the duration of Anne's reign, if you ask me."

Chuckling, Ciar watched as footmen turned the dais into a stage with a lone chair and both full-size and Celtic harps.

The old laird pulled out his snuff box. "There will be a meeting of the Highland chiefs in my solar tomorrow morn."

"I'm looking forward to it," Ciar replied. "Any news of the queen's health?"

"Only that her illness hasn't improved. 'Tis just a matter of time now."

"Who kens." Shrugging, Ciar continued, "She fell ill one

year past, and they all thought she was headed for heaven's gates then."

Lochiel sneezed into a lace handkerchief. "True. Though even one's good fortune eventually runs its course."

Ciar tuned out the laird's comment as his attention was drawn away by the hush of the crowd.

From the side door, Emma entered on the arm of her lady's maid.

"Bonny lass," whispered Lochiel.

Before they reached the chair, Emma stumbled over a fork the footmen had missed when they cleared the stage. The poor lass blushed scarlet, but she quickly regained her composure, grasped the back of the chair, and sat.

"Thank you, Betty," she said quietly before she turned her attention to the harps.

Emma seemed unaffected by the crowd while the maid situated the smaller Celtic harp on a footstool. No one made a sound while Emma moved her hands over the strings.

"'The Selkie,'" she announced right before her fingers began to strike the strings in the happiest rhythm Ciar had ever heard. Both hands plucked multiple strings at once, making the instrument sound as if an entire orchestra were playing.

Even Lochiel tapped his foot.

Though Emma didn't announce the second tune, every Scotsman west of the divide knew it to be "Blind Mary," one of the Highland's most popular folk songs, though a melancholy one.

Ciar had never heard the song performed with such passion before. Her performance was personal and visceral, conveying more feeling than the most heartfelt sonnet. Half-way through, Emma picked up the tempo, turning sad notes into elated music that reminded him very much of the lass herself. She moved with the song as if the harp were an extension of her life, as if she were telling her story to the audience and taking them through the garden on a journey of discovery using every sensation except sight. She slowed the tempo only at the very last, ending on a chord so breathtaking, no one in the entire hall dared breathe.

As the last note rang through the hall, his chest swelled. His mouth went dry.

Please don't stop.

Suddenly the hall erupted in applause. Ciar stood, sure he was clapping the loudest, until Lochiel rose beside him. "Good Lord."

"She's unbelievable," said Ciar.

Emma carefully set the harp upright and rose. Smiling with her eyes downcast, she curtseyed to the audience. Though her lips moved, not even Ciar could hear her over the ovation.

"They're standing for you, lass!" hollered Robert, ascending the stairs with Janet on his arm.

Within a minute, the dais was full of people all swarming around Emma. She was laughing and smiling. Ciar waited and watched for a time. But before he could press through the crowd, Betty escorted the beauty away.

Ciar shook Grant's hand. "Why have you kept your sister's talent a secret all these years?"

Robert grumbled under his breath. "The Highlands abound with superstitious fools. Who kens what would happen if some lout decided to declare her a witch."

"Surely you've enough influence to put such rumors to rest."

"Aye, but only after the damage is done. Och, three years past a mob in Inverness put a blind man's cottage to fire and sword for no other reason but mindless fear."

Ciar had heard the story, and the recollection of it made

his blood hot, just as it had then. "I understand they were tried for murder."

"Tried they were, but not convicted." Robert clapped Ciar on the back. "'Tis why I shall never allow her to perform outside of small recitals among trusted friends."

"Wise of you. If I had a sister such as Emma, I'd want to protect her as well." He gestured toward Lochiel. "Come, your father-in-law has invited us for a tot of whisky and a round of cards in the library."

* * *

"Are you awake?" Emma asked softly, even though she knew from Betty's light snores the woman was fast asleep.

Not a cock crowed, not a bird sang. The only sound was the ticking of the clock on the mantel. Emma quietly slipped out of bed, tiptoed thirteen steps to the hearth, and ran her fingertips along the clock's hands. Gracious, it was only two in the morning and she was famished.

She'd skipped the evening meal because she'd been too nervous to eat. And then after her recital she'd been so wrapped up in answering questions, the idea of eating hadn't crossed her mind.

Now that she'd been at Achnacarry a few days, the castle had grown somewhat more familiar. She was sure she could find her way to the kitchens without having to wake Betty.

Once Emma donned her robe and found her cane, she slipped out the door, but didn't quite close it all the way. By leaving it ajar, she would be certain to find it on her return and not make the mistake of wandering into some unsuspecting person's chamber and crawling into bed with them.

Heaven forbid.

After crossing through the passageway, she found the winding stairs and headed down, around and around, tapping her cane and counting. Certain she'd arrived at the main floor, she stepped out into a dank, chilly cavern. The walls were cool. Something scurried in the distance.

Emma didn't dare imagine what creature had made the noise. Not when she had no idea how she had ended up in the cellars.

I'm certain I counted three flights. She tapped her cane on the stone floor. *Or was it four?*

Quickly, she retraced her steps, expecting to recognize the great hall on the floor above, but the next landing was unfamiliar as well.

Resolving to bear her hunger pains for a few more hours, she climbed two more flights of steps, quietly tapped her way down the corridor, and nudged her door. At least she thought it was her door. However this one was not ajar.

Had it closed on its own? She stood for a moment, rubbing her fingertips together. If she knocked she'd wake Betty. If she didn't knock and this wasn't the right door, she might end up doing as she feared and crawling into bed with a stranger.

Trying not to wake everyone in the adjacent rooms, Emma tapped lightly. "Betty?" she said barely above a whisper.

When no reply came, she cracked open the door. "Betty?"

A clock ticked—a familiar sound. Was this the right chamber? "Betty," she said louder as she stepped inside. "I went below stairs to find something to eat but ended up in the cellars, hopelessly lost."

Behind her, the door creaked and slammed shut. "Oh, dear."

Emma didn't recall the door creaking before. "Betty?" she asked apprehensively.

"There's no Betty here," said a deep, husky voice accompanied by rustling. "Emma, is that you?"

She froze for a moment, clutching her cane over her chest. *Dash it all, this is a disaster!*

"Ciar?" she squeaked. The voice sounded like the Dunollie laird but didn't at the same time because of a gravelly undertone she'd never noticed before.

He cleared his throat simultaneously with the sound of flint striking iron. "Aye. Are you lost?"

"I am," she said as her eyes stung, welling with tears. "I-I'm so sorry. Please do not tell Robert. He'll be furious!"

Good Lord, this was an atrocious state of affairs. She rapidly blinked and swiped a hand across her eyes. "What if someone sees me here?" Her heart raced. "Goodness, my brother would insist you marry me...and of course you cannot...and then he will challenge you to a duel!"

"Wheesht, lass. Not to worry, there's no one here but me." He stepped near and pulled her into his arms and rubbed his palm around her back. "Easy now," he soothed. "You've nothing to fear, nothing at all."

Her head spun. It felt marvelous to have Ciar's arms surrounding her, yet it was terrifying all the same. Had anyone heard her in the corridor?

His big palm continued to circle around her back, making her head whirl in tandem. "Now tell me what happened," he asked softly.

Placing her hand on his chest, Emma took in several breaths to calm herself enough to explain. But his chest was anything but comforting. Beneath a single layer of linen, a strong heartbeat thrummed against her fingertips. Warmth radiated through the cloth, his chest rising and falling with his every breath.

"I...ah..." She slid her trembling hand to his arm. A

very muscular and solid arm clad in the same thin linen, making her no less nervous. "I-I missed supper because of the recital. A-and Betty was asleep, so I tried to find the kitchens, but I ended up in the cellars." She rubbed her hand up and down his enormous, incredibly well-defined arm. "I have no idea how I came to be here. I counted the landings as I passed them. I'm so sorry to have troubled you, but I must be completely turned around—"

"Och, Achnacarry is so vast anyone could find themselves lost."

"Anyone?"

His hand paused. "Aye, so you missed the meal, did you? And why didn't Betty bring you something after your performance?"

Her bare toe turned inward as she scraped her teeth over her bottom lip. "I suppose I wasn't hungry after."

"I see." He stepped back and grasped her shoulders. "Give me a moment to don my kilt and I'll take you to the kitchens myself."

"You?" She rubbed her outer arms to ward off a sudden chill. "I wouldn't want to trouble you any more than I already have. Mayhap if we found Betty."

"Not to worry." Ciar's bold strides padded the floorboards. "Besides, I'm already awake. No use waking your lady's maid. We might end up rousing the entire household, and then there truly would be hell to pay."

She gulped. *Aye, in the form of an outrageous scandal.*

Clothing rustled. Emma gulped. Had he just mentioned donning his plaid? What on earth had he been wearing before?

Merely a shirt? Saints preserve me!

She tapped her cane against the door. "I hate being an imposition."

"Not at all. After your performance this…er…last eve, I ought to do something to express my gratitude." He stepped beside her, lightly brushing his fingertips down her arm, letting her know where he stood. "Are you ready?"

"Aye, but please check the corridor to ensure no one will see us."

"At your service, m'lady."

Emma chuckled. "I'm no one's lady."

"I'm certain Robert will see that rectified one day." He opened the door and stepped out, then returned and grasped her hand. "'Tis clear."

Together they proceeded down the same steps she'd just ascended—she was positive by the echo. "If we keep on this way, we'll end up in the cellars for certain."

"The stairwell splits three ways on the ground floor. It can be tricky for anyone. If you take the wrong turn, you most certainly will end up in the cellars."

"All right, but how did I arrive at your chamber door rather than mine? I ken I retraced my steps."

"You must have wandered up the wrong set of spiral steps. The one on the right leads to the south wing, the one in the middle leads to the west wing, and if you continue downward you end up in the cellars."

"Why in heaven's name did Betty not tell me to mind which stairwell I was using?"

"Perhaps she reasoned you wouldn't be wandering about alone."

"My chamber is in the west wing, then?"

"The south, I believe, given your explanation."

"Och. If I hadn't found you I might have ended up wandering Achnacarry's corridors for the rest of my days."

"I don't know." He chuckled. "Once they realized you were missing, Robert would have sent out a search party."

"Aye, knowing my brother, he would have put up a reward for anyone who had information on my whereabouts."

"A reward? That sounds tempting. How much of a reward?"

Emma thwacked his arm. "Oh, stop."

"Very well, if I must, but it is always ever so fun to pull your brother's leg."

"When it comes to me, his sense of humor is lacking."

"Though I am quite fond of Grant, I must say the good Lord made him a wee bit over-serious."

Emma chuckled. "Truly."

As soon as they stepped into the kitchen, she took in a deep breath. Had she wandered past on her own, she would have recognized the redolence of burning wood from the hearth's fire mingling with the heady odor of a simmering lamb pottage. Warmer air bathed her face. "We've arrived."

"Indeed we have." He ushered her to a table. "Sit on the stool, and I'll put together a snack."

"You?"

"Why not me? I'm no stranger to castle kitchens in the middle of the night."

Emma tapped the seat with her cane and sat. She'd merely hoped to find a bit of bread or a brick of cheese. "Thank you."

"Let's see. A loaf of bread...and what's in this pot?" He sniffed. "Elderberry jam. How would you like slices of bread and butter with jam?"

"Delicious. And here I thought you'd dish up a bowl of the pottage over the fire."

"Would you prefer pottage?"

"When there's jam and fresh bread in the offing?" Emma rubbed her hands. "You cannot tempt me with a tasty treat and then suggest something as bland as pottage."

"I thought as much." Plates and silverware rattled. "Who taught you to play the harp?"

"The vicar's wife took me under her wing when I was quite young."

"I'll wager you were drawn to it like a duck to water."

"I suppose. It wasn't always easy, but music touches the soul in a way nothing else can."

"After hearing you play, I believe you are right."

Emma rocked back as a bubble of happiness filled her. "Did you enjoy the recital?"

"Very much. I was disappointed when it was over. I would have told you, but the dais was swarmed by admirers."

"You flatter me."

"I am merely an honest man."

He set a plate in front of her. "A bit of bread with your elderberry jam, m'lady."

"Thank you. Are you having some as well?"

He sat across from her. "I'd never forgo a sweet."

Emma took a bite. Bursts of flavor both sweet and tart swept over her tongue. "Mm. 'Tis divine."

"'Tis nearly as good as plum tart."

"I love plum tart."

"It might possibly be my favorite, though I'm partial to strawberry, apple, raspberry..."

"Elderberry, of course," she added. "And we cannot forget blackberry."

He smacked his lips. "Who needs anything else?"

"I have no idea."

"Agreed. Plum tart for breakfast, raspberry for our nooning, and what say you for supper?"

"Hmm. Perhaps a variety?"

"Perfect."

Trying not to laugh with her mouth full, Emma pressed

her fingers against her lips. "Och, chatting with you is always so diverting. If it weren't so mortifyingly improper, I would become lost every night just to eat sweets and engage in riveting conversation with you."

"Anytime—as long as 'tis after midnight, lass." His sniggering grew infectious. "I suppose there is something daring about spiriting into the kitchens when no one else is about."

"Agreed." She delicately licked the jam off her fingers, even though doing so was quite brash. "Perhaps a bit mischievous as well."

"Then we must ensure this excursion remains our secret."

"My lips are sealed."

Of course. Holy Moses, Emma would die if Robert found out about this!

Chapter Five

*E*mma's expression grew intent while Ciar led her down the passageway dimly lit by a wall sconce. "Five, six, seven—"

"What are you doing?" he asked.

"Counting the paces from the stairs to the door. I intend to never be lost in this monstrous castle again."

"I think it was a boon that you were lost. After all, that was the best elderberry jam I've ever tasted."

"Please. What if I'd walked in on Lochiel or any of the other guests?"

"That would have been a disaster."

"Have you ever been lost before?"

"Many times, though Livingstone usually manages to set me back to rights."

"He's your man-at-arms, is he not?"

"Among other things. He carries out my bidding, and he's a trusted ally, friend. He's all those and more."

"I'm glad of it. In these times, a chieftain must have men nearby whom he can rely upon."

"Is that what Grant says?"

"Aye."

Emma stopped. "Seventeen steps. I think. Talking can make me err, but this should be my chamber." She pushed on the door and whispered, "'Tis still ajar, just as I left it."

"Well, then you had everything right except for the wing."

"One small error led to one enormous mistake."

"I wouldn't say that at all." He grasped her shoulders, admiring the way her bottom lip was fuller than the top, pouting and begging for a kiss. "Any time you have a yen for a late-night snack, I do hope you'll end up at my door."

She curtseyed, and with her movement, long, thick tresses swung forward. "Thank you for being so kind, m'laird."

Ever since she'd appeared in his chamber, her hair had beguiled him. Brushed out and flowing to her waist, it glistened like copper in the lamplight. "I must bid you good night," he said, his voice suddenly husky.

He dipped his chin to kiss her cheek, but she turned, and her lips skimmed his. That full bottom lip swept across his and along with it came a wee gasp that made his heart melt like sweet cream butter in the afternoon sun.

Within the blink of an eye, he captured that alluring mouth, closed his eyes, and kissed her. Emma's delicate fingers slipped to his waist. Unable to stop, Ciar moved one hand around her back while the other cradled her head. Ever so gently, he swept his tongue inside her silky warmth, asking permission to take more. Her sigh whooshed through him as she returned his kiss.

"Emma? What on earth are you doing?" asked a hushed but shrill voice.

"Betty!" The lass jolted from Ciar's arms as if she'd been seared by a red-hot brand. "You're awake?"

Holding a candle, the lady's maid stared at Ciar, her eyes

wide, her shoulders back as if she were ready to thrash him with the candlestick. "I most certainly am."

"Forgive me." Ciar made a hasty bow and shifted his attention to Emma. "If there's nothing else you require, miss, I'll leave you."

Betty moved in front of the lass. "What else would she require? And why—"

"I lost my way, and Dunollie came to my rescue just like a knight in shining armor." Facing the empty corridor, Emma dipped into another curtsey. "Thank you for coming to my aid, sir."

"'Twas my pleasure," Ciar choked out as he started away. What the hell had he just done?

"Quickly, into the chamber afore someone sees." Betty's curt whisper resonated through the passageway.

Good God, there would be hell to pay come morn.

* * *

"What, exactly, were you doing with Dunollie—at all hours, if I might add?" asked Betty as she closed the door.

Heavens, Emma was two and twenty years of age, and her lady's maid saw fit to scold her? After the most passionate kiss she'd experienced in all her days? The only other time she'd been kissed was when the vicar's son stole an unpleasant, hard-lipped peck in the vestibule of the church. But Ciar's kiss was nothing like that. His lips were warm and soft and...*practiced*. Oh, she could kiss him all night if given the chance. Moreover, when would she ever again have the opportunity to be daring and kiss a man in a passageway in the middle of the night?

It was nigh time to assert herself, and in no way would

she wilt and allow Betty, a servant, chide her. "You may be my companion, but I do not care for your tone."

"*My* tone? Wait until Robert hears—"

Emma shook her fists. "Robert will *not* hear a word about this."

"But—"

Boldly marching forward, Emma grasped Betty's hands. "How dare you immediately arrive at the conclusion that Dunollie was up to no good?"

"I saw you in his embrace."

"So, what of it?"

"I beg your pardon, but your brother has tasked me with your care. I need more of an explanation than he *rescued* you. And from what?" Betty led her to the settee, and together they sat. "How did you end up with that man at our door in the dead of night—in your nightclothes of all things?"

"'Twas my fault." Emma twisted her robe's sash. Oh, dear, what must Ciar have thought of her, bumbling into his chamber with him completely undressed? Her face burned at the thought. Moreover, he'd had to don his plaid—good glory, he most likely had been bare beneath his shirt. If she did not take this incident in hand this moment, her virtue would be compromised.

Heaven help me.

"How was it your fault?" asked Betty, though her tone had softened considerably.

"Ah . . ." Emma mustn't ever think of Dunollie without his kilt again. "I went out searching for the kitchens and ended up in his chamber."

"I am quite certain his chamber is nowhere near the kitchens," Betty said dryly. "Such a thing sounds preposterous even coming from you."

Emma groaned. "I thought his chamber was this one."

She explained the entire debacle with all the stairs going west and south and down to the cellars.

"My word," Betty groaned. "A lesser man might have had his way with you."

"But not Dunollie. He prepared the most delicious elderberry jam spread atop fresh bread. He was so very entertaining. We talked and jested about eating sweets for every meal. I swear I had more fun with him in the kitchens than I've ever had at any gathering. And then—"

"He kissed you."

Gooseflesh rose across Emma's skin. "Aye, well, I think he meant to kiss my cheek, but I turned at the wrong time."

"That's not what it looked like to me. You were swooning in his arms, mind you."

"I was, was I not?" Emma sighed, unable to keep herself from smiling. "Please, Betty. Allow me this one indiscretion. Have you any idea what it is like to be two and twenty and the only exciting thing that has ever happened in my life was when my brother proposed to Janet. And that didn't even happen to me. I want to live *my* life—not Robert or Janet's."

"Hmm." A long exhalation whistled through Betty's lips. "Having been your lady's maid for the past year, I believe I have some inkling of what your situation is like."

"See?" Emma twisted her sash tighter. "Besides, ye ken how hotheaded Robert can be. If he discovers Dunollie mistakenly kissed me, he'll challenge him to a duel of swords, and they both could end up mortally wounded."

"Or His Lairdship might demand that Dunollie marry you," Betty said, as if she were deviously planning.

"No, no, no." Emma waggled her finger through the air. "Ciar would opt for the swords, mark me."

"Hmm... I'm not so certain."

"Oh, please. In no way can you make a stir and blow a wee kiss out of proportion. Now, I must have your word you will remain mum."

Betty harrumphed and took Emma's hand, leading her toward the bed. "Very well, my lips are sealed. As long as you promise to wake me next time you grow hungry in the middle of the night. You cannot ever again entertain a late-night rendezvous with the laird."

"Och, if only."

"Miss Emma!"

Sighing, she slid between the bedclothes. This entire night—not only the kiss, but spending it with Ciar—was the most invigorating evening in all Emma's days. Though at first she had been mortified when she walked into his chamber, his kindness and understanding had made all her trepidation vanish. Now no one would take away this memory. She would lock it in her heart and always dream of her shining knight. "Very well, I'll wake you. But I doubt there'll ever be another opportunity to rendezvous with the likes of Dunollie."

Chapter Six

*T*he following day when Emma ventured below stairs to break her fast, the lairds were already shut away in Lochiel's solar discussing whatever it was Highland chieftains talked about. Aye, she'd heard Robert grumble over the succession enough to know the queen's health was at the top of their agenda. But the queen lived in London, ever so far away. And no matter what laws she passed, they never seemed to have much to do with Emma's happiness.

As the day progressed, she grew more anxious. Neither Ciar nor Robert was in the hall for the midday meal. Once it was over, she had no option but to join Janet, Lady Lochiel, and the other wives in the women's withdrawing room. But it was difficult to idle the time away.

She, Emma Grant, had kissed Ciar MacDougall in the passageway in the wee hours. Would her skin ever stop tingling? She wanted to dance and sing and tell everyone how happy simply being near him had made her. Yet everything she was feeling on the inside was not proper. Worse, speaking of the incident with anyone besides Betty would ruin her.

It might even ruin Ciar. It would hurt him, anyway. And the stolen kiss most likely meant naught to him.

Her fingers fumbled along her row of knitting, dropping a stitch. "Blast."

"Another?" asked Janet.

Emma slid her fingers down, finding the loop of wool. "Here it is."

"Would you like me to weave it through?"

"I can do it."

"It's not like you to drop five stitches in an afternoon." Janet reached in and quickly repaired the slip, sliding the loop over the needle. "You seem awfully nervous. But I cannot understand why for the life of me. Your recital was well received last eve."

"I'm anxious for the ceilidh to begin." Emma resumed knitting and finished the row. "It seems as if the lairds will be in conversation forever."

"We'll all go hungry if they do. We've strict instructions not to light the bonfire until the pipers play for the procession of clan chiefs."

"Perhaps we can wander to the kitchens for some elderberry jam and bread," she mumbled under her breath.

Janet turned a page of her book with a whisper of paper. "What was that, my dearest?"

Emma started a new row. "Nothing."

"If you ask me, there's a great deal more whisky swilling going on than discussion about the state of affairs in Britain," said Lady Lochiel.

"Aye, drinking and boasting about hunting adventures," said Lady Mairi, Dunn MacRae's wife. Clan MacRae was another of Robert's staunch allies.

Everyone chuckled. Even Emma. Though she doubted Ciar would be boasting overmuch. Surely he wouldn't mention anything about their impromptu rendezvous.

Before she reached the end of her row, a man stepped into the room and cleared his throat. "Excuse me, ladies. You are required in the courtyard."

Emma tucked her partially finished scarf in her basket and pushed herself out of the settee. "At last."

"'Tis only half past six. I doubt the march would have started before now regardless." Janet took her hand. "Come along. Are you excited for the dancing?"

"Aye, as long as I don't end up bumping into the lass beside me. 'Tis so embarrassing."

"Not to worry. Everyone will understand. Besides, it is not as if you're the only one who occasionally missteps." Janet tightened her grip on Emma's hand. "We're walking through the doors and then down the stairs."

"I can hear the pipers."

"Follow me, ladies," said the man. "The lairds will start the procession, and the wives will fall in behind them, then everyone else."

The bagpipes grew louder as they stepped through the door. "Three paces to the stairs," whispered Janet.

Emma nodded, walking confidently.

"Excellent. See, you scarcely need me."

"Though you are kind to say so, I fear I will always be in need of a companion."

Janet squeezed her hand. "Then you shall never fear being lonely."

Emma smiled, though she often wished she could be alone. Not that she didn't enjoy the company of others; it would just give her peace of mind to know she could walk anywhere she wanted without the fear of falling. *Or being lost.* Thank the stars she'd wandered into Ciar's chamber last eve. If it had been someone else, the situation might have become quite dire.

"Here we are," said Janet, stopping.

"I hear a crowd."

"Aye, there are swarms of people in the courtyard, and they've made a tunnel for my father and the clan chiefs to walk through."

"Can you see them?"

"Aye, Lochiel just received the torch from the steward, and he's starting down the stairs."

"Do you see Dunollie?"

"He's right behind with Robert. Wave, dearest!"

Emma unfurled her fan and fluttered it through the air, smiling broadly. "Are they waving back?"

"Indeed they are."

"Ciar as well?"

"You…" Janet lowered her voice as she wrapped her fingers around Emma's elbow. "…have a fondness for him, do you not?"

"Dunollie?"

Janet urged her forward. "Ciar MacDougall, one and the same."

How should Emma respond? Her fondness for the laird wasn't new. After all, at this very gathering he'd already danced with her and strolled through the gardens with her. The only thing Janet didn't know about was the kiss. A harmless kiss at that.

Emma raised her chin, trying to appear aloof. "I've always been fond of him."

"Hmm."

Good heavens, *hmm* could mean so many things. Was Janet frowning? Or smiling? Or did Betty tell her about finding them in the passageway in the wee hours?

Unlikely.

"Dunollie has been a friend to Robert since they were lads," Emma continued. "And I've known him for as long myself. Moreover, most gentlemen who visit my brother rarely utter a word to me, but Ciar has always been polite."

"You needn't defend yourself. He's a good man."

Emma let out a pent-up breath. "Betty says he's rugged looking."

"I'd concur with her assessment."

"But handsome all the same?"

"Fearsome, I suppose. He certainly towers over everyone else."

Emma liked that. He was a giant yet gentle.

"Did you sigh?" asked Janet.

"Me? Hardly."

"Good heavens, I cannot believe my father's gall."

"What is it?"

"I thought the tug o' war would be between the clans, not the lairds."

"Truly? Is Dunollie pulling?"

"Of course."

"Well, if he's as fearsome as you said, his side will win."

Janet snorted. "You cannot side with him. He's pulling against Robert."

Emma laughed. "And who else? How are the teams divided?"

"Cameron, MacDougall, Stewart, MacKenzie, Murray, and MacNeill on the left. And there's Grant, MacDonald, MacIain, MacGregor, Gordon, and MacRae on the right."

"Dunn MacRae?"

"Aye."

"Well, he and Robert ought to give Lochiel's team a challenge."

"I hope so," said Janet. "It won't be long now. The referee is moving into place."

"Take up your rope, men!" bellowed a deep voice. "The first team to pull their opponent into the bog shall be the victor."

The crowd erupted in a cacophony of shouts, with everyone crying their favored clans. Beside her, Janet remained silent, so Emma opted to as well, though she crossed her fingers and said a silent prayer for Ciar. He was far too affable a man to end up in a bog.

"Bear down, Grant!" Betty's voice rose over the crowd. "Douse them in the mud!"

Emma inclined her ear over her shoulder. "I hear my lady's maid has come for the festivities."

"I'll have to have a word with her," whispered Janet. "She's awfully brash."

"Och, I don't think we ought to mind. After all, is that not the case with tug o' wars? They're supposed to incite the competitive spirit."

"You're right, dearest." Janet gasped. "No, Robert!"

The crowd roared. The whistle blew.

"Did Dunollie win?" Emma squeaked, clasping her hands together.

Janet groaned. "Aye, and you sound far too happy about it."

She pursed her lips. Goodness, she was bad at hiding her emotions. Everyone told her so. But why should she try to hide her feelings all the time? Such a thing seemed nonsensical. Though...hadn't she denied sighing only a few moments ago? Perhaps she ought to try to be more cognizant of her expressions, especially when it came to Ciar MacDougall, at least while they were still at Achnacarry.

"Forgive me. Is Robert covered with mud?" she asked, this time fully intending to smile.

"You're laughing."

"And why not?" Emma laughed from her belly. "'Tis a rare moment indeed when my brother loses anything."

"Hush. He's heading here now, and he's not smiling."

* * *

Ciar joined his men gathered around the ale keg. "How did I ken I'd find you here?"

Livingstone handed him a frothing tankard. "A man works up a thirst after watching such a riveting tug o' war."

"Aye, and I'll wager you had a good laugh watching the clan chiefs battle."

"I'll say. I don't believe I've ever seen MacRae lose anything requiring a bit o' brawn."

"Do not grow accustomed to it. Should we have another go, the tables could easily be turned." Ciar took a long drink; the ale was just what he needed to quench his thirst. "Did you find the lad?"

Shaking his head, Livingstone rolled his eyes to the skies. "Aye."

"And?"

"He asked a shilling."

"Did you pay it?"

"I balked, but aye. An awful lot to pay for an untried water dog."

Ciar's shoulder ticked up. "Mayhap I don't give a rat's arse if the dog can fish or nay."

"He's a runt." Livingstone licked the ale froth from his lip. "He's not even worth adorning your hall's hearth."

"I disagree. The pup is affectionate."

"What the blazes? Och, if it is affection you're needing, I ken a friendly serving wench."

"Wheesht." Ciar sliced his hand through the air. "Go fetch the dog. And mind you, walk where few will see him."

The man-at-arms snorted, adjusting the dirk in his belt. "That mongrel is more likely to lick an intruder than bite him. He'll be no kind of watchdog whatsoever."

"One never kens. I reckon Albert might grow to be quite protective of his master."

"Bloody Albert it is now?" mumbled the hardened Highlander, walking away.

The pipers played while lads turned the pig on a spit over the fire. Truth be told, the pork had been roasting in the kitchen fires all day, but Lochiel liked it charred by the open fire for a time—said a ceilidh wasn't the same without a pig on the spit. Ciar's mouth watered. He agreed with the old clan chief. There was nothing better than roast pork and warm applesauce. And he'd be eating both soon.

But first he had something important to do.

By the time he finished his ale, Livingstone had returned, leading Albert. "Here's your mop o' wiry fur, and I'll say he's vicious with his tail—wags so fast, he'll knock everything over in his path." The man sniggered. "Is there anything else you'll be needing, m'laird?"

"Nay." Ciar snatched the lead from the jester's hand. "Where are you off to?"

"Remember the serving wench?"

"I should have known." He clapped his friend on the shoulder. "Behave yourself."

"Och. That would be no fun whatsoever."

Scratching the dog's ears, Ciar shook his head. "Are you ready, laddie?"

Albert circled, his tail wagging and swatting Ciar in the knees and shins.

"We may as well head over there." He pulled the dog to heel. "And pray Robert is in good spirits after his hiding in the tug o' war."

Interestingly, Albert heeled well for a dog of nine months. Sam must have worked him on the lead. Ciar skirted around the outside of the gathering. Of course Emma wouldn't be able to see him approaching, but Betty or Janet might say something.

He still couldn't believe he'd let his guard down last eve. Aye, his damned heart had taken over his senses for a moment—long enough to be caught by the bloody lady's maid. Good Lord, he'd felt like a lad of sixteen, smacked on the wrist by his ma. But, since Robert had made no mention of it, Ciar was certain the maid had exercised the good sense to hold her tongue. After all, the last thing Emma Grant needed was to be embroiled in the midst of a scandal.

He stopped the dog behind the lass, who was seated on a plaid with her legs tucked to the side. The firelight made her hair come alive and shimmer.

"Miss Emma," he said softly.

She turned her ear quickly. "Dunollie?"

"Aye, and I've brought a friend."

The dog licked her face and stood expectantly wagging his tail as if he were greeting an old friend.

Emma's jaw dropped as she threw her arms around him. "Albert!"

The pup nuzzled into her with a happy yowl.

"Oh, my heavens, I've thought about you so much, laddie."

Ciar placed the lead across her lap. "He's yours."

Emma's jaw dropped, only to be taken advantage of by Albert's voracious tongue. Sputtering, she coaxed the pup's head aside. "I beg your pardon?"

"I purchased him from Sam."

Janet gaped, looking unamused. "But—"

Robert patted her hand. "I gave my approval this afternoon."

His wife looked none too impressed. Ciar stood between the overactive tail and Her Ladyship. "You what—?" asked Janet.

Robert gave her a wink. "Not to worry. He'll manage the trip to Glenmoriston just fine."

Janet dramatically swept a hand across her brow. "Lord save the rabbits."

"If he chases them, we'll put a lead on him. Besides, once he tires, they will no longer tempt him." Robert prodded his sister's shoulder. "What say you, Emma? Are you happy with the dog?"

She scrubbed her fingers through Albert's shiny black coat. "He's truly mine?"

"Aye, and I reckon he's as thrilled about it as you are— mayhap more so." Ciar lightly brushed her hand as he'd always done to let her know where he stood, though now touching her silken skin made his heart skip a damned beat. "Shall we take him for a wee stroll?"

"But the meal is about to be served," said Janet.

"We'll just venture down to the river and back. We shan't be but a moment."

Emma took his hand and rose as she clutched the lead. "Aye, we *must* go. Albert will adore it."

"We'll save you some pork should it be ready before your return," said Robert.

Janet waggled her finger at Ciar. "Stay in sight, mind you. No ducking around hedges. Lord only knows what other beasties Emma will fall in love with."

He gave her a salute. Now she was a married matron, he mustn't let her get away with too much sauciness. "Yes, m'lady."

Emma started off in the general direction. "Come, Albert, to the river."

The dog stayed at her side, looking up at her as if he'd understood the command. Nonetheless, Ciar hastened to catch up. "Are you confident minding the lead?"

"Thus far. At home I'm so familiar with the grounds I ought to be able to take him for walks on my own."

"You'd like that, would you not?"

"Very much."

Albert surged ahead, straining the lead and making choking noises.

"When he does that give him a tug and say, 'come behind.'"

Emma complied. "Come behind," she said in a stern voice.

"Excellent way to assert yourself and take command. Have you trained a dog before?"

"We had deerhounds when I was a child. Da spoke sternly when ordering them about, and they behaved quite well. He always said a dog responds to one's tone of voice."

"Smart of him." Ciar brushed the tips of his fingers across the ends of the lass's long tresses. She'd worn them down this eve, pulled away from her face by a jeweled comb—such a simple but bonny style. "Albert walks well at heel for a pup. I wonder if he knows any other commands."

Emma stopped and gave the lead a tug. "Sit."

The dog immediately sat and looked up at her, wagging his tail.

She scratched him behind the ears. "Good boy."

"How about 'stay'?" Ciar asked.

"Albert, stay," she said, walking out to the end of the lead, but as soon as she stopped he ran to her.

"You'll have to work with him on that one." Ciar moved beside them. "Are you still confident with walking him?"

"As long as the ground is smooth and there are no obstacles between here and the river."

"'Tis smooth grassland, mowed by Lochiel's sheep."

"Then I'd like to walk him. It makes me feel independent."

"I'm glad of it."

As he eased beside her, Ciar's jaw twitched. Independence was something he took for granted. What must things be like for her, trapped in darkness every day? She certainly coped well—better than many sighted people. And she was always so unabashedly happy.

He glanced over his shoulder. He doubted anyone was within earshot, but he checked all the same. "I must apologize about last eve. It was not my intention to put you in a...ah...*compromising* situation."

"I ken." She looked directly at his eyes. Almost. "Though I'm not sorry about it at all."

With her laugh, Albert started to run, pulling her toward the river.

Ciar followed, ready to pounce on the dog if need be. "Call him to heel!"

"Are we nearly to the shore?"

"Too bloody close to the shore!"

She pulled on the lead. "Come behind."

But she was too late. The mongrel leaped into the water, tugging the poor shrieking lass along with him.

"Emma!" Ciar hollered, dashing into the swells, watching her falter.

With one more step, he swept her into his arms as she howled. "Are you hurt?"

The lass threw back her head and kicked her legs, laughing outrageously. "N-n-naaaaaay!"

The dog splashed around them, yipping as if he'd just caught a fish.

"I fail to see what's so funny." Ciar tightened his grip, raising her beyond the reach of Albert's splashing. "You could have been completely doused."

"But I wasn't. Did you see us? It was terrifying and exhilarating all at once."

"Och aye, terrifying for me."

"Oh? I thought you were a braw chieftain, afraid of nothing."

"Aye, except young dogs hauling blind women into a raging river."

"The current doesn't seem bad."

"You wouldn't think the same if he'd pulled you all the way out to the middle. And there are rapids yonder. You could have been hurt."

She thwacked his chest. "And here I thought you had an adventurer's sprit."

He gave her a look and then burst out laughing himself. Of all the men he knew, he was the most likely to go on an adventure—mayhap barring Kennan Cameron.

"See? I believe this is the most fun I've had since..." A wicked expression crossed her face as her teeth coyly bit her bottom lip. "Since last eve."

Ciar glanced down. Must her face be so radiantly beautiful? God, if Janet and Robert weren't surely watching, he'd kiss Emma again and again...and again. "Och. Fun, aye? We are standing in knee-deep water and Albert has wound the lead around my legs so tightly if I take a step we'll both crash into the river."

"Bad Albert."

"He's wagging his tail."

"Ha!" Emma giggled again. "Whatever should we do?"

"Unwinding is the only option." He pulled her tightly against his chest. "Are you ready?"

"To spin?"

"You want to spin, aye?" he asked, whirling in place to the sound of her jubilant howls of joy while the water dog barked and splashed.

"Leave it to you to make a simple stroll to the river complicated," boomed a humorless voice.

Stopping, Ciar instantly recognized Grant's deep bass. And he sounded about as amused as a vicar pontificating Sunday's sermon.

Ciar took a step toward the shore, except his ankle was entwined with the dog's lead. Stumbling, he cradled Emma as he twisted to protect her from hitting any rocks. Down he fell while they both hollered.

Kersplash!

Something hard jabbed him in the backside as water doused them both. Howling with laughter, Emma squirmed, her elbow smacking him in the jaw. Ciar straightened his arms, keeping her above the water. "I have you."

"Yes, you do," said Robert. "Far too much of her, I'm afraid."

"Let go of the lead," Ciar said, gaining a foothold and standing.

Emma was still laughing as he set her down on the shore. "Oh, my heavens. Naughty dog."

"Dog?" asked Grant.

"Aye." She twirled in place, throwing up her arms. "I love him!"

Ciar blinked for a moment, then looked to the dog, who was now standing in the water, innocently wagging his tail—albeit much slower than before. Oh, aye, the lass loved her new pet. Not Ciar, of course. "He's a Saint John's water dog. Should have thought of that before venturing to the river."

Robert's jaw twitched. "And you couldn't keep him under control?"

"I was leading him," said Emma. She shook her finger, though it wasn't clear at whom. "And do not always be so overbearing, Robert. I'll train Albert, and by the time we reach Glenmoriston, he'll be the most obedient dog in the Highlands."

Grant looked between them. "Well, the pair of you are soaked to the bone. You'd best—"

"Lairds!" hollered Livingstone as he ran toward them at full tilt. "Grave news."

Ciar stepped forward, his fists jamming into his sodden hips. "What has happened?"

"It's the queen. She's dead. Lochiel just received word from Fort William."

"Good God," Ciar said, sliding his fingers over the hilt of his dirk. From here on out he'd need to be armed and on alert. "It begins."

"The news grows worse," said Livingstone.

Ciar eyed him. "Out with it."

"George of Hanover has been named her successor."

Chapter Seven

Seated at the table in Lochiel's solar, Ciar rubbed his temples while he listened to his friends voice their disgust at the prospect of being ruled by a king who'd never set foot in Britain.

"Gentlemen." Ciar pulled out his pocket watch and checked the time. It was well past time for the evening meal, and most every man at the table would need to rise early next morn. "It is time we take matters into our own hands. We must ride at once to unite the Highland armies."

"Do you mean to start a rising?" asked Lochiel.

"I mean to find out exactly who supports us and who does not. And, aye, if we cannot right this wrong peaceably, then we'll have nay choice but to take up arms."

Chisholm nodded emphatically. "Someone must cross the channel and speak to James."

"Mar will do it," said Lochiel. "My son and I set sail for London on the morrow."

"Isn't he away with his bride?" asked Grant.

"Aye, but I ken where to find him."

"Very well, but the rest of us must ride at dawn," said Ciar. "Grant, you take the road to Inverness. MacRae, head for Skye and the isles. Gordon, the Northwest. Murray, take Perth to Dundee. I'll go west and start at Spean Bridge, and ride down through the southwest Highlands."

Lochiel rocked back in his chair. "That's bold of you, Dunollie. Stay clear of royalist Campbell lands. The lot of them can't be trusted."

"I intend to."

"But what of home and hearth?" asked Stewart. "I border Campbell lands. I wouldn't put it past them to attack Castle Stalker."

Ciar rubbed his palm over the pommel of his dirk. "I aim to send my men to Dunollie and keep the peace there. The news will be spreading through Scotland like a brushfire. I expect there will be rioting across the kingdom if we do not stop it straightaway."

Grant scowled. "The imposter from Hanover will learn what a riot is if he dares to cross the channel."

"That's why we must act immediately." Ciar pushed to his feet. "I'm planning to leave tonight since summer days are long. Mind you, if we wait until the man is crowned, it will make dethroning him far more difficult."

* * *

After the announcement of the queen's passing, the rest of the clans moved to the great hall while the chiefs met. The roast pork was served, but Emma could scarcely eat. Obviously, the news meant everything would change, and just when she was growing accustomed to Achnacarry—and all the people—especially one person in particular.

Especially when the gathering was supposed to continue a few more days.

The tension in the hall was as tight as a harp string. "Whatever is taking them so long?" asked Betty.

Janet's knife tapped her plate. "If I ken Robert, they're strategizing for war."

"God save us," Emma said. Albert growled and moved against her leg, his posture rigid. "What is it, boy?"

Just as she posed the question, footsteps resounded from the stairwell.

"At last," said Janet. "There's Robert now."

"Where's Dunollie?" Emma whispered to Betty.

"They're both heading this way, and their expressions are as grim as a pair of men attending a funeral."

"We are riding this night," said Robert. "Each chieftain is to take sections of the Highlands and unite the clans. My dear, I want you to remain here until I send for you."

"Here?" Janet asked.

"Traveling right now is too dangerous."

Albert wagged his tail, gently brushing Emma's calf. By the dog's change in attitude, she guessed Ciar might be near. Interesting how the pup could alert her to things.

"Miss Emma." His gentle voice rumbled beside her as the laird took her fingers between his rough palms. "I did not want to leave without saying goodbye."

"Must you go tonight?"

"Aye, time is of the essence. I'll sleep at the inn at Inverlochy and meet with any allies who happen to be in town, then on to Spean Bridge."

She squeezed his hands, desperately wanting to say something to make him stay. "It seems like madness. Does it really matter to us who sits on the throne?"

"Aye, lass, it does very much. We've bided our time

whilst James's sister was in power. After all, Anne is of Stuart blood. But to usurp James, the rightful heir, a man born in Britain no less, and put a foreigner on the throne is an outrage."

"Aye," Robert agreed. "And if we thought Anne's unfair taxation polices strangled us, we'll be doubly strangled by George. I ken it clear to my bones."

"The English lords in parliament have already run too many families into poverty," said Janet.

Emma knew quite well about the unfortunate. They couldn't make enough mittens, scarves, and gloves to keep them all warm in winter. Nonetheless, she squeezed Ciar's hand. "But if it is nay safe for us to travel, what of you? Should you not stay here as well?"

He tugged her hand, drawing her closer. "It is kind of you to think of me, but my responsibility allays any danger."

"Och, Dunollie can take care of himself like none other," said Robert.

Emma's heart hammered beneath her kirtle. *Don't go!* "Promise me you will have a care."

"I always do." He kissed her hand, his lips warm and lingering longer than necessary. "I will miss you."

Heaven save her, she missed him already. When would she ever see him again? What if there was a civil war? He might be injured or worse. "I want to help."

As he released his grip, she reached out and brushed her hand over his wrist. His skin was covered with downy hair, and it was all she could do not to rub her fingers across it over and over again.

"You must take care of Albert. Teach him well. Mayhap one day he can become your companion so it will not be as frightening to leave Glenmoriston's doors."

"He's already helping me."

Ciar gently patted her wrist. "I'm nay surprised."

"I shall order some white silk," said Janet. "The women will make roses for those loyal to the cause to wear on their lapels."

"Excellent idea," said Betty.

"Aye," Emma agreed. But her heart was breaking. If only she could do more than sit safely within Achnacarry's walls and make silk roses. If only she could find a way to be of help to Ciar. And Robert, of course.

"Will you come see us?" she blurted, not caring if she was being forward. "A-after things have settled."

"I hope the occasion to visit Glenmoriston comes sooner than later. After all, you promised to show me the falls, remember?"

"How could I forget?"

"We must go," said Robert. "Whilst daylight remains."

Emma took Albert's lead and walked to the door with her brother and the man she wished she could marry. "Be safe, both of you."

Robert kissed her cheek. "Take care of my wife," he whispered in her ear. "She's expecting a bairn come late winter."

Emma gasped. "Truly?"

"She thinks 'tis bad luck to announce the news too soon, but I thought you ought to know."

"Thank you. Am I the only one?"

"Aye. She has not yet told her lady's maid."

"Very well, I shall keep it to myself."

"Just do not let her grow overtired."

"Of course not." Emma kissed Robert's hand. "Ciar?"

"Aye?"

She pulled her kerchief from her sleeve. "Take this for luck."

He slowly drew it from her fingers. "Thank you. I will cherish it."

"We must be off afore my sister gives away her heart as well as her kerchief."

Emma affected a smile, though she knew it was a sad one. Evidently, Robert had no idea she'd already given away her heart. And she feared she'd never see it again.

Chapter Eight

We are alone, are we not?" Emma asked as she carefully negotiated the library, a cane in one hand and Albert's lead in the other.

"Indeed we are." Janet was writing a letter, and the scratching of her quill paused. "The castle seems too quiet with the men gone."

"I think 'tis ghostly." Albert stopped before Emma's cane hit the leg of a chair. She altered direction. "But since there is no one else here, I wanted to confide that Robert told me you are expecting."

Janet said nothing for a moment. "I suppose I should not be surprised."

"Not to worry, he swore me to secrecy. However, he felt it best if someone knew. In case..."

"I'm glad of it, I suppose."

"Do you think we'll be home by the time the bairn arrives?"

"Oh, heavens. I do not expect to remain at Achnacarry for more than a few sennights."

"I hope you're right. I miss Glenmoriston." *Though not half as much as I miss Ciar.*

"Bless it, my quill broke," said Janet. The drawer to the writing table jostled. "This is locked. Why on earth would Da lock the silly drawer?"

"Mayhap he keeps coin in there."

"He doesn't. Quills and ink pots only. It has been thus since the beginning of time."

"The beginning of time?" Emma made her way toward the desk and then removed a pin from her hair. "Would you like me to have a go?"

Janet snorted. "I suppose Robert figured teaching you to pick locks would come in handy one day. Who kent it would be in my father's writing table?"

"Robert thought it would keep me amused, especially since my hearing is so acute." Emma held out the pin. "Which drawer is it?"

Janet guided her hand downward. "The top on the right."

She rubbed her fingers across the keyhole. "Ah, yes, it shouldn't take but a moment." Emma loved picking locks. Robert used to bring her locks of all shapes and sizes for her to work with. While she was growing up, she learned to slip in her pin and gently move it until she felt a hint of a cog. And then she would listen, just as she was doing now.

Click, click. A bit farther. *Click.*

She tugged the drawer open. "There you are, my dear."

"Thank you."

"Only quills and ink pots still?"

"Aye. There was definitely no reason to lock it."

"Unless your da kent how crafty I am with a hairpin."

"Perhaps we ought not tell him."

"Very well." Emma picked up Albert's lead. "'Tis ten

paces from the writing table to the hearth and seven to the settee."

"Impressive. You're doing well with the dog. Or had you memorized the entire library already?"

This was the first time Emma had been in the castle's library. "I'm still finding my way, but if I'm not wrong, Albert is helping. I think I'd like to pay Sam a visit in the stables and find out exactly how much my new pet has already learned. When we took our walk to the river, Dunollie mentioned it was clear the lad had done some work with him."

"That's a wonderful idea. Training Albert ought to keep you busy whilst we're here. Let me finish this missive, and I'll escort you."

"I don't think 'tis necessary." Emma fluffed out her skirts. "I'd like to go alone."

"Alone?" Janet asked, the surprise in her voice unmistakable.

Emma was surprised as well, but something had changed, and her confidence was bolstered. Perhaps she'd been at Achnacarry long enough to be more secure with her bearings. She positively hated to be a burden to anyone. "I'll have Albert to help, and the library is just off the great hall, so there isn't a labyrinth of corridors to negotiate. Once I'm outside I'll be able to find the stables by the smell."

The drawer closed. "Do you find stables foul?"

"Not at all. But horses and hay have an unmistakable scent. I can find a stable at fifty paces or more."

"Well, I'll say it is very brave of you to venture outside on your own."

"I visit the stables at home, and since we're going to be here a time, I may as well try."

"But I'm not so certain you ought to be taking Albert. He could see a grouse and dart away. Why not leave him with me and use your cane?"

"Pardon, but he is why I'm paying a visit to the stables in the first place. Besides, this dog has stopped every time before my cane has touched each and every obstacle. I believe he is brilliant."

"Perhaps he's able in the library. But what if something distracts him? He might pull you into a hedge, or a stone wall for that matter."

"That's precisely why I need to speak to Sam about his training."

"You can do that without the dog, dearest."

"I think not."

"Very well." Janet groaned. "I'll go with you."

"No. I absolutely insist on doing this myself." Emma had circumnavigated the chamber enough to find her bearings, and she headed toward the door. "'Tis the middle of the day. There are plenty of people about to ask should I lose my way."

After all, she'd learned a great deal about Achnacarry since being lost in the middle of the night. All the bedchambers were above stairs, so she wasn't likely to enter a room she shouldn't.

"Come behind, Albert." She gripped the latch on her first try, which made her grin. "We will find the stables if it takes us all afternoon. And if, perchance, I do not return by the evening meal, you may send a search party."

As soon as she stepped into the great hall, a footman appeared. "May I help you, miss?"

"If you would point me toward the door, please."

"A quarter turn to your right and straight ahead. Follow me."

She and Albert followed the sound of the man's footsteps and stopped with the creak of the door.

"Do you need assistance descending the stairs, miss?"

"I think I'd like to try it alone, thank you."

Emma's stomach squeezed when she stepped outside. For a moment her palms perspired, making the lead slip. Stopping, she took in a deep breath and tilted her nose to the sky. The warmth of the sun caressed her face while a slight breeze whirred through her hair. She shifted the cane into the same hand as the lead, holding it horizontally to ensure it didn't smack Albert. Finding the rail, she gulped. "Here we go, laddie."

The dog remained at her side, his coat lightly brushing her skirts as they descended the six steps without faltering.

Just yesterday she had needed Betty to help her, but Emma felt inordinately secure with Albert. She took another breath, almost laughing, but with her inhalation came a myriad of scents. Straight ahead was grass and the freshness of the river. To her left she identified the sweet scent of hay and horses.

Returning her cane to the other hand, she started toward the stables. As they neared, the dog pulled, gagging on his collar. Emma tugged him to heel. "No."

Albert yowled.

"Come behind," she said in a stern voice. "We shall walk to find Sam, not run."

At the mention of the lad's name, the dog snorted and yipped, though he did come to heel.

"You know Sam's name, do you not?"

"*Yawol*," Albert agreed.

"Well then, we shall find him together."

"Good afternoon, Miss Emma."

"Sam?" she asked.

"Aye."

"Thank heavens. You are just the person I've been looking for."

"Is Albert causing trouble?"

"No, on the contrary, he's marvelous. I can tell you've done some training with him."

"A bit. Taught him to walk at heel and fetch. That sort of thing."

"Have you had much experience training dogs?"

"I suppose. I trained his mother to sit and fish. Fetch birds as well."

"Wonderful. Do you think you would be able to help me train Albert to be my eyes?"

"Your eyes?" the lad asked incredulously. "I'm not certain he can do that."

"I think he can. Or at least he can help me. Today I was working with him in the library, and he stopped before my cane hit each obstacle. If he can do that every time, I think it would help immensely."

"I suppose it's worth a go."

"And he also needs to learn to stay when he's told. Would you like to help?"

"Aye. As long as it doesn't interfere with my chores, I can."

"Excellent. When can we start?"

"I wake with the crow of the first cock and climb down from the loft and—"

"The loft?"

"Aye, miss. I sleep in the hayloft. Da says it is the most comfortable place in the world."

"Truly?" Emma slid Albert's lead through her palm. "Do you not have a bed of your own?"

"Nay. Besides, I reckon me father's right. I sleep sound near every night except in the dead of winter."

"And when do you finish with your morning chores?"

"I usually have time to meself after the midday meal."

"Very well, let's start on the morrow after our nooning."

* * *

"Thank you, my friend," said Ciar, shaking MacLean's hand outside the Inverlochy tavern. "Keep your men on alert. You shall be hearing from us in due course."

"The sooner the better."

"Agreed," said Ciar, mounting his horse and tipping his cap. "At long last 'tis time to take matters into our own hands."

Staying the night in Inverlochy had been a boon. He'd found and recruited the leaders of two staunch Jacobite clans, men who would bring substantial armies to the table.

But Ciar's work had only begun. He cued his mount for a trot and headed northeast. The road to Spean Bridge was boggy and rutted even on the best of days. The foliage of massive sycamores blocked the view while twists and turns up and down craggy hills made the going arduous.

Not many traveled this route. Nonetheless, it was the only road to Clan MacDonnell's lands. And Coll of Keppoch was one of James's staunchest supporters.

Ciar had been riding for about an hour when the birds stopped chirping. He chuckled to himself. Emma would have noticed the change sooner for certain. But Ciar was no stranger to the wilds of the Highlands. He pulled his horse to a stop and listened.

Aye, there was no mistaking voices ahead, though he couldn't make out what was being said. Dismounting, he led his horse off the path and secured the reins around a branch, then crept up the side of a hill.

At the crest, a flash of movement caught his eye.

Redcoats.

He crept a bit closer, careful not to make a sound.

Down below, two dragoons rifled through the clothing of a dead Highlander with a blade buried in his back.

"Jesu, Riley. You're the best man with a blade I've ever seen. Hit him square from, what, thirty paces?"

"I'd remember that, Manfred. I'll bury a dagger in anyone who tries to cross me." The man who answered to Riley retrieved his blade and wiped it on the dead man's kilt. "Find the coin, ye wastrel."

"Give us a moment." Manfred, a scrawny man, slinked to a garron pony and unlaced a satchel from the empty saddle. "Mm. You'll like this, Riley. By the weight of it, we'll be living high on the hog for ages."

Thieving bastards.

The last thing Ciar needed at the moment was to ride into the middle of a crime. But he'd never be able to live with himself if he turned tail and rode around.

Gritting his teeth, he pulled a flintlock from his belt and primed it. One against two—not bad odds, though he'd be a hell of a lot happier if Livingstone had accompanied him.

He crept closer—nearly close enough to touch their backs. "Why am I not surprised to find the crown's dragoons are murderers and thieves?" he growled, clicking the hammer of his pistol. "Raise your hands slowly. Ciar MacDougall of Dunollie here, and I'll tell ye now, the first to make an errant move will enjoy a lead ball in his arse."

"The highwayman attacked us," Riley said as he raised his hands.

"Aye?" Ciar sidestepped around them. "Is that why the poor soul with your blade buried in his back was toting a satchel full of coin?"

Keeping his flintlock trained on Riley, he untied a length of rope from one of the horse's saddles and tossed it at the smallest. "Manfred, tie up your partner and make the bindings nice and tight. I'll be watching."

The little man's eyes shifted from Ciar's face as he caught the rope. Then the corner of his mouth ticked up. "Nay, I haven't a mind to, governor."

A creeping sensation shot up the back of Ciar's neck . . . just before the world turned black.

Chapter Nine

*D*rip...drip...drip.

For the love of God, every time the water dropped it echoed like a cannon inside Ciar's skull. His teeth throbbed with the unbearable pressure, but the relentless noise refused to stop.

He shifted his head a bit, the agony making his eyebrows pinch together.

Where am I?

The sharp odor of piss mingled with earthy dirt.

His shoulders ground into a cold, hard floor.

Hell's gate it must be.

His coughing made the back of his head pulsate with painful hammering. "Whisky," he groaned, slinging an arm across his forehead.

"Och, it looks as if the great Dunollie may survive to swing from the hangman's noose."

"Ye'll not be tasting any spirit where ye're headed," said another.

Ciar opened and closed his eyes. The voices were unfamiliar and sounded menacing. "Where am I?" he croaked, the saliva in his mouth thick and sticky.

An ugly chuckle rumbled in the chamber, feeling like a snare drum in his head. "Ye're a guest of Governor Henry Wilcox. In the bowels of Fort William with the rest of us wretched sops, ye are."

Shite.

He remembered now. There must have been a third redcoat, and the bastard struck him from behind. "I was ambushed."

"Och, were ye now? Did ye hear that? Dunollie claims he was ambushed."

Ciar ran a hand across his belt. Dirk gone, pistol gone, sword gone, sporran gone. "I was." He forced himself up with his elbow, which only intensified the tortuous throbbing in his head. "Came upon three murdering dragoons. They'd dirked a man and stolen his coin."

At the sound of laughter, he opened his eyes. These bastards were all enjoying themselves at his expense.

"He's blaming Tommy MacIntyre's murder on the redcoats."

"Aye," Ciar said, his throat still arid and grating. "A bull of a man named Riley and his accomplice, Manfred. Never saw the third. He's the one who bludgeoned me from behind."

He sat forward and shook his head while three filthy, ragged tinkers surrounded him, the whites of their eyes piercing through the dim light.

"Sounds a likely story."

"We've all been backstabbed by slippery dragoons."

"It doesn't matter if he speaks the truth, he'll be hanged for certain once Wilcox returns."

"Wilcox is away?" Ciar asked, wondering how long he'd been in this hellhole.

"Aye."

He rubbed his temples. "Bloody ballocks."

"Why should it make a difference? Even if ye were the king, ye'll never set eyes on the man's polished brass buttons."

"Aye, he'll hear the dragoons' testimony, and that'll be enough for him."

"Too right. It matters not whether ye're innocent or guilty. All the soldiers are backbiting bastards, and Wilcox is the most ruthless of the lot."

Ciar groaned, dragging himself against the stone wall. Condemned for a murder he didn't commit. "When will the governor return?"

"Who kens? The longer he's away, the better."

* * *

"Stay," Emma said, slicing her hand downward in front of the dog's face. She walked to the end of the lead, set it down, then proceeded around the hedge and stood while Sam used his father's pocket watch to keep track of the time. By the ticking she knew exactly where the lad stood, not but a pace away.

They remained agonizingly silent as Albert sat alone in the middle of the grass. He yowled, making her bite her lip to keep from uttering a sound. They'd been practicing the stay command for days, and the dog had done so well. But Emma was his worst problem. She hated to make him stay behind while she disappeared. How he must fret. And she knew all too well what being in the dark was like.

"Time," Sam whispered.

Emma stepped out from around the shrubs. "Albert, come!" she called, clutching her hands to her chest while the patter of his paws neared. "Sit."

She could sense him obey by the burst of excitement in the air and the swift brushing of his tail on the grass. Finally, she reached out to give him a scratch. "Good boy!"

"I think he has it. But you'll need to keep practicing until he's able to sit for a half hour without becoming distracted."

"A half hour?" She dropped to a knee and snickered with the slurp of Albert's tongue. "That is unbearably long for him."

"The better trained he is, the happier he'll be."

"Truly?"

"The dog loves the attention. And look at you pair—you've only been at it a sennight. In a year imagine all you will have taught him. Ye ken, dogs want to please their masters."

"And they adore praise."

"Everyone does, I reckon."

"Aye." She brushed her hands over Albert's coat and stood. "You are an excellent trainer, Sam. I thank you."

"I hope to train Lochiel's hunting dogs one day."

"Then I shall do my best to put in a good word on your behalf."

"You would do that for me?"

"Absolutely. Lady Janet has taken a keen interest in our progress, and she is Lochiel's daughter. I'm certain His Lairdship will listen to her when he returns from his journey to London."

Emma's attention shifted toward the sound of a horse cantering over the courtyard cobblestones. "I've urgent news from Fort William!" shouted the rider.

"Who is it?" Emma asked.

The lad stepped out from behind her. "'Tis one of the guardsmen."

"Come," she said, grasping Sam's hand and hastening to hear the guard's report.

As soon as her feet hit the cobbles, she asked, "What has happened?"

"'Tis Dunollie," said the guard. "They're holding him in the gaol. Nearly a week ago he was taken into custody for the murder of Tommy MacIntyre on the road to Spean Bridge."

Emma gasped. "Murder?"

"Aye, miss. In broad daylight, and there were witnesses— soldiers of the crown saw it all." Shod horseshoes tapped the cobblestones. "They say he murdered the MacIntyre man for coin. Dirked the poor blighter in the back, he did."

Emma's blood turned icy. Ciar would never commit murder. And for coin? That made no sense at all. Dunollie was one of the most prosperous lairds in the Highlands.

"He'll hang for certain," the guard continued.

"No." Emma's strangled whisper caught in her throat.

She clutched her hands around her neck. Lochiel had sailed to London with his son. Robert was in Inverness. She inclined her head toward Sam. "I must speak to Janet straightaway. Albert, come."

With the dog at her side, Emma swiftly climbed the stairs into the keep and found Janet in the library. "Dunollie is in Fort William's gaol, charged with murder!"

"What in heaven's name?" Janet's voice shot up. "It can't be."

Emma hastened through the door. "One of your father's guards just returned with the news."

"Dear God." Janet's voice warbled as the gravity of the situation became clear. "Robert said things would be riotous, but I never thought something like this would happen. Dunollie a butcher? Nay, nay. It smells of skullduggery."

Emma dug her fingers into a chair's upholstery. "Of the worst sort."

Janet strode across the floor. "I'll dispatch messengers to intercept Robert. But my father and Kennan might be another matter. I'll wager they're at least halfway to London by now. We must also send word to Braemar Livingstone straight away."

"Let us hope they have already been informed. Surely someone in Fort William has carried the news to Dunollie Castle."

Emma dropped into an overstuffed chair and gripped the armrests. How could this have happened? Ciar had been on his way to Spean Bridge. Alone. "He has no one to speak for him."

The quill tapped the ink pot. "Dunollie can take care of himself."

"In Fort William's prison?" Emma pushed to her feet and stumbled over a footstool. "They'll hang him for murder before your letter reaches Robert. We must take action straightaway. We absolutely have to make haste. We'll request an audience with the governor and testify in favor of Dunollie's character."

"Oh, no. Have you lost your mind? We cannot possibly leave Achnacarry."

"But we must do *something*. What if…" Emma couldn't finish, could not allow herself to imagine the worst.

"Do not even think it. Dunollie is one of the most respected chieftains in the Highlands. Wilcox kens that for certain."

Janet's words did little to ease the bitter roiling of Emma's stomach. There must be something more they could do than send messengers and write letters.

Chapter Ten

*F*eeling like a rat plucked from the dregs of the middens, Ciar walked with his hands and ankles in manacles, a length of chain linking them together. God's stones, he'd never committed a crime in his life, and there he was being escorted by four dragoons, the rear arse prodding him in the back with his musket.

"Keep pace, ye maggot," said the arse. "You're lucky I haven't my bayonet attached."

Ciar ground his molars as his eyes shifted. He could take the lot of them even in irons if he'd had a decent meal in the past... Lord, how long had he been in this hellhole?

They passed a placard reading *Governor Wilcox, Fort William's Dragoons*. Ciar didn't need to read it to know where they were headed.

Even his knees ached as he climbed the wooden stairs, the man behind him shoving him into a small room. The lead dragoon knocked on the far door. "Ciar MacDougall here as requested, governor."

The door opened and a small man peeked out. "Bring him in."

Ciar wiped his mouth with the back of his sleeve. He reckoned he had one chance to plead his case, and this was it.

A prod came from behind. "Move, ye flea-bitten swine."

It would take but a heartbeat to spin around, grab the damned musket barrel, and feed the butt end to the arse. But that would do nothing to further Ciar's plea of innocence.

He shuffled through the door, throwing his shoulders back and holding his head high.

Wilcox bent over a map with two other officers. Ciar had encountered the governor before when the man rode through his lands on one of the army's peacekeeping visits. He had a long nose and an unpleasant frown etched into the weathered lines of his face. He straightened, frowning deeper. With an arch of his brows, his gray periwig shifted a bit. "Well, well, Dunollie, I smelled you before you ascended the stairs."

"Mayhap you should provide a wash bowl for the poor blighters in the pit. A cake of soap might help as well."

The arse with the musket jabbed him. "Shut it."

"That's enough, sentinel." Wilcox pointed to the lead man. "Taylor, you remain. The rest of you wait in the entry."

Ciar smirked at the man over his shoulder.

Wilcox sauntered around his table, shoving a wooden chair aside with his knee. "The evidence against you is overwhelming."

"Aye, after I'd been bludgeoned from behind, I figured your men would fabricate a story against me."

"You mean to say that three of the king's dragoons are lying? Each of them has testified under oath that they witnessed you mercilessly killing a man in cold blood and taking his purse."

"Lies." Ciar started to spread his palms, only to have

them halted by rigid iron. "I was taking a message to Coll of Keppoch when I found two men standing over a dead body. A reedy cur named Manfred was congratulating a redcoated bastard he called Riley. I should have kept going, but my conscience wouldn't allow me to pass, and when I confronted the murderers, a third struck me from behind."

"Hmm." Wilcox smoothed his hand over his immaculately groomed periwig. "I didn't expect such a compilation of drivel from the great chieftain of Dunollie. Though I don't know why. All condemned men profess their innocence, no matter their station."

The corners of Ciar's mouth tightened. He and his clansmen did their best to stay clear of government troops for this very reason. For years the government troops had "kept order" in the Highlands by sending regiments out on peacekeeping sorties, when all they really did was instill fear in the hearts of kindly folk. People were untrusting and suspicious, and was it a wonder why? English officers like this man claimed to be ridding the Highlands of lawlessness when in truth they were seeding it.

Wilcox smirked then held up a piece of parchment. "I signed this document this morning. Do you know what it is?"

Ciar's gut squeezed, sending bile up his throat, but he said nothing.

"'Tis your writ of execution."

He'd expected as much, though the words slayed him as if the governor had plunged a blade into his heart. Was this it? His life over? Dear God, there was so much left undone.

"However, hanging you now would only serve to create anarchy at a time when the kingdom cannot afford it." The governor tossed the writ onto the table. "My duty is to keep the peace in this ungodly place. Therefore, I have no choice but to hold you until George has been crowned."

As he jolted, the chains between Ciar's manacles rattled. "Without a trial?"

Wilcox smirked, tipping up his chin and making his nose appear inordinately long. "Do you really want to parade before a jury of my soldiers and listen to the evidence against you? What evidence have you to refute the testimony of, must I repeat, three soldiers?"

"I have my reputation. I have my honor."

"Of course." The governor rolled his eyes and smirked. "Very convincing argument, that."

The officers in the chamber chuckled.

Wilcox motioned to Taylor. "Take him away."

The dragoon prodded Ciar's shoulder. "Out."

"And one more thing," said the governor. "I'll be sending a retinue to your lands to establish a clear message. If any of your men are seen within twenty miles of Fort William, they will be shot."

Ciar met the man's gaze with a steely-eyed stare. "'Tis not my men you should worry about. 'Tis every Highlander in Scotland."

"Why do you think you are still breathing?" Flicking the lint off his red doublet, the man snorted. "I will not be remembered as the cause of a rising. My duty is to keep the peace above all else. Though if I were to set you free, my superiors would sever my cods."

Ciar's eyes narrowed with his scorn. "Lovely thought that."

Wilcox moved around the table as if he were dancing a minuet, the fop. "As you are a member of the gentry, I am bound to concede and move you to a private cell—one reserved for officers."

"Most accommodating of you."

"I wouldn't advise being smart with me. I can easily throw you back into the pit with the animals."

Ciar scowled. He'd rather be in the rodent-infested bowels of this shitehole with the prisoners than in present company.

* * *

"Are you still awake?" Emma whispered, though she knew Betty was fast asleep and had been for quite some time.

The mantle clock chimed twice as she slipped out of bed and tiptoed to the garderobe. Last evening, Emma had sent Betty to fetch a glass of wine and a plate of biscuits and, while she'd had a modicum of time to herself, she prepared everything, ensuring her cloak and kirtle were at the top of her trunk.

Albert's toenails clicked on the floorboards as she shrugged into the dress and tied the laces. She found the dog's lead right where she'd put it beside her boots. After she put them on and pulled her cloak around her shoulders, she clipped the clasp to his collar. She took her satchel with her coin, an iron pick, and the biscuits from last eve, then held very still for a moment, not daring to inhale. Only when confident Betty's light snores filled the chamber did Emma allow herself to breathe.

"Come," she whispered and led the dog out the door, careful to ensure it closed without a sound.

Once they passed through the corridor, she loosened her grip on Albert's lead a tad. "Take me to Sam."

The pup had learned his lessons well and, rather than tug against his collar, he rubbed his body along Emma's leg while walking at heel. He took her straight to the big oak door, and as she opened it a whoosh of frigid wind bit through her cloak. She clutched the neck tighter and pulled up the hood. "Walk on, laddie. We're nay about to let a wee jolt of cold stop us."

As they entered the stable, the air grew warmer without

the breeze. Hay crunched beneath her feet. "Where is he, laddie?"

A horse nickered. Another kicked the wall of its stall.

She let the dog pull her forward. When he stopped she reached out, her fingers meeting with the rungs of a wooden ladder. "The loft?"

"Arf!"

"Sam?" she called. "Are you up there?"

Emma wrapped her fingers around the rung and raised her foot, only to be hindered by her skirts. "Sam?" she asked, louder.

Rustling came from above. "Miss Emma?"

"Aye, 'tis me. I need your assistance straightaway."

"But it is in the wee hours. You should be abed."

Her spine shot rigidly straight. "Not when Dunollie is at the mercy of Governor Wilcox."

Emma stepped away while the lad climbed down the creaking ladder. "Do ye ken the governor?"

"I know of his reputation, and that is enough."

Sam hit the ground with a thump. "Good, because I reckon you do not want to meet him. No one does."

"On the contrary."

"Huh?"

"I need you to take me to Fort William straightaway."

"Ye mightn't have noticed, but 'tis black as ink outside. Besides, I'll have to ask for permission to do that."

She'd thought he might balk, but if she didn't take charge and do this immediately, Janet would be sure to stop her on the morrow. "No, we cannot possibly wait. If we leave now, I will pay you a gold guinea."

"A guinea?" the lad asked, sounding more interested. "That's more than I make in a month. More than I make in two months."

"Will you take me?"

"Come first light I will."

"It must be now."

"Now? Can you ride?"

She'd have preferred to ride in a cart, but hitching up a rig would cause too much of a commotion, not to mention take too much time. "I'll ride double with you." After all, she'd ridden double with Robert plenty of times. "But we must leave at once."

"I suppose I'm awake now, but ye make no sense at all." Grumbling a Gaelic curse, the boy moved away. "Give me a moment to saddle a mount."

Emma waited while he brought a horse out of a stall, the muffled clop of hooves approaching. "Thank you for indulging me."

"I hope it will not be for naught," Sam said. "By the saints, what do you intend to do in Fort William when you can't...?"

"Can't see?" she asked, running her hand over Albert's coat. "You'd be surprised what a blind woman can manage when she sets her mind to it."

Mayhap he's right. But if I do not do something, who will?

A myriad of scents filled the air as the lad worked—the musky smell of wool from the blanket, oiled leather. Emma even detected the sharp trace of iron from the bit.

Sam took her hand. "Step over to the mounting block."

She tugged the dog's lead. "Albert must come with us as well."

"Not on the back of the horse. The animal will spook for certain."

"But I'll need him," Emma insisted.

"If you want to bring him he'll have to walk."

"How far is it?" she asked.

"Twelve miles, near enough."

"That's awfully far."

"He's a dog. He'll be fine," Sam said.

She bent down and removed the clip from Albert's collar. "Are you certain?"

"Positively." Sam urged her up the two steps. "Climb aboard."

Emma ran her fingers over the smooth saddle with one hand and found the stirrup with the other. "I'll sit astride." She swung her leg over the horse's back and quickly did her best to straighten her skirts and cover her knees with her cloak. She'd ridden astride with Robert at home. He always said it was safer. "If Albert begins to lag, we'll have to find a way to let him ride."

Sam mounted behind her. "Och, next you'll be asking me to throw a sheep over the gelding's withers as well."

He reached around her and took up the reins. "Come behind, Albert. We've a long journey ahead of us."

Chapter Eleven

The ride was slow going as Sam let the horse pick its way through night's darkness. But at least they were on their way.

"We're approaching Fort William now," Sam said as he tapped the reins.

Emma sat a bit taller. She'd heard the dog's gait when they'd crossed the bridge over the River Lochy five or so minutes ago, but she didn't hear him now. "Where is Albert?"

"Still beside us."

"Are we on grass?"

"He is. The road is packed earth."

"Very good." She ran her fingers through the horse's coarse mane. "I'd like you to take me straight to the fort."

"Are you certain? The sun rose only an hour past. 'Tis still early."

"The sooner we arrive, the better. Let me tell you what I need you to do."

When Emma had slipped out of her bed and gone to the

stables, all she'd had on her mind was finding a way to free Ciar. Obviously, pleading with the governor was at the top of her list. She was the first to admit it was a rather paltry plan and, though it might still be her best option, after four hours of riding, she'd decided that once she entered the fort, she must learn everything about the layout as quickly as possible.

Sam nudged her with his forearm. "Why do I suddenly have a feeling a guinea wasn't enough?"

"Wheesht and listen." She shifted against the lad, her backside already sore from sitting astride for hours. "Once we're inside, I need you to be my eyes. Take note of where the sentries are posted, where the gates are, and especially if you see any..."

"What?"

"Well, Robert always says every fortress has a weakness."

"Like the postern gate at Achnacarry?" Sam asked. "If I were to lay siege to the castle, I'd attack from there. 'Tis not heavily fortified, and there are more guards posted near the front gate."

"Exactly. You will act as my footman, but in truth you will be my spy."

"That sounds exciting, except I might remind you that you're blind, and I'm no spy. Together we'll be about as useful as Albert."

"Albert is very useful." She ran her fingers through the horse's mane, letting the coarse hair slide over her palm. "After the dragoons take me to meet with Wilcox, I want you to learn all you can about Fort William's weaknesses. Can you do that for me?"

He gulped. "I'll give it a go, but they mightn't like me wandering about."

"I don't think they can arrest you for that. If they give you a difficult time, tell them you were lost."

They had no trouble being admitted by the sentry at the fort's main gate, but gaining an audience with Governor Wilcox proved to be a challenge. They ate the biscuits Emma had brought while waiting on a bench outside the officer's rooms.

Albert pawed Emma's knee.

She gave him a nibble. "Forgive me. I suppose we should have stopped at the inn to break our fast."

"This won't tide me over for long," said Sam with his mouth full. "For breakfast I usually eat three eggs and a helping of bacon and toast with Cook's elderberry jam."

Emma's mouth watered for the delicious jam. If only she were sitting in the kitchens across from Ciar now. "We'll eat after we've finished here."

Two hours had passed when she was finally called. "Wait and observe," she whispered.

"Excuse me, miss, but you cannot take a dog into the governor's chamber."

Affecting her most haughty expression, Emma gripped the lead in her fist. "I can and I shall."

The sentinel grumbled something uncouth under his breath. "This way."

"Walk on, Albert," she said, urging the dog forward and stretching to her full height. If ever she needed to draw upon the Grant fortitude and tenacity, now was the time.

When the door creaked open, she moved through with an air of complete confidence, walking until Albert stopped. No matter how much she quaked on the inside, after years of studying Robert as he assumed and grew into their father's role, she knew in her bones she must not cower in the face of adversity. "Good morning, governor. I am Emma Grant, sister to the chieftain of Clan Grant, and I am here on grave matter."

A man cleared his throat to her left, and she immediately turned toward the sound. "I knew Dunollie was likely to have visitors, but a woman?" he asked. "And one with..."

"I assure you, sir," she said, in a voice so confident, she had no idea from whence it came. In no way would she allow him to discredit her because she was unable to see. "My blindness has no effect on my mental capacity."

"I rather doubt that," he mumbled rather sardonically. "Won't you sit?"

Since the man hadn't the decency to touch her arm and hold the seat, she'd look even more inept if she fumbled around trying to find a chair. "I'd prefer to stand, thank you."

"If you don't mind, I'll take a seat and finish my coffee."

Nodding her assent, she moved farther into the chamber and gave Albert a silent command to sit. "I understand Ciar MacDougall has been falsely accused of murder."

"Hardly." A cup tinked against a saucer. "There are three witnesses to his crime."

"And these are honorable men?"

The governor groaned. "I cannot abide Scottish High-landers and their all-encompassing honor." Wilcox belched. "Indeed, if you must know, the men are the king's dragoons, highly trained members of the fiercest army in Christen-dom."

That can be debated. "I see. However, I have been acquainted with Dunollie all of my life and not once have I known him to lie. Most certainly, the man is no murderer. And he is definitely not a thief. I can confidently attest to his character and will bear witness as such."

Emma's fingers tightened around Albert's lead to keep her hands from shaking. *Heaven give me strength.*

Wilcox snorted. "All Highlanders are thieves. It is inher-ent in their blood."

A bolt as hot as a branding iron shot up her spine. Perhaps the answer to her little prayer had come with fire. "Is Scotland not a part of Britain? Tell me, sir, how did you come to this ill-begotten opinion of my countrymen? I'll have you ken we are renowned for our hospitality."

"Hospitality? Hmm. You are speaking to a decorated veteran of the War of the Spanish Succession, not to mention my many military exploits in Ireland. I am well aware of the traitorous nature of Highland clans, and I'll tell you I've found in no uncertain terms that they are exactly like the Irish. Your *kin* cannot even manage to get along with each other, let alone the government that upholds the laws of the kingdom."

"So, you condemn a man without bothering to investigate?"

"Not when I have three, I repeat, *three* witnesses within my own ranks."

"I see." Unfortunate that Robert hadn't taught her to wield a dirk, else she might show the man just how inhospitable Highlanders could be. And such a pity she hadn't thought to teach Albert to attack on command. "I trust you will at least grant me leave to visit the prisoner."

"You may. However..."

"Yes?"

"I expect you and your footman to leave Fort William by dawn on the morrow. None of Dunollie's men or *women* are allowed within twenty miles. And I warn you, if you should return to the fort, I will have you arrested for disturbing the peace."

Could the man be more discourteous? "I assure you I have no intention of remaining in this...this...this *foul-smelling pigsty* any longer than I must." She tugged the leash. "Come, Albert."

As the dog guided her out the door, Emma held her chin high. Though her hands shook with the intensity of her convictions, she did her best to project an air of undaunted confidence. Never in her life had she been so quick-tongued, nor could she recall a time when she'd stood her ground with such assertiveness. Perhaps she had inherited the renowned Grant backbone after all.

* * *

Ciar's new accommodations were substantially better than the pit. At least the tiny shed they'd locked him in wasn't damp with rats scurrying about. It even had a wood floor, though that was the only comfort. Along the back wall was one barred window. Across from it, the black door had a small barred hole about the size of his family Bible.

He'd slept in worse conditions in the mountains. He'd weathered snow, rain, sleet, hail. At least this roof didn't leak, though he'd not turn away a bit of hay to ease the pressure on his hips should anyone care to offer it.

It had been so quiet, he jolted when a sharp rap came at the door. "You have a visitor."

Ciar pushed to his feet. Livingstone? But Wilcox had sent a retinue to Dunollie—he'd said MacDougall men would be shot if they set foot in Fort William. It couldn't be one of them.

His question was answered as the hinges of the door screeched open.

He blinked in disbelief. "Miss Emma?"

A nervous smile tightened at the corners of her lips as she stepped inside, leading Albert. "I came as soon as we received word."

"Wait a moment," said the guard. "You must leave your satchel and the dog." When the sentinel reached for Emma's bag, the dog growled like he intended to eat the man for breakfast.

"Come behind." Emma held out the strap of her bag. "You may take this, but unless you want to have your hand bitten off, I suggest you leave Albert with me."

The sentinel eyed Ciar. "Ye ought to put a muzzle on him."

Stepping between the two, Ciar put Emma at his back. "That will not be necessary. The pup is harmless."

The man straightened his grenadier hat. "Orders are your visitors are allowed no more than five minutes."

"Duly noted," Ciar said, backing Emma into the chamber.

As soon as the door closed, he spun around and grasped her shoulders. God, it was so good to see her, yet infuriating as hell. "You are the last person I expected to visit."

Within the blink of an eye disappointment reflected in her features. "The last?"

He dropped his hands, peering through the tiny window on the door. "Who's with you? Surely you didn't come alone."

"Alone? I wouldn't have made it beyond the gate." She ran the lead through her hand. "I asked Sam to help. He's acting as my footman and my guide."

She'd brought a child? Ciar raked his fingers through his hair. "But why are you here? I cannot believe Janet allowed you out of her sight. Ye ken how dangerous it is to leave the castle. 'Tis the reason Robert had you stay at Achnacarry. The roads are full of lawless fiends and will be until..." He couldn't bring himself to say "until George of Hanover is crowned." Such words rubbed against the grain.

"After everyone was asleep I slipped out of my chamber, found Sam, and away we rode through the night." She moved a hand to his cheek. "One of us had to do something. All the men are away. Janet sent missives to Robert, her father, and to Mr. Livingstone, but I didn't feel it was enough."

"Who else kens I'm here?"

"I have no idea. We received word of the charges against you from one of Lochiel's men who was returning from Inverlochy with supplies. I imagine the news has spread by now." Emma slid her fingers to his chest, the soothing sensation almost making him sigh. "Livingstone has taken your men back to Dunollie, has he not?"

"Aye. But Wilcox has sent half his army there as well. He told me if one of my men sets a foot in Fort William he'll be shot."

"Goodness, the man is vile."

"Aye, and he believes a handful of contemptable scoundrels' testimony over my word."

"He told me the same, but I don't accept a word of it. Tell me, what happened?"

Ciar relayed the details about finding the dragoons on the road to Spean Bridge after they'd killed Tommy MacIntyre. "I didn't get a good look at the victim's face at the time, but once I heard the name of the poor sop, I realized I'd met him. Had an ale with MacIntyre and MacDonnell at the Inverlochy tavern last year."

She pulled a kerchief from her sleeve, making him realize he'd lost the one she'd given him when they'd taken his sporran. "Good heavens. There must be something we can do to prove your innocence."

"There is, but I'm powerless caged in this box."

"What if . . . " Emma inclined her ear to the door.

"What if?"

Her eyebrows arched with intelligence as she wiped the kerchief along his jaw. "I have an idea."

He caught her wrist and stilled her hand. What was she doing? "I cannot abide your involvement in this mess. I'd never forgive myself if you were caught up in the middle of it."

"But I can help."

How in God's name could a sightless wisp of a lass be of any help? She'd already taken too much of a risk in coming. "Nay. 'Tis too dangerous."

"You already said simply riding on the roads is dangerous." She pulled her hand from his grasp and moved the kerchief to Albert's nose. "Ciar." She shook it. "Ciar."

The dog sniffed and wagged his tail.

"Ciar," Emma said again and then tugged the dog's nose toward the hem of his kilt. "Ciar."

"Arf!"

"He seems to like this game," Dunollie growled. "But this is nay child's play, and Albert is not keen enough to break me out of this fortress if that's what you're thinking. You'll be arrested and locked in the pillory if you try it."

The guard rapped the door. "Time's up, miss."

Emma clamped her hands to his cheeks and pulled his face downward.

Ciar's breath caught as he pursed his lips. But she didn't kiss him as he expected. She pressed her lips to his ear and whispered, "Tonight. Be ready."

"Did you not hear what I just said?" Before Ciar could ask what in God's name she was planning and put an end to her well-intended but ludicrous ideas, the door swung open.

"Aw, now isn't that nice," said the sentinel. "A kiss for the condemned."

Emma backed away, holding her head high like a queen. "Come, Albert. Thank you so much for allowing us a modicum of time, sir. Would you do me the kindness of accompanying me on a walk of the perimeter? This wee beasty needs to stretch his legs."

Ciar smacked his head with the heel of his hand. The lass was astonishing. Good Lord, Emma would be nice to an asp. He gave her hand a squeeze before she was ushered out the door. "Always remember your safety is all that matters to me."

The door shut in his face and the lock screeched into place, and he watched through the tiny window as she walked away, chatting with the guard.

God save she do something we'll both come to regret.

* * *

"Do I hear the gentle waves of a loch behind us?" Emma asked as the sentinel's keys jangled.

"Aye, Loch Linnhe," he said.

"Let us start there, shall we?"

"I'm here, miss," whispered Sam, following. "The fort is surrounded by stone ramparts. 'Tis as sound as they say it is."

Emma had assumed as much. Regardless, she continued to persevere. "Do you receive your stores by water?" She counted three steps from the door to the corner of the building, then eight to the rear.

"Some," said the sentinel.

They stepped off a gravel path onto grass. Albert stopped when they reached the wall.

The man's steps slowed. "This way."

"Why turn right and not left?" she asked innocently.

"Because the pit is south. No lady such as yourself ought to venture near it on account of the smell."

Emma sniffed. "I smell horses."

"That's because the stables are on our right."

She counted forty-five paces to the corner of the ramparts—and it was hidden by the horse barn. How fortuitous. "Since the wall abuts a loch, is there a sea gate for unloading supplies?"

"Aye, 'tis just up here along the north wall."

"North? Isn't that odd?"

"Oh, no, the River Narin empties into the Linnhe, and the inlet is a good place to moor our galleys."

"Does the governor have a galley?"

"Several royal boats owned by the crown, of course." The sentinel stopped. "Here it is, we call it the sally port—on account of its security."

There were eleven paces from the corner to this gate. That summed up to seven and sixty steps from Ciar's cell to the sally port, which was much better than the one hundred twenty she'd calculated from the main entrance.

"How interesting. Have a look at that, lad," she replied. "The fortress is very secure, is it not, sir?"

"Indeed, miss. 'Tis the most secure garrison in the Highlands."

She affixed a genuine smile. "You must like it here."

Sam grunted. Evidently he didn't care if the sentinel liked his situation or not.

"The cold annoys my rheumatism a bit," replied the man. "But it isn't a bad post for an old soldier."

"I imagine your knees ache terribly after standing guard outside Dunollie's door hour upon hour."

"He's not going anywhere. His cell is sound with bars on the windows. Besides, this is a fort, miss. After sundown the gates are closed, and the wall is patrolled at all hours."

"I see. Very impressive, indeed."

Emma gave the soldier a polite curtsey. "Thank you ever so much. I truly had not realized how monumental Fort William is."

Chapter Twelve

*A*re you certain no one can hear us?" Emma asked, listening to differentiate the myriad of sounds around them.

Sam's spoon tapped his bowl. "We're alone at the rear of the alehouse, and the crowd at the bar is making such a ruckus, I can scarcely hear you."

"Good." She ate a bite of stew. "Mm. This is delicious."

"It is. But I'm so hungry, I'd eat anything at the moment."

She washed down her bite with a sip of ale. "I'm going to need your help tonight."

"After we return to Achnacarry?"

"We're not going back. Not tonight, anyway."

Emma slipped her hand into her satchel and pulled out a pouch of guineas. "First, I need you to purchase a horse."

"For you to ride? How will you—"

"The beast is not for me," she cut him off. "Ye ken who."

"Dunollie?"

"Wheesht."

"But he's behind bars, guarded by an army."

"Aye." She found the lad's arm, shifted her hand upward, and patted his cheek. "And that's why I asked the sentinel to give us a wee tour of the fort."

"Ye cannot be serious. I'm only sixteen and have never been more than twenty miles away from the stable at Achnacarry. And you, holy hellfire, Miss Emma, you are not thinking clearly."

"I am of sound mind, and if we do not act, that horrid governor will hang an innocent man—an upstanding member of the gentry, no less." Emma sipped her ale, scrunching her nose at the bitterness. "I have it all planned. We shall use the sally port. Remember, the sea gate? I told you to have a look at it as we passed."

"I do, but—"

"Can we lead a horse down there?"

"I think so. The shore of the river is lined with sand and stone."

"Excellent." Emma took another bite of stew. "But to be certain, after you purchase the horse, ride down the path and make sure."

"Does Dun...er...the laird have a plan?"

"Aye."

"What is it?"

Emma dabbed the corners of her mouth. She didn't want Sam in any deeper than he already was. She'd told the sentry at the gate the lad was her footman, and that's all they knew of him. If something went wrong, they'd have no idea where to find him. "'Tis best if I only tell you what you need to know."

"Ye ken the sally port is barred and locked."

"What kind of lock?"

"How should I know?" Sam asked with his mouth full. "A black one."

"All right."

"Do ye have a key?"

"Aye, of sorts." She grasped his hand and squeezed. "Mention this to no one."

"But do you not think one of Lochiel's men will be looking for us soon? At least for you. We ought to be heading home, else they'll take a pound of flesh out of me hide, they will."

"This is all my doing, and I shall vouch for you if need be. But Achnacarry is so large, it will take them half the day to figure out I'm not there. By the time anyone may or may not reach us, I'll have taken care of what needs to be done. I'm certain of it."

* * *

The church bell struck twice, piercing through the night air like the first call of a tern at dawn. Keeping close to the wall so they wouldn't be seen, Emma and Albert followed Sam while he led the horses over the boggy land. Beside them, the river gently trickled. Ahead, the lake water slapped the shore. An easy breeze stirred the seagrass.

"The sea gate's just ahead." Though he spoke softly, the lad's voice carried with the resonance of a deep F from a harp string.

"Is there a guard?" she asked.

"None I can see."

"Can you please direct me to it?"

"It will be on our left. But aren't we close enough?"

Emma brushed her fingers over her chignon, locating three hairpins. "I need to pick the lock."

"You what?" he asked, the tenor of his whisper shooting up with disbelief.

"Secure the horses as close to the wall as possible so the patrol on the wall-walk will not see them, then follow me. I need your eyes." Emma urged the dog across the uneven ground until he stopped at the wall. She reached for the gate, but placed her hands on cold stone.

"Three feet to your right," whispered Sam, bless him.

She paused for a moment and held very still. *No sound of anyone approaching as yet.*

When she found the gate, she tied Albert's lead to one of the bars and grasped the lock between her hands. Goodness, it was heavy. A hairpin wasn't going to be strong enough for this monster.

Digging in her satchel, she found a slender iron pick at the bottom—one Robert had given her during his lock picking lessons. She inserted it into the keyhole and turned her ear. A padlock this size ought to have two shackles, and the trick was finding the second one. Working the pick forward a fraction of an inch at a time, she patiently listened.

Clink.

Stopping, she tightened her grip. *There's the first.*

Emma bit her lip and levered the pick upward ever so slightly. Another clink came when she tried to move it forward, but the sound didn't have the right resonance. She needed to hear a hollow, unmistakable chime, a noise no untrained person would be able to distinguish.

Levering the pick a mere fraction, she tried again. This time the tool slid easily.

Clink.

She dared to inhale.

"Will Dunollie meet you here?" asked Sam.

"Shhh."

If she wasn't successful now, she'd have to start over.

Footsteps approached on the wall-walk above, coming from the direction of Loch Linnhe.

Every muscle in Emma's body tensed, her heart suddenly racing. "Haste," she whispered. "Clamp your hand around Albert's muzzle and crouch in the gateway."

"Stay," Sam growled with a bit of rustling.

The dog wriggled and grunted while the soldier paused right above them. Had he seen them? Could hc hcar the dog's impatient snorts?

Dear God, please let him pass!

Emma's breath rushed in her ears as she willed Albert to remain calm. Her head spun. In the next heartbeat all could be ruined. The padlock slipped in her sweaty palm, and the fingers of her right hand twitched from holding the pick steady.

Help!

The soldier marched on, moving toward the loch until his steps faded into the sounds of the breeze and the lake lapping the shore.

"That was too close," whispered Sam.

"The sentry had no idea we were here," she said with more confidence than she felt.

"May I release Albert now?"

"Aye." With a flick of her fingers, the metallic clack of the padlock opening rang like a bell in the night air.

"Holy smokes, you did it." The lad's voice was filled with disbelief.

Emma held out the pick. "This is one skill my brother taught me that once seemed nothing more than an idle pastime. But at long last it has proved quite valuable." She slipped the tool into her satchel and untied Albert's lead from the bar.

"It seems like we're a fair bit lower than the fortress grounds." She inclined her ear upward. "Are there stairs?"

"Seven of them. You do not want me to go in there, do ye?"

"Nay. Can you whistle like a blackbird?"

"Aye."

"Stay hidden in the stairwell, but if you see any danger, whistle ever so quietly."

"What if they see you?"

"Then I'll have to pretend I'm a ghost, will I not?" She smiled, though no one need remind her she was about to enter the lion's den. Drawing in a deep breath, Emma faced the most perilous seven and sixty paces she would ever cross. With luck, this might be the one time in her life when darkness was her friend.

"Ye're either brave or mad, I'll say."

"Perhaps I'm a bit of both." She climbed the stairs, running her hand along the stone wall.

At the top she stopped and held the kerchief to Albert's nose. "Find Ciar."

"He's nay a bloodhound," Sam whispered a bit too loudly.

"At least he's a dog." Emma turned toward the sound of Sam's voice. "Stay hidden."

"I will."

With a tug of the leash, she slipped against the north wall and headed west toward Loch Linnhe. Eleven paces took her to the corner. The smell of horses and hay reassured her.

Only forty-five paces to reach the rear of the officers' hold.

Halfway, a gentle whistle came.

She pulled Albert against the ramparts and held his muzzle. "Stay," she commanded, barely whispering.

The footsteps clapped the wall-walk again. Heavier this time, but still she heard only one guard.

She froze, imagining herself bathed in light, terrified she'd be seen.

Albert squirmed.

"Shhhh!" she whispered with her heart flying to her throat.

Emma's mind ran the gamut as the dragoon neared. How would she respond if he spotted her? Apologize? Tell him she was lost? Admit she was taking a lock picker to Ciar? What about a pastry? She was blind, after all. How could she know if it was day or night? Bless it, if she had thought, she might have stopped by the baker's and purchased a tart or something to make her excuse more plausible.

But the guard continued along the wall, not even pausing this time.

She allowed herself to breathe. *Thank heavens.*

Hearing no other movement, Emma continued counting her steps. At forty-five paces, her hands started trembling uncontrollably. She'd need to move away from the wall now. Out of the shadows. She'd be even more vulnerable.

Eight paces to the front.

But when she turned and reached out, Ciar's cell wasn't there. How far off track was she? Had she turned the wrong way?

Help! I ken I counted correctly.

After forcing herself to take a calming inhalation, she smelled the horses. Perhaps she hadn't walked far enough? A soft neigh came from her left. She held the kerchief to Albert's nose again. "Please, laddie, take me to Ciar!"

The dog walked on, his tail slapping her knee. Beneath her boots was the familiar sound of gravel crunching. Was she close?

Three paces to the door.

Emma let Albert lead her the few paces. He stopped and nuzzled her hand.

"Here?" she asked, reaching out, her fingers brushing wood. Tears welled in her eyes as she drew a breath of relief. "You are brilliant."

She found the padlock right below the latch. This model was easy, nowhere near as large as the lock at the postern gate.

"Ciar?" she whispered. "Are you ready?"

Pulling a hairpin from her chignon, she set to work on the lock, praying she'd found the right door.

"Emma?" A healthy dose of disbelief reflected in Ciar's voice.

Nonetheless, the sound made her heart jolt like a spark from a fire. " 'Tis me."

She released the lock with a flick of her wrist and opened the door, reaching inside. "We must hasten. A guard walks the ramparts every few minutes."

"Aye, I've noticed that as well. But how did you slip through the gates?"

She found his hand and pulled. "A wee iron lock pick. A gift from my brother, six years past."

"Wait." Ciar didn't budge. "When did the guard last walk by?"

"At pace twenty-two behind the barn."

"A few minutes ago?" he asked.

"Possibly. My heart's been hammering so, it seems as if hours have passed."

He pulled her inside and closed the door. "Let us wait here until the next sentry makes his round, then we'll go."

She nodded. "Very well. Good thinking."

Ciar kept hold of her hand as they silently stood, the sound of his breathing making her heart soar. Just standing here with him made the danger and the terror of venturing into the unknown worthwhile.

Good heavens, she'd done it! She'd spirited inside the most highly guarded fortress in the Highlands and found him. If only she could tell this man how much he meant to her. She ached to wrap her arms around him this very minute and never let go.

"I cannot believe you took such a grave risk." His warm breath skimmed her ear while the deep, bass resonance of his voice made a shiver course across the back of her neck.

She squeezed his big palm. "There was no other way. If you stay here, Wilcox will hang you for certain."

"You've come now, and that's what matters. But I should not have told you the only way to prove my innocence is outside Fort William's walls."

"I spoke to the governor, and it is the truth. Everyone kens you're innocent except Wilcox."

"And his army."

She gulped. "Aye, you would mention that."

Albert growled at the sound of an approaching soldier. Emma quickly pulled him to her side and held his muzzle. "Shhh."

This time two guards came past, the murmur of their voices rising over the sounds of the night. They stopped and chatted for a time while Emma hardly dared to breathe. Albert jerked his head, trying to free himself.

"No!" she whispered, fighting him and keeping her fingers clamped. "S-stay!" she hissed, and the dog immediately settled. For heaven's sake, "stay" had worked before; she shouldn't have changed the command.

After what seemed like an eternity, the soldiers continued on their watch and Emma released her fingers. "That was close."

"The dog's young."

"But he's smart. And he helped me find you."

"Bless him." Ciar tugged her fingers. "Let's go."

"Skirt around to the left, 'tis eight paces to the wall, and then we'll have the shadows of the stables to keep us hidden."

"You will never cease to amaze me," he murmured, taking her hand and moving into the lead.

Chapter Thirteen

Ciar held tight to Emma's hand, praying the dog wouldn't see a rabbit and bark, let alone charge off and make chase. It was a miracle the lass had managed to spirit inside with the pup and not be caught.

She never should have risked entering the stronghold at this hour, let alone traveling to Fort William with but a boy as her escort. Nonetheless, she possessed a backbone hewn of steel. Hands down, Emma Grant was the bravest, if not the foolhardiest, woman he'd ever encountered.

As they reached the edge of the stables, Ciar stopped.

"There's eleven paces to the sally port," she whispered.

Thank God. He could barely discern the shadow marking the gateway. The moon illuminated the clouds above. It was dark but not dark enough.

"Are you ready?"

"Ready never to set foot on Fort William's soil again."

"I'll second that." Though Ciar knew he'd return. It was the only way.

Emma's estimation of eleven paces hit the mark. He squeezed her hand as he checked all sides to ensure they were alone. "The first step to the gate is here."

"The first of seven."

"How—?"

Sam's shadowy face peered through the gateway. "There you are."

"Arf!" barked Alfred. "Arf, arf!"

"Hush," Emma squeaked as voices rose, coming from the gatehouse.

Out of the corner of his eye, Ciar spotted a flash. "Get down!" he shouted as a musket fired from across the grounds. "Run!"

"Sam!" Emma called. "Fetch the horses."

Ciar started to pull her toward a moored skiff. A boat would take them home faster, but a good marksman might shoot them dead before they could row out of gunshot range. In the blink of an eye, he changed directions and headed for the horses.

A cacophony of bangs and shouts came from the barracks as the troops stirred. God save them, the entire regiment would be upon them in seconds.

"Haste!" Ciar roared, spotting redcoats with muskets racing atop the wall-walk.

As the lad approached with the reins in his fist, Ciar grabbed Emma's waist and hoisted onto a saddleless steed. Taking the reins, he took two steps back and vaulted into place behind her. "Come, Sam!" he bellowed, digging his heels into the horse's barrel. "Ride close to the wall and follow me."

Bellows of "Dunollie" and "Grant" rose as he galloped the horse for the road, leaning forward and shielding Emma with his body. "Keep your head down," he hollered back to Sam.

The lad stayed right behind, handling his steed like a

jockey, exactly what Ciar would expect from the son of a coachman. As they hit the road, Ciar ignored his urge to head south and led the way north—far enough to confuse anyone who made chase.

Before he crossed the river, he led them upstream to hide their tracks, then turned at an old croft and followed a rutted road through the byways of town.

"Where are we headed?" asked Emma.

"Somewhere you'll be safe."

"But we need to prove your innocence."

"Correction," he growled over his shoulder. "Only I can prove my innocence."

"But they'll be looking for me as well. You heard them. They were shouting my clan name as well as yours."

Ciar clamped his molars until they hurt. It would be a risk to send her back to Achnacarry and even riskier to send her home to Glenmoriston—not to mention in entirely the wrong direction. He knew of only one place in the Highlands where he could provide her with sanctuary. Only one place where he could ensure her safety.

"Does Janet ken where you are?" he asked.

"Most likely she has figured it out by now."

Gnashing his teeth, Ciar demanded more speed from his mount, as if he was in the race of his life. "Good God, she's doubtless worried out of her mind."

"It wasn't to be helped. She would have stopped me had I mentioned what I was up to." Emma shifted against his chest, turning her face toward him. "Regardless, we must send word straightaway. The last thing I desire is to upset her."

If Ciar knew Her Ladyship, she'd already be beside herself with worry.

Sam reined his mount up to their flank. "Are we past the danger?"

After checking over his shoulder, Ciar slowed the pace to a fast trot. "We won't be past danger for sennights. And mark me, Wilcox will never rest until he has my neck in a noose."

"Or you prove your innocence," added the lass.

He couldn't agree more. "Aye, God willing."

Emma yawned and shook her head. "Will we ride throughout the night?"

Sam did the same, wiping his brow in the crook of his elbow. "I've no idea how long I'll be able to keep me eyes open. We rode all last night as well."

"Ballocks," Ciar swore under his breath. Too many things could go wrong. They needed help—mayhap send the boy home or find a boat or bloody hide. "All right, then. I've a friend in Corran who owes me a favor."

"Isn't it too dangerous to stop?" Emma asked. "The red-coats cannot be far behind."

"Mark me, if we stop, our chances of making it safely out of here will quadruple."

It was still dark with no sign of sunrise when Ciar reined his horse to a stop in the shadows of an enormous sycamore outside Dicky MacIain's cottage. The old crofter ran a few head of sheep as well as the ferry across the narrows of Loch Linnhe.

"The pair of you stay on your mounts whilst I rouse him." Albert followed as Ciar started off, but he dismissed the dog with a flick of his wrist. "Och, go wait with Miss Emma."

She followed with a sharp "stay." If only she had left the laddie behind, they might have fled without an army on their heels.

But hindsight was always the best teacher.

Ciar didn't knock on the door. Dicky had a reputation for being a sound sleeper, and time was not in his favor. Instead, he climbed through a window, lit a candle from the coals in the hearth, and headed straight for the back room. Raucous snores led him to Dicky's bedside. Thanks for small mercies, the old fella was alone.

He nudged the man in the shoulder. "Wake up. I'm in need of a favor."

Dicky sputtered and gasped, reaching for his dirk.

As a slight glint of steel flashed, Ciar pinned his friend's arm to the bed, dripping a bit of candle wax on the man's forehead for good measure. "'Tis me, ye angry bear."

The old crofter sputtered. "Dunollie?"

"Aye."

"But I thought—"

"You thought nothing," Ciar growled. "I need you to ferry a lad across the loch, and I'll be trading a gelding for the lend of your skiff."

Bloodshot eyes grew round. "Lend?"

"I've no time to haggle. The horse is sound. Whatever you reckon is a fair difference in price, send a note to my factor and it will be paid." Ciar spotted an old sword propped in a corner and examined it in the candlelight. "And add this piece of rusted iron to my accounting."

"That was me granddad's."

Smirking, he rubbed his thumb across the blade. It was duller than a butter knife but better than nothing. "I'd reckon he was the last one to run it across a sharpening stone as well."

"Bloody miserable Highlander waking me in the dead of night. A man needs to be shown some respect. I ought to charge a shilling just for the pain in me backside." Mumbling curses like a peg-legged sailor, Dicky rose and belted a plaid around his waist. "I thought Wilcox was aiming to hang ye."

Ciar set the candle on a table and shoved the weapon into his belt. "He won't if I can prove my innocence."

"Good luck there." Dicky shoved his feet into his boots. "Everyone from Tarbert to Inverness kens ye're innocent."

"There are three scheming dragoons who ken it as well. The same three who murdered MacIntyre and pointed the finger at me."

"Good God, ye'll never win against such odds."

"Not behind bars I won't." Ciar marched through to the main room. "Haste. Redcoats aren't far behind."

"That would be right, bring a retinue of backbiting government troops to me door, ye thoughtless whelp."

Ignoring Dicky's grumblings, Ciar led the way to the sycamore. "Emma, Wilcox kens who ye are, but what about the lad?"

"I told them Sam was my footman."

He grasped the lad's bridle. "Did ye speak to anyone? Tell them where you hailed from?"

"No, sir."

Ciar turned toward Emma. "Did anyone ken you rode in from Achnacarry?"

"No." She shook her head. "No one asked."

"Fortunate." He slapped Sam's knee. "Dicky will ferry you and your horse across to Ardgour. From there it's a straight ride up to Lochiel's fortress, but I do not recommend making the journey at night. Lord kens where Wilcox is sending his troops."

"Ye intend for me to go alone?" asked the lad.

"Aye." Ciar stepped away from the horse. "You said you were tired. Once you're across, ride into the hills and take a bit of rest. Dicky will give you some food."

"I will?" asked the old man, pulling Sam and his horse toward the loch. "Next ye'll be giving away the plaid off me back."

"Do you have a spare?" When Dicky responded with an

audacious scowl, Ciar chuckled. "Thank you, friend. I'll nay forget your kindness."

The old man beckoned the lad. "Come, there's a parcel of dried meat in the boat."

Ciar's humor faded in the blink of an eye. He reached up to help Emma dismount. "We'll be rowing a skiff from here."

"Will that be safer?"

Rather than set the lass on her feet, he cradled her in his arms. "Faster. I reckon safer as well."

She patted her hip. "Come, Albert."

Ciar looked toward the rickety wooden pier where the skiff was tied. Dicky had already shoved off. "Blast, I should have had Sam take the pup with him."

"But he's my dog."

"And he nearly got us killed before we had a chance to flee." Ciar hurried down to the pier and helped her to the bow seat of the boat. "You'll need to keep him quiet."

"I will. I promise." She patted the bench, and Albert hopped into the hull, sat, and put his head in her lap. She ran her hand along his fur. "You mustn't bark."

Ciar untied the rope, then climbed onto the rowing bench and took up the oars.

"Och!" Emma gasped, her back stiffening while Albert's ears pricked. "Riders are coming."

Ciar's gaze darted northward toward the road. Seeing nothing but the outline of trees through the darkness, he whispered, "Can you hear them?"

"Two horses...no, three."

"Ballocks," he growled. "Duck your head, I'm pulling the skiff under the pier."

She bent forward, grasping the medal around her neck. "Saint Lucia save us."

Ciar released his grip on the dock's slats long enough

to move the sword into his lap, but quickly grabbed hold again to ensure the skiff remained hidden. "Can you keep Albert quiet?"

"Aye." Emma slid an arm around the dog's back. Holding him firm, she gently clamped his muzzle closed. "Sh, stay," she whispered in the dog's ear so quietly it was barely audible. "Good laddie."

With Ciar's next breath, horses' hooves thudded against the compact dirt road like the steady drums of a death knell. They almost beat louder than his heart.

Too many things could go wrong. And there he sat with Grant's sister and a half-trained dog.

"Look there—Dicky has a passenger," shouted one of the riders.

Ciar's gaze darted to the far shore. The clouds had parted, and the moonlight illuminated Sam's outline as the lad walked the horse off the ferry.

"But he's not MacDougall. Look at the size of him—he's a scrawny bastard like you, Landry."

Ciar's fingers dug into the rough wood. If only the man's name had been Riley or Manfred, he might end this debacle here and now.

"We may as well wait until the old man returns. Mayhap he knows something."

"I doubt it," said a third. "If you ask me, MacDougall rode for the mountains. They all hide up there like rats."

"I reckon the Highlanders transform into ghosts, I swear. We chased Grant and his men up the slopes of Ben Nevis in a snowstorm, and the bastards vanished while we ended up with frostbitten toes."

"Well, it isn't snowing now. We'll find the renegade. Mark me."

Albert squirmed, giving off a squeak and making the skiff

rock, slapping the water. After a few jerks of his head, Emma blew softly in the dog's ear, as she smoothed her hand up and down his coat. Ciar could have sworn she was repeating the word "stay" over and over again, but he couldn't be sure.

"Ate too many peas, did ye, Rutford?" asked Landry.

"Shut your gob," came the reply.

Ciar dared to breathe. *The dog will be the death of us.*

The men chatted while what seemed like an eternity passed.

"Throw us a rope, and we'll tug you ashore," hollered Landry.

Boots clambered across the pier, making it tremble while Ciar shifted his fingers aside a heartbeat before a black boot trod on them.

"My thanks," said Dicky, his gaze flickering beneath the pier as the coil unraveled.

Ciar bared his teeth—a half grimace, half smile. The blood had drained from his fingers, and they'd already gone numb. His arms were shaking from keeping the boat steady in a constant fight against the wind rippling across the water.

Another set of boots clomped onto the dock. "Who the devil needed a ferry ride at this hour?"

"'Twas a young coal mine worker," Dickey explained. He must have dreamed up the story on his way back across the river. "His ma died. Told me his father perished in the mines, and the poor sop was worried about the children left alone."

"Where's he headed?"

Ciar's gut clamped into a hard ball. *Don't say Ardgour.*

"Pollach."

Again Ciar let himself breathe. It was unlikely the soldiers would follow. If Dicky had said Ardgour, they'd ask for a ride across the loch and demand to question the lad.

"Where's that?" asked a dragoon.

"Through the glen on Loch Shiel. I reckon the boy ought to reach home by dawn."

"Have you seen anyone else this night?"

"Until that lad beat on me door, the only thing I'd seen was the inside of my bloody eyelids. And that's exactly what I intend to stare at until well after the sun rises." Dicky strode toward the shore, the heel of his boot smashing Ciar's finger.

Snapping his hand away, Ciar shook his fingers, making the skiff totter.

Bloody miserable festering maggot!

Thank God, the redcoats followed the crotchety old coot. If it had been Sam's finger Dicky stepped on, the lad would have bleated like a lamb in a castrating pen.

"Did the coal miner mention any word about Ciar MacDougall?"

"Dunollie?" asked Dicky. "Isn't he your guest at the fort?"

"He was."

"It appears Robert Grant's blind sister helped him escape."

"You mean to say the king's dragoons had the wool pulled over their eyes by a blind woman?"

Emma's shoulders began to shake while Albert squirmed.

Ciar braced himself, ready to dive across the boat and smother the damned canine if need be.

"If she's Grant's sister, then she's a ghost," said the same one who'd admitted to following Robert two years past.

"I suppose we'll leave you be for the night," said a dragoon, the leathers of a saddle squeaking as if he'd mounted. "But if you hear news of anyone catching sight of MacDougall, send a runner to the fort."

"I'll do that," Dickey replied. "But he'd be daft to show his face in these parts."

Ciar held the skiff steady while the soldiers started off to the tune of the old man slamming his front door.

Emma continued to methodically pet Albert and didn't release him until the sound of retreating horses faded. "My lands, that was close," she whispered.

"Too close." Ciar peeked over the pier, checking all directions, before he shoved the skiff into deeper water and picked up the oars. "The faster we row away from here, the easier I'll breathe for certain."

"How far do we need to go?"

"We ought to pass Castle Stalker in about an hour— a Stewart keep. Then I'm hoping we slip by Dunstaffnage before dawn."

"Why?"

"'Tis held by the Campbells now, and I don't trust them any farther than I can throw a twenty-stone rock." As he pulled on the oars, he scanned the loch's eastern shore. "Dunstaffnage once was ruled by my kin when the MacDougalls were Lords of the Isles."

"Once? Did they lose it in a feud?"

"A major feud of sorts. My ancestor, John MacDougall, fought Robert the Bruce and lost."

"How unfortunate." Emma tilted her face to the skies as if she were thinking. "But you have Dunollie now."

"Aye. And it's but three miles south of Dunstaffnage as the crow flies."

"So, will we be there by first light?"

"Nay, lass. I'm not taking you to my keep. The risk is far too great."

Chapter Fourteen

*E*mma stretched. The pillow cradling her head was so soft, she wished she could sleep forever. Intending to do her best, she rolled to her side and smoothed her hand over exquisitely fine linens.

"Yowl," came a happy, though unwelcome, sound from the foot of the bed.

"A few more minutes, Albert."

His tail beat against the mattress as he scooted up and licked her face.

Emma pushed his head aside. "Go on."

Then reality dawned. Bolting upright, she wrapped her arms around the dog's neck. "Ciar?" she shrieked. "Are you here?"

"Aye, lass," came a raspy reply, one sounding as if they were in a tunnel.

"Where are we?" She clutched the blanket beneath her chin. "H-how did I end up in a bed?" It was a very comfortable bed, but she had absolutely no recollection of anything beyond Ciar rowing the skiff and talking about the landmarks they'd pass along the way.

"Forgive me." The sound of his boots brushed over a solid floor. "You were asleep when we arrived, and I hadn't a mind to wake you. We're on the Isle of Kerrera in my sanctuary."

"We're in a church?"

"Nay." The bottom of the bed depressed as he sat.

Still clutching Albert, Emma drew her feet away and tucked them to the side. Ciar MacDougall had just sat at the foot of her bed. The mere thought befuddled her mind.

"We're in the cellars of Gylen Castle," he calmly explained as if it were perfectly normal to be in an unmarried lass's bedchamber...sitting on her bed, no less.

"Cellars?"

"Aye, the keep was built by my grandfather's grandfather. But during the Wars of the Three Kingdoms, the Covenanters besieged the castle. Clan and kin put up a brave fight until they ran out of provisions and had no choice but to surrender or starve."

Emma pressed the heels of her hands to her temples. "I still do not understand why you have a bedchamber in the cellars."

"Well..." Ciar's voice grew haunted. "After my ancestors laid down their arms, the Covenanters burned and sacked the castle. They massacred everyone, including the women, save my grandfather's father, another ancestor named John. On that day the wee lad became the Seventeenth Chieftain of Dunollie."

Good heavens, she hated barbarity. "My word," she whispered. "Such mindless violence."

"After, the castle stood in ruins—still does. However, when William and Mary ascended to the throne, usurping the rightful heir, my da kent civil war would come again. We set to clearing the rubbish out of the cellars and turning it into a place of refuge. Mark me, Gylen still looks lonely and ruined on the outside, and any treasure seekers or soldiers who come snooping about would never find the entrance to this hiding-hole."

Emma lazily swirled her fingers behind Albert's ears. "'Tis a refuge in plain sight, then?"

"Aye. I keep general stores stocked. Nothing fancy, mind you, but there's dried meat and apples, and a barrel of oats. We've plenty of whisky, and there's a spring with fresh water amongst the remnants of the outer bailey."

"It sounds ideal."

"Far from it, but it ought to keep us alive until I can settle this charge against me."

"Us?" Dare she hope? "Do you mean to keep me here with you?"

"Och, Emma, I apologize from the bottom of my heart, but I can see no other way. If Wilcox found you, he could do unimaginable things to ferret me out. And I cannot take a chance on seeing you hurt."

"But I want to stay. I want to be of use."

"For now I need you to remain out of sight whilst I visit a crofter in Balliemore."

"Where?"

"The tenant who tends my sheep on the isle lives two miles north of here. He'll take a message to Livingstone, and I'll dispatch one to your brother as well—let him ken you are safe and unharmed."

"Robert," she whispered, clamping a hand over her mouth and trying to blink away a tear. "He'll be angry with me."

"No, lass." Ciar scooted up the bed until his big arms surrounded her shoulders. "This is all my doing, and I doubt your brother will ever forgive me. If I had kept riding to Spean Bridge and ignored the crime, I wouldn't be in this dilemma. Neither of us would be."

"It isn't like you to keep riding. You did the honorable thing, and you will prove your innocence. I know it right down to my bones."

"Thank you, lass. I need such words of encouragement."

Emma closed her eyes and sighed as Ciar kissed her forehead, his beard a tad prickly but alluring all the same.

He slid his fingers down her arms and grasped her hands. "Before I go, I want to show you the lay of the place."

"I suppose it sounds awfully crude to call it the cellars."

He pulled her to her feet. "Mayhap, though that is exactly what Livingstone and I call it—either that or the vault."

"Who else kens of it?"

"Only Braemar and the crofter, Archie. His wife, too, I suppose." Ciar gently took her hand and brushed her fingers over a wooden table. "The bed is at the rear of the cellar, and there's a washstand beside it—chamber pot beneath. The floor is covered with a rag rug that I can roll up if you prefer."

Emma patted her thigh, telling Albert to follow. "It shouldn't cause a problem as long as I grow accustomed to it."

"There are two wooden chairs and a table straight ahead, and to the left there's a wee hearth with brushed sheepskin on the floor before it."

"I can feel the warmth on my face. But isn't it dangerous to have a fire?"

"We'll need fire to cook over the iron hob, but I use only lignite coal from my mine in Northern Ireland. It burns clear."

"Truly?"

"Aye, but only in small amounts."

He led her past the chairs. "On this side you'll find the cellar door. In the passageway to the right are the vaults with stores, and to the left is the way out. 'Tis a long affair of about three hundred feet, tunneled through earth and rock."

"We don't exit into the remains of the keep?"

"That would be far too obvious. The outlet is covered by heather rushes and is only paces away from the eastern beach. I've hidden Dicky's skiff in the gorse just beyond the beach, covered my tracks as well."

"Heavens, no one will ever find us here."

"Not likely. But I have no intention of staying any longer than necessary."

"What do you intend to do?" Emma asked.

"First thing is to notify Livingstone of my whereabouts."

"And then?"

"And then you shouldn't worry about how I will bring my accusers to justice. 'Tis nay pretty, but it must be done. You'll soon tire of this place, as will I." He pulled out a chair and urged her to sit. "There's dried meat, apples, and an ewer of water on the table. I ken 'tis not much, but I'll return with some more substantial fare."

"Thank you."

"Is there anything else you need before I go?"

"Ah…" She went through the map of the chamber in her mind, then scraped her teeth over her bottom lip. "Is there but one bed?"

"One large bed, but not to worry. I slept on the sheepskin pelt before the fire. 'Twas by far more comfortable than Fort William's hospitality."

"Oh." A moment of awkward silence filled the chamber.

Of course he would have slept elsewhere. She ought to be relieved. "Must you leave now?" she asked, grappling for something to say to encourage him to stay a bit longer.

"I'm afraid I must."

She brushed her fingers over the table, finding the plate of food. "I'd like to go with you."

"Not this time. I expect Wilcox to have men combing every inch of my lands, at least at the moment. For the next sennight or so, I do not want you to leave the cellars unless I am with you, understood?"

"Aye." She nibbled a bite of dried meat. "How long will you be?"

"A few hours. I hope to return in time for the noon meal."

"And what of Albert? He needs to step outside soon."

"I took him out not long before you woke, and he knows the way now. I doubt anyone will suspect a dog traipsing about, but you must remember there are ships sailing the seas around Kerrera, and some are not friendly. You won't hear them when they're a half mile out, but they will most definitely see you, and that we cannot risk."

* * *

An old sheepdog rushed across the grass, barking like a savage as Ciar approached the croft. Preparing to defend himself, he gripped the hilt of the rusted sword, hoping there'd be no need to use it.

Just in time, Archie bolted out of the cottage. "Come behind, ye flea-bitten mop o' fur."

His wife, Nettie, was right behind, wiping her hands on her apron. "What's all the commotion?"

"Just an old friend," said Ciar as he continued forward.

Both of them gaped as if they'd been surprised by a visit

from royalty. "What the blazes are ye doing on Kerrera, m'laird?" asked Archie.

"I've something to speak to you about." Ciar gave the man a pointed look. "In private, though I'd be much obliged for a basket of eggs, bacon, and anything else you have to spare, Nettie."

She thwacked his arm. "Is that all the welcome we'll see? Why not come inside and have a smoke and a pint? Ye look as if ye've been in the wars."

He gave her shoulder a squeeze. "Perhaps some other time. At the moment I've business with your husband."

"You men, always so serious. Trouble with the Hanoverian king?" Nettie asked as she returned to the cottage.

Ciar chuckled. "You've heard about that, have you?"

"Visited the mainland four days past." Archie cupped a hand to his mouth so Nettie wouldn't overhear. "Heard about your unfortunate turn of events."

"I'm surprised you know."

"Brought a few new head of sheep over from the mainland yesterday. There are redcoats everywhere."

"Have they been here?"

"Why would they come to an island with one cottage, a few hundred sheep, and a ruined keep?"

"I have a feeling they'll befall Kerrera soon."

"Oh? I'm guessing you didn't depart Fort William amicably."

"You'd be right." Ciar escorted the crofter to the old barn. "I need your help, friend."

"Ye ken where my allegiance lies. If ye want me to take up my sword, I'll stand beside ye through thick and thin. There's nothing I'd like better than to feed those redcoats a serving of my icy dirk."

Kicking a bit of straw, Ciar gave the man a sincere smile.

"I appreciate your candor, but I'd rather not start a war with the crown at the moment. Not over a trio of murdering rats who tried to pin their crime on me."

"They meddled with the wrong man, I'll say."

"I hope you're right." Ciar brushed the dust off an oxen yoke hanging from a pillar. "I need you to find Livingstone and tell him I must see him straightaway. Tell him to come alone and to bring ink and quill."

"Ye aim to fight this with a pen?"

"Nay, but there's a woman with me, and—"

The crofter's eyes bugged wide as his mouth dropped open. "I'll be damned. A woman has tamed the wild beast?"

"Bless it, if you would listen." Ciar punched the yoke. He'd always been called "the beast" on account of his appearance, but he didn't like anyone referring to Emma as anything other than a delicate flower. "She's the reason I'm walking free at the moment, and I'll not hear a word against her."

Archie grinned, his teeth crooked and brown. "So, ye like her a great deal, do ye?"

"No...er...yes." Ciar looked to the rafters. "She is a very bonny young lady. She also happens to be Grant of Glenmoriston's sister."

"And that's a problem?"

"Presently he doesn't know she is...*ah*...with me."

"Oh, dear."

"Aye, and I need to rectify that as soon as possible."

"Are ye certain? If I ken Grant, he's more likely to sever your balls afore he lets ye explain."

Ciar adjusted his stance. At no time did he or any man relish being told his cods were at stake. "Hence the quill."

"Very well. What else do ye need?"

"Weapons—dirk, sword, pistols. And we need food.

Plenty of it, but I'll fetch it from here at night. I don't want either you or Nettie coming to the cellars. You must act as if nothing whatsoever has changed on this island in the past fifty years. Understood?"

"Aye, sir. Er..."

"Hmm?"

"When should I set sail for Dunollie?"

"Straightaway. And if anyone asks your purpose, tell them you've come for oats and flour."

Chapter Fifteen

*B*efore Ciar stepped into the tunnel, he scanned the sky above the craggy, half-ruined tower and saw not a wisp of smoke.

About halfway to the door, Albert met him, wagging his tail. "You've decided you like me, have you, laddie?" He scrubbed his knuckles through the dog's fur. "Or was it the meat I gave you this morn?

"Come along. Let us find out what your mistress is up to."

As they proceeded toward the dim light, the air grew comfortably warm. He'd tested the lignite coal but had never stayed in the cellars. Thank God it was working now.

The sound of trickling water came from within. Ciar stepped inside and abruptly stopped, his heart flying to his throat. "God's bones," he growled under his breath while Albert yipped and dashed across the floor.

Bare naked, Emma turned away from the washstand and stooped to pat the dog. "What is it, ye wee beasty?"

Heaven help him, she was a vision to behold. Her auburn

locks tumbled about skin as silky smooth as polished marble. And she was formed like a goddess. Shapely legs. Perfectly rounded buttocks. Gloriously slender arms.

She straightened. A triangle of tight red curls drew his gaze, framed by creamy, sumptuous hips. Her waist was so small, Ciar ached to wrap his fingers around it to see if the tips would touch. As his gaze meandered upward, his mouth grew dry with the racing of his blood. There he stood, a gruff, grisly beast of a man with a twice-broken nose, staring at the most perfect breasts he'd ever seen in his life. Nay, they weren't large, but rounded and right-sized for Emma's form. Rose nipples stood proud, calling to him, begging to be suckled.

"Holy. Bloody. Hell." The words tumbled from his lips before he thought.

The lass immediately snapped her arms across her chest. "Ciar? I-I-I didn't expect you back so soon!" she squeaked, turning left then right and left again, as if she were uncertain of what to do or where to go. "I'm so sorry. I thought I'd have enough time to bathe."

Chastising himself for his lustfulness, Ciar hastened forward. "There's nothing to apologize for, lass."

Her clothes were neatly piled on the bed, and Emma scooted nearer until her thigh touched the coverlet. But as she reached for her shift, it slipped to the floor. "Oh, blast," she cursed, her face apple red.

Ciar quickly picked it up. "Here."

She snatched the linen from his fingers and clutched it over the front of her body. "Heavens! You, you must turn away at once."

"Of course." He did as she asked. "Do you need help?"

"I am perfectly able to manage." The shift whooshed, making a puff of air caress his calves. "Please, never tell anyone what you saw. Especially Robert." She was right. Her brother would find no humor in the situation whatsoever.

"Och, I'd be the last person to utter a word to a soul."

She drew her kirtle from the bed, the wool giving an even greater whoosh. "I'm so embarrassed."

"Please don't be." His words came out low and raspy. "Next time I'll be certain to call out and announce myself before I step inside."

"Thank you." Her voice was breathier than usual as well. Was it her embarrassment or something else?

Ciar clenched his fists. He'd behaved like a rake, standing in the doorway and staring as if he'd never seen a naked woman before. Ballocks, he was daft. No matter what he thought or how tempting Emma might be, he was a fugitive on the run from government troops. He was in more hot water than ever before, and the poor woman had been dragged into this because of her kindness. She was more precious than all the diamonds in the world and, by God, he would treat her as such.

"I've sent word to Livingstone," he said, mostly to ease the tension in the air.

"When do you expect him?"

"Today. Evening, perhaps." Ciar glanced over his shoulder. "May I turn around now?"

"I must don my stockings first."

"Why not allow me?"

"Because it would be indecent."

Of course it would, you ignoramus. "Forgive me. I only thought to help."

The rustling behind him stopped. "Oh, flay it all, these miserable things are twisted beyond reason."

Ciar turned.

Seated on the bed, the lass had a woolen stocking partway up her calf, the seam wound around her ankle every which way, and to top it off, the toe was knotted. But the hose wasn't what drew Ciar's gaze. The bare flesh of her leg was akin to the call of temptation, pleading for a caress—just one wee stoke of his fingertips across pure satin.

Blinking, he shook his head and pushed away his thoughts, lightly brushing the back of her hand. "Please. Allow me."

"But—"

"No exceptions. You have my word I will never speak of this." He drew the pink hose away from her grasp. "Since Betty isn't here, I will play your lady's maid whenever you should require it."

"Humph." Propping her hands behind her, she raised her foot. A fine-boned, slender foot. Even her wiggling toes were bonny. "I was flustered is all. I am fully capable of dressing myself."

Ciar shook out the stocking and rolled it down, then slipped it over her lovely foot. "I'll venture you rarely do."

"Nonetheless, I've donned my stockings many times."

He rolled it up her leg, his knuckle brushing skin every bit as soft as he'd imagined. Such a travesty to cover such beauty. "But not when a man was standing but four feet away whilst you were trying to rush."

Another blush sprang to her cheeks as he reached for a pink ribbon. "Do not remind me."

He quickly tied the garter in place and started on the second stocking. "I thought I'd take you and Albert for a stroll. There's quite a bit to see...er...the way *you* see."

She laughed out loud. "I'm certain there is. And do not assume just because I'm blind I don't see. The world is what we make of it, and to me it's a labyrinth of maps, a treasure trove of textures, tastes, and sounds."

He slipped on her boots. "After spending the afternoon with you in Achnacarry's garden, I have no doubt."

"I've been blind all my life. And therefore I don't miss it like people who can see and lose their sight. I ken I'm not the same as everyone else, but I've found my way." She took his hands and slid to her feet.

"Agreed. Though I recall you were not comfortable at Achnacarry and preferred to be at home."

"How could I forget? I thank you for being thoughtful and showing me the chamber before you left. While you were gone, Albert and I counted steps."

Ciar remembered her calling off the number of steps at Fort William. "How did you memorize all those paces at the fort? Had you been there before?"

"Nay, after I visited you I asked the sentinel to take us around the perimeter to exercise Albert."

"And he didn't gripe?"

"It is all in the asking. If you are polite, people will usually be friendly in return."

Ciar led her to the passageway. "I wouldn't be so certain, especially when it comes to dragoons. They're an ornery lot."

"I shall keep that in mind the next time I pick the lock to your gaol cell." Emma chuckled. "Come, Albert."

* * *

As soon as they stepped out from the tunnel, Emma felt as if a heavy weight had lifted from her shoulders. A cool breeze washed over her face while a tern cried overhead. "Is the day fine?"

"Pleasant, though there's a cloud covering."

Ciar kept hold of her hand and led her down an incline. "Would you prefer to practice walking with Albert?"

"Why not let him run?" She smiled, hoping he wouldn't know how much she wanted to feel Ciar's strong fingers around hers. He made her feel so secure. Wanted. "If you don't mind leading me about."

"Not at all."

"I hear the rush of the sea—it must be only paces away."

"'Tis just down the slope. Would you like to walk on the shore?"

"Is it safe?"

"Aye, the cove is hidden, though I'll still keep a watchful eye for ships."

"I love the smell of the water."

"How would you describe it?"

"Clean with an overtone of salt, and today there's grass and a hint of coal intermixed."

"You smell the coal?"

"A bit, aye."

He stopped and turned. "She's still burning clear."

"Thank heavens."

When they stepped from the grass onto the stones, she teetered against Ciar's arm. "Pardon me."

"I should have told you we were about to step onto the beach."

"Is it not sand?"

"Not here. 'Tis covered with smooth rocks. Would you prefer to return to the grass?"

"Nay." Once Emma steadied her footing, the going was fine, especially with a braw Highlander at her side.

When they stopped, she faced the rush of the waves, raised her arms, and took in a deep breath. Albert splashed through the water and then came and sat beside her, his tail brushing the rocks. She knew he was wet from head to toe. After all, he was a water dog.

"What do you see?" Ciar whispered behind her, his breath warm on her neck.

"I see endless possibilities, the miracle of nature surrounding us abundant with tranquility." The wind picked up her hair. "What do you see?"

"Waves rolling capped with white foam. The craggy banks on either side that protect this wee strip of stony beach. In the distance to the right is the grand Isle of Mull, where MacLean's Duart Castle stands. And to the left is the mainland."

"Your lands?"

"The end of my lands is beneath our feet. Dunollie sits to the north."

"Then . . . are we on the southern end of Kerrera?"

"Very good." He took her hand and continued on. "Come see the keep."

Albert yipped, shaking and spattering droplets of water.

Laughing, she dabbed the moisture from her cheeks. "I think he likes it here."

"He likes to run."

Emma didn't much care for running at all. Doing so usually ended with pain, though she might give it a go with Ciar. "When you hold my hand I feel confident enough to run."

She bit her lip. Had she just spoken her thoughts aloud?

Aye.

And so what if she had?

He'd just seen her naked. Moreover, she'd allowed him to help her don her stockings. To have his gentle fingers whisk over her skin made her heart soar, her breath tremble.

What had he felt when he stepped inside the vault and saw her backside? Did he feel the same as she? His voice had grown gruff. Had he wanted to kiss her again?

Though Emma had been mortified when he'd found her bathing, she'd suddenly had an overwhelming urge to kiss him.

But well-bred women didn't ask important lairds to kiss them. Such a thing wasn't done.

Not ever!

She gripped his hand tighter as he pulled her up a slope.

"We're coming to a set of stairs."

"How many?"

"Five." He stopped. "Are you ready?"

Emma found the rail with her free hand. "Lead on, sir," she said, though her mind was anywhere rather than the steps. She was far more interested in the coarse calluses on Ciar's palms. Like all Highlanders, he practiced swordsmanship daily. He was a respected cattleman like her brother, which required a great deal of backbreaking work.

"Here we are." His voice echoed as if they were between the walls of a narrow glen. "This was once the hall."

"Was it a large hall?"

"Big enough for kin, I suppose. My ancestors oversaw the shipping trade from this post."

"Fascinating."

The coo of pigeons and the squawk of gulls swarmed above. "There's no roof."

"The ceiling and floorboards have rotted away, and now you can see up through the walls of all five stories and watch the clouds pass overhead."

"Not much use in the rain." Emma turned her ear. "But the pigeons like it."

"That's because they're roosting in the masonry. They've made nests in what remains of old hearths."

"The hearths are still intact?"

"They're hewn of stone and mortar. They look odd, though, depressed into the walls high above our heads. Lonely, waiting in vain for someone to kindle a fire within them."

Shivering, Emma scooted closer to Ciar. "Do you think ghosts are here?"

"Nay." He snorted. "If they were, they've been supplanted by the pigeons."

She laughed at his humor, as she felt his nearness, felt the warmth radiating off him. Would it be too audacious if she mentioned their kiss? Could she ask him if he enjoyed it?

What if he did not? What if he didn't even remember kissing her?

Goodness, she could be ruined merely by her thoughts. *But aren't I already ruined?*

After all, she'd ridden to Fort William with a lad she barely knew. She'd broken into a government fort and freed an important prisoner. And now she was in hiding with that very man. A braw, handsome, loving Highlander.

Dunollie.

She'd been so fond of Ciar all her life. "Since I am ruined," she blurted, "I'm happy it is with you."

"I beg your pardon?" he asked as if she'd uttered a blasphemy.

"You cannot think for one minute Robert will be able to arrange my marriage after all I've done in the past two days."

"If any man utters a word about ruination, he will face me."

"No one need speak it. 'Tis a fact." Emma almost smiled. What did it matter if she was ruined? She'd already known her destiny was to live out her days at Glenmoriston. In fact, this adventure was the most exciting time of her life.

It might be the only exciting thing that would ever happen to her.

She tilted her face toward the sound of his voice. "I want..." Her stomach squeezed. *What if he refuses?*

"What do you want, lass?" he asked, his voice low, soothing, making her feel as if she could say anything to him.

Just out with it!

Her tongue tapped her upper lip as her skin tingled, especially her breasts. They felt as if they craved some forbidden desire smoldering deep inside. "Will you kiss me again?"

Chapter Sixteen

Stunned, Ciar froze for a moment. Ever since they'd been caught by Emma's lady's maid, it had taken a great deal of restraint not to wrap the lass in his arms and show her a real kiss—one unfettered, intentional, and utterly heart-stopping.

And now the beauty had asked him to kiss her?

His eyes widened as he raked his fingers through his hair. When had he last blinked? "Are you certain?" he croaked like an adolescent lad.

She took his palm and brushed her fingers over his knuckles, her caress as gentle as a downy feather. "I'm two and twenty years of age, and before the eve when I wandered into your chamber at Achnacarry I had never been kissed—at least not *really* kissed. I have been isolated and sheltered all of my life. Most men fear me as if I am cursed, but you have never been afraid. Moreover for once, I, Emma Grant, am on a great adventure." She grinned, wickedly waggling her brows. "I am even a fugitive of the crown."

Holy hellfire, Ciar felt terrible about that. "I will make it right. I give you my word."

"Mayhap you will, but this is *my* adventure! I want to be reckless and daring. I—"

Unable to control his actions for one more second, he wrapped her in his arms and captured those tempting lips in the rawest, most unapologetic kiss he'd ever given. God's stones, a man could only resist temptation so much. As the lass melted in his arms, he plunged his tongue into her mouth and took his plunder.

And, bless it, she plundered him back. Never in his life had a woman imparted so much emotion with a kiss. What she lacked in experience, she made up for with pure, unadulterated passion.

She moved into him, pressing her body flush to his, matching his fervor and urging them higher. His heart hammered as she rubbed against him like a hellcat bent on seduction.

Och aye, Ciar wanted this woman with his entire being. As hard as an iron rod, his cock pulsed. There was a stone shelf right behind them. All he needed to do was lift her up, raise her skirts, and expose those creamy thighs that had tantalized him. Oh, how she'd tempted him when he'd found her nude. In seconds he could be inside her. He could take her to heights of which she'd never dreamed.

But Emma hadn't asked to be ravished. She'd asked for a wee kiss. And then his mind had instantly plunged into the gutter.

I'm a rogue of the worst sort.

He forced himself to pull back and wipe a hand across his mouth. "Forgive me."

Hurt contorted her features before she whipped around

and hid her face in her palms. "I'm sorry. I-I-I thought you *liked* kissing." A peal of tortured anguish ripped from her throat.

He placed a hand on her shoulder. "'Tis not that. I pushed you too far."

She batted his fingers away. "No, you did not! I asked you."

"I did. Too much. You released my wicked beast within. I wanted to—" He cut himself off before he proved exactly how barbaric his thoughts had been.

"Wanted to what?"

"Don't ask," he growled, scowling as if his hard and dark features would make her stand down.

"I'm so confused. Why is my entire body trembling, yet you are angry?"

"I'm not angry."

"Do not try to tell me you are anything but. I hear the ire in your voice."

"I may be cross, though it is not you with whom I am irritated."

She threw out her hands and started away, right for a break in the wall, leading to a sheer drop to jagged rocks. "There are only the two of us here."

He hastened forward. "Stop!"

Albert barked, clamping her skirts in his teeth as Ciar wrapped a hand around her wrist.

Emma shrieked as he yanked her back and swept her into his arms. His heart nearly exploded in his chest. "Good God, woman, you were about to fall to your death."

And judging by the dog's hellacious barking, Albert agreed.

She jabbed the heel of her hand into his chest. "Then why did you stop me?"

"Because I—" Damn, every time he opened his mouth he

dug himself deeper. "Because I cannot bear to see anything bad happen to you."

"Put me down."

Ciar obeyed.

Wrapping her fingers around Albert's collar, she walked in a circle, took a few steps, then stopped. "It appears I am entirely at your mercy." A tear slid down her cheek. There she stood, the bravest woman Ciar had ever met, and she was devastated.

Because of him.

She wanted an adventure. She wanted to be reckless, as she'd put it, be free of the shackles of her disability. And now he'd smashed her dreams and made her feel undesirable.

I should be strung up by my thumbs.

He took her hand, trying not to squeeze it too hard—not to let his emotion show in his touch. "It is myself with whom I am angry. You stirred a fire deep within me, and it would be wrong of me to take advantage...of you."

* * *

"These oatcakes will fill our bellies," said Ciar, his spatula tapping the iron hob over the fire.

Emma picked up two wooden plates from a basket by the hearth. "I wish I were able to help with that."

"You have. You mixed the oats."

She pursed her lips as she set the table. Any other woman ought to be able to manage the cooking, but she'd been involved with only meal planning at Glenmoriston. "Where did you learn to prepare meals?"

"A man must eat when he's driving cattle to market. If he doesn't learn a few tricks, he'll starve."

"But do your men not tend to the cooking when you're droving?"

"Aye, mostly. Though when I was a lad my da ensured I prepared most of the meals whenever we were away from home's hearth."

"You're lucky."

He chuckled. His deep, resonate laugh always made her feel warm inside...even if he didn't like her as much as she adored him. "Few would see it that way."

As soon as Emma sat, Albert put his head in her lap. Petting him made a wee flicker of warmth spread through her insides. The dog had a way of lifting her spirits, bless him.

"You're managing to find your way around the chamber well," said Ciar.

"As I mentioned before, Albert and I counted paces after you left this morn." She should have opted to bathe first; then she would have been finished before Ciar returned.

Good heavens, it had been a day of mortifying humiliation. As least she ought to be mortified with herself. Truly, Emma had been embarrassed half to death when he'd found her stark naked. But he didn't seem to notice her awkwardness. His actions were so incredibly gentle, his voice soothing. She couldn't recall a maid being so meticulous, so careful or tender with the donning of hose. Rolling stockings up one's leg was an everyday occurrence done with efficiency if not haste.

But when Ciar helped her, it was as if someone opened a window on a spring day to the beautiful songs of birds, and scents of fresh flowers and rain. If she allowed herself to believe it, she would say Ciar applied himself to the task with affection. But perhaps she had imagined it.

Yet it seemed so genuine, did it not?

Bubbles floated in Emma's stomach. Her breasts tingled along with a yearning deep inside her body, one she couldn't describe. The same yen had been overwhelmingly intense when they'd kissed in the corridor at Achnacarry. Goodness, that fleeting, stolen moment seemed so long ago.

She tapped her fingers against her mouth. Why were her lips still buzzing from the delight of it?

Emma mustn't allow herself to dream. What promised to be wonderful had ended badly.

I'm so confused!

Why had Ciar grown so angry after she'd asked him to kiss her? Yes, he said he was upset with himself, but was he truly? Emma knew she'd broken every etiquette rule imaginable in being so forward. And she must never, ever do so again or risk infuriating him all the more. Oh, dear, what if he thought her an insufferable trollop?

She pondered the idea while she shifted her fingers from her lips to her neck. If he was not attracted to her, then why had he kissed her in the first place? Also, his words had directly conflicted with his actions. Something greater than a frivolous kiss had passed between them. She knew it. *You stirred a fire deep within me.* Those words affected Emma more potently than anything he'd ever said to her.

Did Ciar have any idea of the enormity of the bonfire he stirred within her breast?

"Here we are." He set the food on the table. It smelled nutty, and the heat of it warmed her face. "We'll have to live with this simple fare until Livingstone arrives. Two oatcakes or three?"

"Two should suffice, thank you."

"Would you like a slice of apple as well?"

"Please."

Her mouth watered as he cut into the aromatic fruit and put it on her plate.

The oatcake was bland and rather tasteless, but a bite of apple helped to make it more palatable. "This is delicious."

His knife tapped the plate as he snorted. "And here I thought you weren't one to tell tall tales."

She slipped a morsel of food down for Albert. "'Tis better than going hungry."

"Aye."

"Hello inside!" bellowed a deep voice.

Albert launched into a maelstrom of barking.

Emma snapped her fingers. "Come behind."

As the dog obeyed, Ciar's chair scraped the floor. "Livingstone, 'tis so late I didn't think you'd come until the morrow."

"Had to wait until dark, and then I made like I was sailing to Mull and tacked around behind Kerrera. The mainland is crawling with redcoated bastards. Uh...pardon me, Miss Emma."

She held out her fingers. "No apology necessary. They *are* bastards."

The gentleman gave the back of her hand a rough peck. "Beg your pardon, but how the blazes did a wee lassie end up rescuing this enormous bull of a man from a fortress like Fort William?"

Heat rushed to her face while she considered the utter incredulity in his tone. "It seems Robert's lessons in lock picking finally came of some use."

"Truth?" asked Livingstone as if he still had difficulty believing it. "Leave it to Grant to teach his sister to pick locks."

"She risked a great deal," said Ciar. "More than I would expect of any man."

"Well, I'm glad of it. Needless to say, somehow or other we would have found a way to slip inside, mark me."

"Pull up a wine cask and join us." Ciar's chair creaked. "And what news aside from the redcoats infesting my lands?"

"Nothing new, I suppose." A barrel made a hollow echo through the vault. "The kingdom is up in arms about the succession of the Hanoverian king."

"And are there murmurs of civil war?"

"Clans from Glasgow to Skye are ready to take up arms."

"'Tis as I thought." Ciar heaved an enormous sigh. "Will you join me in a dram of whisky?"

The cork popped from the bottle. "Don't mind if I do. Would you like a spot, Miss Emma?"

"Of whisky?"

"Why not?" asked Ciar. "You're a fugitive as am I and on your greatest adventure. A dollop in your water might do the trick."

Before she uttered an objection, the spirit plopped into her glass. Robert enjoyed the drink, why not give it a try? She raised the cup and sniffed and then took a timid taste. "Mm. It has a rich, peaty essence."

"Exactly how I like it," said Braemar. "Though it burns like hellfire when ye drink it straight."

She sipped and swirled it in her mouth. "If it burns, then why not always mix it with water?"

"Once one grows accustomed to the fire, diluting such a delicacy seems like a sacrilege," said Ciar. "Livingstone, did Archie tell you to bring my weapons?"

"Aye, and food as well. A dirk and sword are wrapped in the leather parcel, and food stores are still in the boat."

Emma leaned forward on her elbow. "You didn't happen to bring along a skein of wool and some knitting needles . . . or a harp perchance?" Of course she didn't expect a positive response, but it would be nice to have some things to occupy her thoughts. Especially after today.

"Are you weary from the tedium already?" asked Ciar.

"Nay, but I like having something to occupy my hands."

"Ye could practice picking the locks on the cellar doors," said Livingstone. "It seems it is an indispensable skill—one which may come in handy should we need to march on Kensington palace."

Laughter resounded through the cellar accompanied by a raucous yip from Albert. But the joviality gradually faded until the chamber was filled with slight hisses from the coal fire. A chill coursed down the outsides of Emma's arms. It was as if the three of them suddenly realized the gravity of their situation.

The whisky cork popped again on Ciar's side of the table this time. He poured thrice—even adding another dollop to her cup. "Three red-coated dragoons ambushed Tommy MacIntyre on the Inverlochy-Spean Bridge Road. The poor man hadn't a chance—dirked in the back he was."

Livingstone's cup thudded on the table. "The murdering asps."

"I couldn't ride around and let it pass."

"No bloody chance. I wouldn't have been able to, either."

"Hellfire and damnation," Ciar cursed. "When I confronted them, a third struck me from behind. I never saw him."

"How convenient for the backbiters."

Ciar heaved a long sigh. "Wilcox would have already put a noose around my neck if it weren't for the unrest."

The man-at-arms scoffed. "Thought hanging ye would cause a riot?"

"Aye."

"Well, the governor was bloody right—for a host of reasons. But they're looking for you everywhere. Both of you. And they'll be here next, mark me."

Emma clutched her arms across her midriff. "Nonetheless, they won't find us, will they?"

"Not if we remain hidden." Ciar gave her a reassuring pat on the shoulder. "Livingstone, I need you to locate the Irishman, Kelly. Wilcox and the others will not ken he's my man. Have him strike up a friendship with the sentinels named Riley and Manfred—a close friendship."

Ciar sipped his whisky before slamming the cup onto the table. "And the third—I want to sever that bastard's balls."

Covering her mouth, Emma snorted. "I daresay, that is what he deserves."

"Forgive my vulgar tongue, lass."

In truth, she liked that he felt comfortable speaking so freely in her presence. It made her feel more a part of the solution. Besides, it wasn't as if she hadn't heard such things from her brother's lips.

Ciar stood and began to pace. "Once Kelly kens their comings and goings, we'll nab them all at once."

"We, sir?" asked Livingstone. "But you mustn't be seen."

"Did you reckon I'd hide away whilst you and the men have all the fun?"

"Aye, and I recommend it as well."

"I agree," said Emma, breaking off a bit of oatcake and swirling it in her mouth.

Ciar hit the table, making everything rattle. "Enough. Send word to Archie once Kelly wheedles his way into their confidence. I want to personally flay those bastards."

Livingstone stood as well. "Before or after they've confessed?"

"Wheesht. Keep the supplies coming, and if you can manage it bring some knitting needles and wool—keep mum and tell no one who they're for."

"My word is my oath."

"Thank you," Emma said, offering her hand. "But do not risk bringing anything here for me if there is any danger that doing so might reveal our whereabouts."

Chapter Seventeen

*W*ith powerful strokes, Ciar pulled himself through the water, willing the iciness to cool the flame burning just beneath his skin. Back and forth he swam, each lap stronger than the last.

Three days had passed, and he was already restless beyond all imagination. He hated waiting for anything. Worse, biding his time while the bonniest lass in the Highlands pattered about trying to keep amused was all but killing him.

Emma's intoxicating scent wafting through the cellars tormented him with his every breath. The lass need only walk past and she turned his head with her floral bouquet. She was happy and affable and everything he'd ever dreamed of in a woman. She hummed with the most alluring alto voice he'd ever heard. And she grew more and more irresistible by the moment.

By his blood, he would exhaust the lust coursing through his body. He was close friends with the lass's brother.

They'd marched into more brawls and battles together than he could remember. In no way could he ruin their alliance—handed down from their forefathers.

Ciar's jaw twitched.

Bless it, he would not ravish Grant's sister. Not ever.

Then his eyebrow arched.

Not unless she agreed to be his wife.

Ciar stopped kicking, treaded water, and looked to the shore.

Emma sat on a log of driftwood rubbing a clamshell between her fingertips and ignoring Albert, who was splashing through the water, chasing fish and yipping as if he was pleased to remain on Kerrera for the rest of his days.

God's bones, she was a vision.

A wave crashed over his head, and he kicked his feet against the pull of the undertow.

Emma had good breeding for certain. The Grants and the MacDougalls were both powerful clans. But could Emma bear him an heir? She'd been born without sight because she had come too early. Hadn't Robert said so?

Mayhap she can.

It was Ciar's duty to continue the Dunollie line. He had no siblings to step into the role. And he'd be obstinate enough to defy death if his cousin were still in line to inherit. Truth be told, Ciar needed an heir posthaste with all this business of being falsely accused on top of impending war.

But then again, he mustn't give the idea a second thought. Not until he cleared his name.

A mammoth wave smacked him in the back of the head and dragged him under, sending his body tumbling downward to the chilly depths. Pushing off the sandy sea floor, he fought for the surface, coughing like a seal as he let the surf carry him to the shore.

Worry stretched Emma's features as she stood and clutched her fists to her chest. "Are you all right?"

Completely naked, he trudged onto the beach, his cock just as hard as it had been when he'd started. "Aye." He coughed. "Swallowed a bit of seawater is all."

She seemed to watch him, though her eyes were eerily vacant as they always were. Glittering blue, they were recessed a bit, but Ciar always felt the color made her look more mysterious. Moreover, when Emma Grant smiled, everyone followed, because the happiness she carried in her heart bore enough light to illuminate the great hall at Edinburgh Castle. Her smiles were infectious and addictive.

She stepped toward him. "Are you finished with your swim?"

He glanced downward, ever so glad he didn't need to hide his nakedness from her. God's stones, would he be hard for the rest of his days? "I am," he said, turning his back and reaching for his plaid.

"I've been collecting shells." She gestured toward a pile. "I'm not sure what to do with them now, but they are the most amazing shapes. If you hold the large ones to your ear, you can hear the surf."

Ciar dried himself then tucked the tartan around his waist. "Can you?"

"Aye, we have an enormous shell in the library at Glenmoriston, and Robert says it sounds like being adrift in the midst of a calm sea."

"Poetic of him."

"Indeed. He doesn't usually mince words." She laughed, picking up the clamshell. "I think I'll keep this one and put it on my mantel. That way I will always remember Gylen Castle by the shore on a wee isle, and my great adventure."

"I doubt you will ever forget this . . . *mishap*."

"Do not say that. It is an experience of a lifetime, and I intend to enjoy every moment."

"Well then, let us pray you're not captured by redcoats and sent to the gallows." Ciar winced. He shouldn't have said such a thing.

"Oh, no, that cannot happen. You said we were safe."

He slipped the shell from her fingertips and held it to his ear. "Och, you're right, the sea is quite prevalent in this one."

She grinned, making rays of sunlight fill his chest. "Albert loves it here."

"Perhaps Albert and I have a great deal in common."

"But I thought you were going mad."

"Did I say so?"

"Nay, but you've fidgeted enough."

He returned the shell. "I don't fidget."

"Very well, oiling and sharpening your weapons three times a day isn't fidgeting, it's . . . hmm . . . it's . . ."

"Being prepared." He grasped her elbow, the gesture becoming second nature and comfortable. "What shall we eat for supper? The lamb pottage, or would you care for more of my delicious oatcakes and dried beef?"

"Let us make it interesting and have oatcakes *and* pottage."

"Excellent idea."

He started for the tunnel, but Emma didn't budge. Bending forward, she hooked the leash onto Albert's collar. "I'd like him to lead me."

"I don't mind helping."

"Aye, but you won't always be nearby to take my hand. And it has been liberating to have the dog to train. I cannot thank you enough for giving him to me."

"He's already been more useful than I'd ever dreamed he'd be."

Honestly, Emma had been so instantly taken with Albert that Ciar had purchased the dog as a companion. But even though he was still young and excitable, he'd become invaluable. Ciar walked beside them, ready to catch Emma if she should stumble. The ground was craggy and uneven, and there were stones strewn about, covered by slippery moss. Amazingly, Albert walked slowly and picked his way around obstacles while the lass intently followed him as if the pair were a team working in harmony.

* * *

"The wine is fruity," Emma said, drinking her second glass. Livingstone had brought a new cask along with the stores, and she preferred it to whisky, which made her head swim much too quickly, though she mustn't overindulge in any spirit.

Ciar sipped, followed by a soft but guttural swallow. "It *is* nice."

Oh, how she adored the sounds he made. "What shall we do this eve?"

"You could sing for me."

"I think I'd rather listen to you sing. Besides, I prefer to play the harp."

His cup tapped the table. "But your voice is so lovely. 'Tis soothing."

She batted her hand through the air. "How do you ken?"

"I've heard you humming and quite enjoyed it. Your voice reminds me of an effervescent yet mellow viola—similar to when you played 'The Selkie.' "

Butterflies swarmed in her stomach, which they had been doing far too often of late. And Emma didn't really want to sing, she wanted to enjoy something *with* him. "I have an idea. Do you have a chessboard?"

"I do. In my library at Dunollie. 'Tis quite nice, made of walrus ivory."

"I'd like to see it someday, though the board will do us no good at all at the moment." She drummed her fingers on her cup. "We ought to play a game."

"Hmm. What kinds of games do you know?"

Emma thought back. She liked chess because she could feel the pieces and picture the board in her mind's eye— though Robert always became overtly irritated when she knocked over his king...on purpose, of course. The mere thought brought a snigger to her lips.

She couldn't play cards unless she had a partner, and never had any luck at dice. Oh, yes, a brilliant idea came to mind. "At Yuletide when we were trapped indoors we used to play questions and commands."

"Is not the game played with a group of people?"

"Aye, including cousins and clan, we always had a large gathering at Christmas when Da was alive."

"And now?"

"Not as many visitors, though I reckon that will change..." Oh, dear, she'd almost said *once the bairn is born,* and she'd promised Janet she'd not mention it. "Um...once Robert and Janet have children. Have you played?"

"If I have, I do not recall the rules."

"Well, there's a commander, and everyone else is a subject. The commander asks a question of one of the others, and if the subject refuses or cannot answer satisfactorily, the poor commoner must pay a forfeit or have his or her face smutted."

"Smutted?" Ciar asked, laughing.

"Indeed, fouled with all manner of vile things, like mint

sauce and whipped cream or even dust from the floor. Once Robert had his face blackened by charcoal."

"And he stood for it?" Another deep laugh rumbled through the cavern. "Now that I would have liked to see."

Oh, how Ciar's laugh could make everything shine with happiness. "It was quite some time ago. He couldn't have been more than seventeen, and I think he rather fancied the lass who smutted him."

"That explains it. Your brother would only humor a woman—never a man." Ciar shifted in his seat. "What constitutes a forfeit?"

"The subject must do something of the commander's bidding."

"For example...?"

"Well, there was the time Lewis Pratt had to drop to his knees, put his head under Mrs. Tweedie's hem, and low like a cow." She tapped a finger to her temple. "Or there was the time I had to waddle around the drawing room squawking and pretending I was a duck."

"What a sight that must have been." Ciar snorted as if he was holding in an urge to chuckle. "I imagine it is best for the poor subjects just to answer the commander's question in the first place."

"Exactly. However, it is much more fun if they do not." Though feeling a wee bit tipsy, Emma took another sip of wine. "Shall I assume the role of commander first?"

"By all means."

In a heartbeat, heat spread across her cheeks. There were so many questions she wanted to ask and just as many she didn't dare. Perhaps another cup of wine would help her to relax. As she poured, she squared her shoulders and assumed a practiced air of composure. "Let us start with something simple. If you had three wishes, what would they be?"

"Hmm. Are the wishes for myself, or can they be political?"

"Yourself, of course. Bringing politics into it would turn an enjoyable game into something far too serious."

Pacing herself, she took only the slightest of sips while she wriggled in her seat ever so anxious to hear what he had to say.

He took his time drumming his fingers. "To begin with, I'd wish to have the false charges brought against me dropped and stricken from the record."

"A seriously important subject. However, given the circumstances it's exactly what my first wish would be." She leaned in, unable to help the grin stretching her lips. What would he say next? Wish to marry a princess? Wish for the sturdiest and fastest horse in the Highlands? "And the second?"

"I'd ask for health and happiness of clan and kin."

Unamused, Emma sat back, almost teetering. "Dull but important. I suppose I'll grant you that."

"And lastly I'd like the harvests to be prosperous for the rest of my days."

"Alas, I do not think you have the gist of it as of yet. Here I was champing at the bit thinking of all the fantastical things you might wish for. You could have been far more creative."

"What would you suggest?"

"Perhaps a new fleet of sea galleys or a magical sword that never needs sharpening." She looked away. *Or a bonny wife who will love you forever.*

"But I asked for things that are important to me. Did I satisfy the commander's wishes, or must I pay a forfeit?"

"Nay, I believe your last two wishes could have been far more astounding. You must do better at surprising me.

I am afraid you'll have to pay a forfeit...but not one too dastardly, since you are new to the game." Emma swayed in place as if she were playing a cheery folk tune. "You must kiss Albert on his belly, and I want descriptive details of every step."

The dog's toenails tapped across the stone floor when he heard his name mentioned.

"His belly, aye?"

"Mm hmm."

"I suppose a kiss is better than having my face marked with charcoal." Ciar grumbled something not even Emma could hear, and then added, "Come, ye overgrown urchin."

Albert moved between them.

"Put your paws up here." Ciar thumped his chest. "I've taken hold of the dog's arms. Now I'm diving for his under-belly. Mmmwa, ye hairy beasty!"

Albert yowled and shook, his tail slapping Emma's knee.

Emma clapped then scrubbed her knuckles through the dog's fur. "It seems the laddie enjoyed the attention."

"Aye." Ciar pounded the table with three quick raps. "Now I'm the commander, am I not?"

"You are." She sipped again, letting the fruitiness of the wine tantalize her tongue. "Give me your worst."

"Very well." His voice turned serious, and then he hesitated. "If your eyes were opened, what is the first thing you would want to see?"

Emma's breath seized in her throat. Oh, Lord in heaven, did he not know how often she'd prayed for the gift of sight, if only for a day? She would rush outside and take in all the colors from the grass to the sky to the flowers.

Ciar sat very still. He expected an answer. And though she wanted to experience everything, from nature to the colors of silks and fire, there was one thing she desired to see most of all.

"You," she blurted as her face burned. Clapping her hands over her cheeks, she was absolutely certain her blush had nothing to do with the wine. Had she really spoken such a shameless thing aloud? Goodness, if she kept flirting with him, he might make her stay in one of the ruined, dank vaults.

The rough pads of his fingers swept across her hand. "Och, I'm not a handsome man, lass. You may not like what you see."

"To me you're handsome. You're beautiful. And Betty says by the girth of your shoulders Robert was smart to make you an ally of Clan Grant."

"Betty? What remarks has your lady's maid uttered about me?"

Emma's head swam with hundreds of responses, most of them unutterable. "Um . . . you're rough-hewn but robust." *And such a man attracts me like no other.*

"And you? Are you of the same mind?"

"I told you I was." Before she thought better of it, Emma leaned forward and placed her hands on his cheeks. With a sharp inhale, he stiffened and grabbed her wrists. Cringing, she drew away. "Apologies. I should have asked permission first."

"The err is mine. I wasn't expecting you to 'see' me at the moment." His grip eased as he drew her fingers back to his beard. "I must ask Livingstone to bring a razor."

"The hair feels softer than a few days ago. And so thick. I'd wager it makes you look fiercer than before." She couldn't help but explore more. "You have a prominent nose, but I think it suits the ridges of your cheeks."

Ciar closed his eyes as she moved upward, the lashes

tickling her fingers. His brow was broad and framed by a great deal of hair, soft, but masculine.

"It is decided. You are inarguably handsome, and there is nothing you can say to change my mind." She forced herself to draw away, lest she let the wine take over her sensibilities and kiss him, which she absolutely must not do. "The first thing I want to set eyes on is you. And that was not an easy question to answer, mind you. You could have laughed in my face or, worse, ridiculed me. Therefore, I will *not* be smutted, no, no, no."

"Agreed, though I didn't realize subjects could be so insistent," he said, chuckling. "I'm afraid you are far better at this game than I."

"My turn." She cleared her throat. "Did you swim... um..." Good heavens, how could she finish? And why the devil hadn't she considered the nature of her question before she opened her mouth?

"You are well aware I swam this day."

"That wasn't my query."

"Very well." He cleared his throat. "Did I *swimmmm*...?"

"Naked."

Silence.

Emma wiped a hand down her face as the air in the soundless room grew more uncomfortable. She didn't need to touch him to sense the intensity of his stare boring through her.

"Am I utterly shameful for asking?" she whispered, hoping he heard, but praying he hadn't.

"What did you think?" he asked, blast him. He was supposed to answer directly, not pose a question.

Emma bit her lip, her mind racing. *I thought you disrobed and walked into the surf without a stitch of clothing on your person. That very moment was exactly when I would have*

*given my soul for a brief gift of sight. Och aye, to see you—
the brawny Highlander who preoccupies my dreams—to see
all of you would have granted me a memory to cherish for
all my days.*

"You were bare, were you not?" she asked, trying to
sound unperturbed, trying not to reveal how fast her heart
raced between her breasts. But the ensuing silence made
her so very self-aware. In an effort to mask her mortifi-
cation, she pounded the table. "The commander demands
an answer!"

"I was," Ciar said boldly before he drank, though his
cup scarcely made a noise when he set it down. Why had
he been reluctant to tell the truth? "I...ah...er...I must
apologize for my vulgarity, disrobing in your presence. I
didn't think..."

Emma clapped a hand over her chest to prevent her heart
from leaping across the room. "Did you speak true when
you said I stirred a fire deep within you?"

"Ah..." He audibly gulped. "That is two questions,
commander."

"Did you?" she demanded, pounding her fist once more.

"If you believe I would lie about something so deeply
personal that was uttered with the gravest of humility and
intended only to be heard by your ears and yours alone, you
are quite mistaken."

Unable to sit for a moment longer, Emma grasped his
shoulder and stood. Slowly, she slid her fingers down the
length of his arm, stopping only to swirl a gentle touch over
the back of his hand.

Never in her life had she felt so bold or so empowered.
Might it be the wine? Nay...not this night.

He felt something for her—something affectionate, just
as she did for him. She refused to allow any other doubts

to cloud her mind. The only thing that mattered was being there alone with Ciar MacDougall, a man who had always treated her with respect. A man she had admired all her life.

She slid onto his lap and laced her arms around his neck. "You may have spoken true, but the commander demands you pay a forfeit for wounding me this afternoon."

Not waiting for his response, she moved closer, first finding his lips with the pad of her thumb, then sealing her lips with his.

Ciar gripped her waist powerfully, his mouth softening against hers. Fresh in her mind was the stolen kiss in the corridor at Achnacarry, and as she swayed against him, she pulled on that experience to impart the most determined, passionate kiss she could muster.

Encouraged by his shudder, she plunged her fingers into his hair and explored with her hands. She adored the natural curl. His sturdy neck. His powerful shoulders.

She adored him kissing her.

As his lips gently slid away, she embraced him, caressing her cheek over his. "You have no idea of the torch I carry in my heart for you."

"Och, *mo leannan,*" he purred. "I am not a saint. Being intimate with you makes me crave more—so much more."

"I never assumed you were anything but a man, flesh and blood. I've said it before and I'll say it again, I am on the only adventure of my life. I want to experience everything. I may die a spinster, but I intend to have the memory of this time with you to cherish in my heart for the rest of my days."

His lips gradually moved over hers. His tongue swept into her mouth with slow, languid strokes. His mouth was silky and warm, and she never wanted this moment to end.

Emma's head swam, whether from the wine or from the

hot desire coursing through her blood she did not know. She needed, craved more. More kissing, more of him.

She gasped as his lips trailed to her neck. "Show me what happens between a man and a woman. I want to know. I *have* to know."

He froze, his body rigid against her. "Och, I cannot take your innocence."

"Not even if I give it to you freely?"

"I must respect you," he whispered. But he didn't push her away. Instead, a big arm braced her back while the other swept under her knees. "However...I can no longer resist you," he growled as he stood.

Emma sighed as she curled into him, smoothing her hand over his chest.

Ever so gently, he set her on the bed and slid in beside her. "Are you certain you want me to bed you?"

She cupped his cheek with her hand then slid it down over his hammering heart. "Please. I want this. I want you."

"Then lie back and I will show you what it means to be worshipped."

She rolled her shoulders into the pillow. "You tease me."

He tugged open the lace on her kirtle. "Never."

Emma gasped as she caught his fingers. She had some understanding of how it all worked. She'd heard enough comments by the servants, but otherwise, she was two and twenty and totally clueless as to how men and women actually made love. "What are you doing?"

"Untying your bodice so that I may kiss you..." He brushed his lips over the top of her breast. "Here."

She shivered with delight. "Oh."

"Does that meet with your approval?" The rumble of his voice vibrated across her skin.

"Aye."

"No stays?" he asked.

Scraping her teeth over the corner of her mouth, her shoulder inched up. "There wasn't time."

"All the better," he said.

As he tugged her shift away from her breast, she felt no bashfulness. The fire in her skin was too hot to be shy. She arched her back as he took her nipple into his mouth and swirled his warm tongue around it.

"You need no stays. Your breasts are perfect," he said as he licked her tender flesh.

Perfect? He is perfect.

His hands trailed down her body and lower over her thighs and to her calves.

She writhed with the allure of his touch. "What are you doing now?"

He pulled off her one boot and then the other. "I intend to strip you bare."

She crossed her hands over her naked breasts. "Completely?"

"How else can I feast my eyes upon all of you?"

"But—"

"Hmm?"

"What if you don't like what you see?"

"Och." He pulled the ribbon on her garter and tugged away her stocking. "There's no chance of that. I'm certain of it."

Yes, he had seen her once before. *Fair is fair.* "Then I must see you bare as well."

"After you," he growled, removing her second stocking.

Smiling with the anticipation of running her hands over Ciar's naked body, Emma moaned as he kissed the bottom of her foot. "Every place your lips touch makes the fire within me burn hotter."

"Mm," he agreed as if he knew exactly how she felt.

The mattress depressed as he crawled upward, grasping her skirts. In a heartbeat, he tugged them up her back and over her head.

"My God." Those two words came out low and breathless.

Emma instantly crossed her arms over her body, but he caught her wrists. "No. You mustn't cover yourself. I-I've never seen such a beautiful sight in all my days."

"Truly?" she whispered.

"Och, if no one has told you that you are a goddess, then allow me to be the first."

"And you are a magician."

His lips nuzzled her neck. "Why would you say that?"

"Because only you can make me feel as if I am indeed a goddess."

"My goddess."

Floating on a pillow of happiness, she untied and tugged away his cravat. "Now you."

"I'm easy." He pulled her up to sit and guided her fingers to the circular brooch at his shoulder. "Release this, unfasten my belt, and remove my shirt, and I'll be bare."

"What about your hose and garters?"

"Already gone."

Scraping her teeth over her bottom lip, she carefully unfastened his brooch and let him slip it from her fingers. Her heartbeat raced as she slid the plaid from his shoulder, then traced her hands downward and found his belt. "Are you ready?"

"Aye," he said hoarsely.

It only took a tug and he was right, the wool pooled around them.

After dropping the kilt to the floor, she clutched the hem of his shirt and pulled it over his head. Sitting before him, she was scarcely able to breathe. "You're bare to me like you were outside?"

He took her wrist, turned it over and kissed her palm. "I am."

She braced her hands on his shoulders, quite unsure of how to proceed. Instead, she allowed her instincts to take over and urged him down to the bed. "Then let me see you."

Chapter Eighteen

Never in all his days had Ciar allowed himself to be utterly prone to a woman. But then he'd never worshipped a woman the way he did Emma. He reclined into the comfort of the mattress and closed his eyes.

"Where should I begin?" she asked.

"You've seen my face. How about starting there?" he asked, wondering how she would react when she discovered he was harder than an oak branch.

She kneeled beside him and cupped his cheeks. "My bonny man."

Her hands brushed and swirled down his arms, tracing the lines of his muscles. "I already ken how strong you are."

"Some call me a beast."

Back up she went, rubbing her palms over his hairy chest. "You are no beast."

He shuddered as she closed her mouth over his nipple. "Mm."

"Do you like me to kiss you here?"

"Aye," he croaked, unable to utter another word. His cock tapped his stomach, and if her warm tongue continued to tease him, he'd soon lose his seed.

Ciar allowed himself to breathe as her hands continued down his stomach. "Is every inch of you hard?"

"Yes," he managed, his voice strained.

And then her fingers brushed his cock.

As they both gasped, Emma grew very still. "What is that?" She didn't know?

"My . . . *sex*."

Understanding crossed her face while she boldly took hold of his shaft. "I . . . ah . . . never realized a man's member could be so rigid." Ciar's eyes rolled back as she stroked her fingers along the length. "Is it always like this?"

"Of late." He chuckled, stilling her hand. "But not usually. Whenever my cock grows hard, it means I want to be inside you." Unable to stand the torture a moment longer, he coaxed her to her side, traced his finger along the curve of her hip and into the soft, coppery curls.

"Inside?" she asked.

"Here." He slipped his finger through her parting and found the channel. Jesu, she was so wet, so ready, and he wanted her more than anything. "Like this, but the fit is much tighter."

Gasping, she arched her back, her body shuddering. "Am I falling ill?"

"Nay, lass. You're only beginning to experience the heat of passion."

"There's more?"

He moved over her, angling his shoulders between her legs. God, she smelled tempting. "The best is yet to come."

She curled up, her fingers finding his hair and tugging. "I'm certain you shouldn't be *there*!"

"Och, this is exactly where I ought to be." He rubbed the pad of his thumb over her tiny button, gazing up the length of her. Such a stunning image—womanly hips tapering to a slender waist and breasts just large enough for his mouth. "Now lie back and allow pleasure to take you on the wildest adventure yet."

The lass's fingers released as she collapsed against the pillows.

"That's better," he purred.

Sliding his finger inside her, he tempted her slowly, watching her lips part with her stuttered breathing. In and out, around and around, deeper into her hot, wet core.

True to the lass's adventurous nature, soon she draped her arms across her forehead and moved her hips with the rhythm. Tantalized by the seductive dance, Ciar's cock throbbed and leaked a bit of seed.

Keeping his eyes upon her body, he continued stroking his finger as he licked her.

Gasping, Emma bucked. "My God!"

"Ride with it, *mo leannan*," he growled, licking again.

When her hips worked faster, he clamped his mouth over her and suckled, rapidly moving his finger.

"I see . . . !"

But he didn't stop to ask.

"I see staaaaaaaaars!" she cried with one final arch of her back.

His heart thrumming with wonder, Ciar gradually slowed the tempo, placing his hand on her mound of curls. "Stars?" he asked.

"Light darted through my eyes. I'm certain of it," she gasped. "Is that normal?"

"Aye." He crawled up beside her and traced a finger

around her breast. "You described it perfectly—stars shooting through your vision. I've seen it before myself."

"'Tis a miracle."

"The joining of a man and a woman is God's greatest gift."

She rolled to her side and stroked his arm, her eyes closed as they oft were. "Is it like this every time?"

"It can be, but..."

"What?"

"I believe there is nothing in this world as staggering as when a man and a woman join in passion."

Her beguiling fingers moved to his chest, and he shuddered at the lightness of her touch. No woman had ever brought him so close to losing control merely with caresses. Every time she touched him, he was moved by the deeply curious and intense exploration of her hands.

"You have not been pleasured," she whispered.

Ciar tensed his muscles, willing away his lust. "One thing at a time, lassie. Your pleasure comes first, and I will not take you until..."

"Until?"

"Och, I am a wanted man. I'm in no position to make an offer of marriage. And mark me, lass, I ken you will marry one day, and that honor should be reserved for your husband."

Emma said nothing for a long while, her fingers exploring.

She slid her fingers lower, down to his abdomen. "Well, then. 'Tis time you showed me how I can bring you pleasure just as you did for me."

Ciar's breath seized in his chest. "Nay, you are a gentlewoman. I'd never ask you to lower yourself in such a way."

Her fingers tickled their way down to his navel while

she bit the corner of her mouth. "I think we ought to make a truce."

"Oh?" He brushed a kiss over her forehead. "What is that brilliant mind of yours thinking up now?"

"Whilst we're tucked away in this fantastical place, I am merely a woman and you are a man. All societal rules and superstitions that surround us do not play a part in here. What matters is you and..." She slipped her hand to his cock, wrapped her fingers around it, and squeezed. "*Me*."

Ciar groaned. "When you have hold of me like that, I am powerless to resist."

Her fingers eased. "Am I hurting you?"

Wrapping his hand around hers, he showed her how to pleasure him. "Having your hands on me sends me wild—but 'tis the most tender place on a man. When you hold it gently and slide your hand up and down, it is almost like being inside you."

Ciar's eyes rolled back as the student took to her lessons with utmost precision.

Emma turned up her face as her lips parted, making her appear as seductive as sin. "May I lick you?"

"God, woman."

"May I?"

"Aye," he croaked. "But only if you so desire."

"Mm," she purred while she scooted down and licked his throbbing tip. "Like this?"

He grunted with his thrust. "Yes."

"You like it. I can tell."

Baring his teeth, he tried to maintain control, but it had been too bloody long.

As Emma slid him into her mouth, he guided her with light caresses and moans of pleasure, showing her what he needed.

In moments his breathing sped. Emma sensed his desire mounting and matched his pace.

"Yes, yes, yes," he growled, thrusting with the licks of her wicked tongue. One day he would have her on her back with her knees spread wide. One day he would watch the ecstasy on her face while he plunged deep inside her over and over again.

With a sharp intensity, the world around him shattered. His knees locked as his cock exploded.

Emma's grip tightened as she pulled away her mouth. "God's grace," she cursed. "You are astonishing!"

Chapter Nineteen

*E*mma came awake as Albert's nose skimmed her face. She blinked and brushed him away, much too comfortable to rise as of yet. Behind her, Ciar sighed, his arm draped across her waist. Had she ever been this content? And in such tumultuous circumstances.

Spending last night in his arms was the most wonderful experience in her life. If he asked her to marry him, she would do so this very day without hesitation.

She liked that he respected her, but the words that she replayed over and over were *I'm in no position to make an offer of marriage.*

Did that mean he intended to make an offer once he was able?

She dared not ask. In no way did she want to say or do anything to stanch the euphoria thrumming through her blood. This was her time—*their time*—and once Ciar had been cleared of any wrongdoing, they would hide no more.

She prayed Livingstone and Kelly would figure a way to bring the culprits to justice without a battle.

"Are you awake, love?" he whispered, kissing her neck.

A soft chuckle pealed from her throat. "Aye, and Albert is anxious to go out."

Ciar's arm released as he rolled to his back. "I'll tend to him."

"No." Reluctantly, she slid to her feet. "I'll do it."

She pulled a blanket around her body, counted the paces, and opened the latch. Albert brushed her wrap as he trotted past. "Come straight back, laddie."

The bed creaked, followed by Ciar's barefoot gait. "Perhaps we ought to go with him."

Emma tightened the blanket around her shoulders. "Now?"

"There's nothing like a wee dip in the Firth of Lorn as the sun rises," he said, clanging the pots by the hearth. "I'll put a kettle of water on, and by the time we've returned it will be piping hot."

"Returned from out of doors?"

"I have no idea where else we might enjoy the firth."

"But I cannot swim."

"Then we'll have to rectify that, will we not?"

Emma gulped. She'd waded in the surf before, but she had been wearing her shift at the time. "Outside without our clothing?"

"'Tis a good way to keep your things dry, lass. Besides, you are well aware I swam yesterday in the raw." Ciar took her hand. "You have a blanket, and we'll stay hidden in the cove just as I did."

Though not enamored with the idea, swimming with Ciar piqued her interest. In seclusion. Without clothing.

An adventure.

He pulled her outside, where they found Albert already in the midst of taking a dip, yapping and splashing through the waves as he chased a flock of irascible terns.

Ciar slowed the pace. "We're about to step off the path onto the beach stones."

Emma slid her foot forward. "Will they not hurt without my boots?"

"They're smooth as the tiles in my great hall."

"Hmm." She stepped, the rocks soft and cool under her toes. "Do you realize I've never been to Dunollie Castle before?"

"No? Well, that's something I hope to rectify."

She grinned. Wouldn't it be fantastical to visit Ciar's castle? Mayhap find herself lost in the corridors and wind up in his bedchamber. Oh, how naughty she had become overnight. And to think, only a handful of sennights ago when they'd arrived at Achnacarry she had abhorred leaving Glenmoriston.

He stopped, wrapped her in his arms and kissed her. "We can leave our blankets here on the driftwood."

"I reckon I like it better right here," she said as a chilly breeze curled around her legs. "Are you certain 'tis a good idea to swim so early in the morn?"

He urged her to release her grip on the blanket. "There is no better time. Besides, the water feels warmer when there's a bite to the air."

As soon as he pulled the plaid away, Emma's teeth started chattering. But she let him lead her into the surf, the water washing over her toes.

"See? It is refreshing."

"If you s-s-say so."

"Come deeper."

She followed willingly until the water slapped her thighs.

"I think this is far enough. 'Tis so cold I'm surprised there's not ice floating in the surf."

"Ice? It is August, lass. There's nay chance of ice." He gave her hand a tug. "Do ye ken the only way to brave the Highland sea?"

"Naaaaay," Emma said, positively certain she did not want to know.

"Like this!" he shouted, sweeping her off her feet and hurtling her into the surf.

"Aaaaaa!" she screeched while saltwater filled her mouth as she plunged downward. Flinging out her arms, she grappled for Ciar, kicking futilely while she sank. As water enveloped her, she fought harder, straining to keep her head above water, gasping for air.

Just as the waves pulled her under, the Highlander's powerful arms slipped beneath her and pulled her flush against his bare chest. "Refreshing, is it not?"

Shaking her head, Emma coughed. "I-I-I thought I—" She gasped. "Was going to drown."

"I'd never let you drown." He laughed, spinning her around, his deep voice resounding off the cove's walls. "I will always be here to catch you."

"Stop!" she hollered as he pulled her through the freezing surf. "Stop, you barbarian!"

But he didn't. Instead, he urged her to climb onto his back. "Wrap your arms around my neck."

"Why?" she asked, clinging to him with all her strength.

"Mayhap not quite as tightly as that," he croaked.

She loosened her arms, her teeth chattering. "S-sorry."

"I'm taking you on a wee swim across the cove. Lesson one."

"N-no, wait!"

But before the words escaped her lips, she was riding

on his back as Ciar worked his arms and legs, making the water splash everywhere. When he stopped, he wrapped an arm around her waist and coaxed her around to his front—skin to skin, her breasts molding into his chest. "Are ye still cold, lass?"

"Aye, though not as much as before." Unable to touch bottom, she wrapped her legs around him, needing warmth, needing him. "Y-you?"

"Invigorated. Och, I reckon the water on the hob ought to be steaming by now. What say you we go fill a half barrel and warm our bones?"

"Oh, yes." Her teeth chattered. A warm bath never sounded so good—as long as they were together. "We mustn't delay a moment longer!"

* * *

"Stand in front of the fire whilst I fill the half barrel," said Ciar, ushering the lass forward by the shoulders.

"I-I'm soooo c-cold."

Her lips were blue, and her entire body shivered as Albert dashed in circles around the chamber, acting as if he'd never been so happy to be dripping wet.

Ciar tucked his plaid around his hips, fetched the tub from the storeroom, and rolled it into the center of the room. "I'll just pour in the hot water and temper it with a wee bit of cold."

Clinging to her blanket, Emma nodded. "W-we have the rose soap that Nettie sent over."

"Aye."

Archie's wife had also provided a spare shift for Emma, hazelnuts, and a leg of roast mutton, bless her.

He used a folded cloth to pull the pot off the hob and

waddled across the floor so not to burn his thighs. Thank God Emma couldn't see his duck walk, nor anyone else for that matter. He'd never hear the end of it.

Once he'd readied everything, he stepped back. The soap and sponge were in a bowl beside the tub. Drying cloths were draped across a chair where they wouldn't be splashed. And Emma's lips were almost pink again.

He took her hands. "Are you ready?"

"Is it warm?"

"Aye." The dog dipped his nose into the bath and sputtered while Ciar led her across the floor. "Albert thinks so as well."

Emma snorted. "You'll have to wait your turn, ye hairy mop."

He dropped his plaid with a whoosh. "Will you mind if I step in first?"

"Will we both fit?"

"If I dangle my legs over the edge."

"Will that be comfortable for you?"

Ciar brushed her cheek with his knuckle. "With you in the bath with me, it will be like floating on a cloud."

"You say the nicest things."

"Only because you bring out the cordial ogre in me."

"Why ogre?"

Ciar submerged himself into the tub backside first. Warm water sloshed up to the center of his chest. "Because I am a beast, agreeable or nay."

"You've never been anything but pleasant toward me— pleasanter than anyone else."

"That's because kindness breeds kindness, and you're the most affable lass I've ever met." He tugged her fingers. "Can you step in and straddle me?"

"Like a horse?"

He liked the image she conjured—Lady Emma on the back of a horse wearing nothing but wild, flowing, auburn tresses. "Aye," he said throatily, his cock already so hard it tapped his stomach.

Ciar eased back and feasted his eyes on the idyllic pose she made. It made him want to be a painter simply to capture the beauty of a nymph preparing to bathe. Her medal of Saint Lucia swung forward while she braced her hands on the edge of the tub. With her eyes half-cast, she carefully climbed in with one foot and then the other. A bonny grin spread across her lips. "It is delightfully warm."

"Mm hmm." As she began to lower herself into the water, Ciar caught her wrists and stopped her. "Allow me a moment to gaze upon perfection."

Her expression grew uncertain as she tried to cross her arms over her breasts. "But it isn't natural for me to flaunt myself."

"When we are alone, there is no reason why you should not. One man, one woman, remember?" He kissed her fingers. "You're beautiful, Emma. From porcelain skin to hair of burnished fire. And whether you like it or nay, you have the figure of a goddess."

"Now I know you are telling tall tales."

Ciar tugged her onto his lap so she faced him. "Oh, no, lassie. You may be as sweet as a sugared date, but your body is made for sin."

She wriggled, making her mons slide flush against his erection. Within a heartbeat, her expression changed from one of happiness to that of seductress. "Oh, my."

"Mayhap now you understand exactly what you do to me."

"Me?"

"Yes, lass, you."

He clamped his big hands on either side of her face and

kissed her, let his tongue lazily sweep into her mouth as he rocked his hips, brushing himself along the intimate channel that would bring her undone.

Her hand searched to the side. "Should we not wash whilst the water is hot?"

Ciar collected the soap and placed it in her fingers. "If we must."

"Mayhap we can make it fun." She grinned like a contented cat as she slowly swirled the soap over his chest. He closed his eyes and breathed in the scent as Emma worked the slick bar lower and lower until she lightly brushed his member.

"May God have mercy on my soul," he growled.

"And mine," she added, wrapping her arms around him and rubbing the soap with her breasts.

Ciar dropped his head back and moaned.

Emma stiffened. "Am I hurting you?"

"Lord, no."

She scooped a handful of water and let it dribble atop his shoulder. "It feels good, then?"

"Like I'm drifting among the stars."

"I think the lather is—um—*sensuous*."

"Do it again."

This time Emma took even longer, exploring every part of his body, first making him sit forward so she could wash his back. She ran the cake under his arms and around his neck. Then she rocked away and covered herself with rose-scented bubbles. A pink tongue slipped to the corner of her mouth as she drew the soap around her breast torturously slowly. "It feels…"

"Hmm?"

"Good."

"Have you ever touched yourself like this before?"

She shook her head. "You bring out the Jezebel in me."

He *tsk*ed his tongue. "You are shameless, and I adore it."

Laughing, Emma pressed her soapy body against him and buried her face in his neck. She trailed kisses along his jaw until Ciar tilted her chin upward and captured her mouth. Still, Emma set a fervent tempo as she writhed against him. Back and forth and, holy Moses, when she rubbed herself up and down along his length, his eyes crossed.

Somewhere in the midst of the frenzy, she took hold of his shaft and rose to her knees, teasing herself, teasing him.

Ciar wanted to thrust into her so badly, he tried to think of anything to keep himself from taking her. The cattle, the accounts, Wilcox, the bloody bastard dragoons... *Emma's wet quim sliding around my cock.*

God yes, he wanted her now. He palmed her breasts and suckled each nipple, thrusting his hips upward while hot, wet woman surrounded him.

"Aaaaahhhh." A high-pitched sigh squeaked from Emma's throat—one of utter ecstasy yet of pain as well.

Ciar opened his eyes and froze.

Oh, God.

She'd done it so fast.

And he'd let her.

His bum cheeks clenched. "Are you hurting, lass?" he asked, barely able to utter a sound.

"A bit," she peeped, clinging to him, her eyes squeezed shut.

"But we agreed not to..."

"You deemed it so. I do not recall agreeing." She moved a bit. "Are you angry with me?"

How in God's name could he ever grow irritated with this selfless, talented, effervescent creature? "Never."

"T-then show me what to do next."

"Relax," he whispered, letting the muscles in his arse ease. Emma's grip softened while she exhaled with a long sigh.

"Better?" he asked.

"Mm hmm." She wriggled a bit. "What now?"

"I think it comes naturally to you, lass." He sank his fingers into her hips. "If you want to ride me, rock your hips to and fro as you were doing. But ride slow, like you're on a well-broke horse, not a colt fresh off his ma's teat."

Emma moved slowly at first, the corners of her mouth drawn downward.

"You don't have to keep going—not if it hurts."

"Sh." She plied him with a kiss, her hips working faster.

Ciar tried to let her take the reins, but when she took his nipple between her fingertips and tempted him, a shot of seed burst straight through the tip of his cock. He needed to thrust, to bury himself deep inside this woman and take her to heaven. He grabbed her hips and urged her faster, urged her to rock and swirl and...

As Emma cried out, he roared with the power of his release, clinging to her as if he'd never let go.

"God, woman, you have bewitched me mind, body, and soul."

"Och..." Still panting, she collapsed onto his shoulder. "I wish this adventure would never end."

Chapter Twenty

*T*he days blurred together. They took Albert for long walks through the cover of the glen, and Ciar even let Emma accompany him on a visit to Archie and Nettie's cottage. The passionate nights made it seem as if they were living in a dream. He chuckled every time he thought about how long he had known Emma and how he'd always pushed aside his feelings for her. Had he been in love with the woman since she was a wee lass of seven?

Most likely.

No woman in all of Scotland was remotely like Emma Grant. She was curious about everything and looked at the world as though every day held something magical. And it did because she was alive in it.

Ciar almost forgot about the charge of murder hanging over his head until Livingstone returned.

Emma was practicing with Albert on the lead. The dog stopped in front of a log, but rather than tap forward with her walking stick, she stood very still and turned her ear. "Is a storm brewing?"

The sky was unusually clear, but when Ciar looked to the cove, one of his sea galleys tacked through, manned by a crew of his men with Livingstone at the tiller.

Emma's suggestion of a storm began a roiling in Ciar's chest. What he wouldn't give for a few more days of enjoyment in her company. "We have visitors."

"Who?"

"Livingstone and a few of my men."

The lass gripped her lead with both hands, her face stricken. "Oh."

Ciar grasped her elbow and walked with her to the shore as the crew hopped over the side of the galley and dragged the hull onto the beach. He frowned at his man-at-arms. "I'm surprised to see you in broad daylight."

Livingstone jumped down from the bow, keeping his boots dry. "There's been unrest in Crieff. Wilcox has sent a regiment across the Highlands, and we've been fortunate to have a bit of respite at Dunollie."

Ciar still didn't like it. "He kens I'll stay away with an army watching my gates, but he has spies about, mark me."

"We took precautions. Sailed up to Mull first like the last time. No one will ken we ended up here."

"Would you like to come inside for a cup of wine?" Emma asked. "It would be much more pleasant to chat in there away from the roar of the surf and the squawk of the seabirds."

"Don't mind if I do," said Livingstone, motioning for the men to wait.

Ciar was so anxious for answers, he would have preferred to ask questions right there on the beach. But Emma was right. They'd be able to speak more freely inside.

She even placed a plate of oatcakes on the table and poured the wine. "It is ever so good to see you, Braemar," she said, though not in her usual cheerful voice. She, too, knew his visit meant an end to their utopia.

Ciar gestured for Livingstone to take the second chair while he stood with his fists on his hips. "What news?"

The Highlander sipped and licked his lips. "The dragoon who cuffed you is named Brown. He's a braggart and an ox of a man. He and Manfred are still posted to Fort William, but Riley has been transferred to the garrison at Dunbarton."

"Fie." Ciar threw up his hands and paced in a circle. "What else did my man Kelly uncover? I need something that proves their guilt beyond any doubt."

"Och aye, Kelly did as we asked—had them in their cups at the Inverlochy alehouse. Brown was all too happy to boast about his crimes. He admitted to striking you from behind with a branch as big around as his thick arm. Moreover, he waved MacIntyre's sgian dubh beneath Kelly's nose—says he carries it for luck."

Ciar slammed his fist into his palm. "I'll show that bastard luck."

Livingstone arched his brows and shifted his gaze to Emma, but she only smiled serenely and asked, "What of Manfred? Does he keep any of the spoils?"

"Indeed. It seems he's fond of boasting as well—flashed MacIntyre's pocket watch."

"They need to pay, the lot of them." Ciar continued to pace. "Where's Kelly now?"

"I told him to wait at the inn in Connel."

"Excellent. Send Archie there and have him tell Kelly to fetch MacIntyre's son. Tommy Jr. will be able to identify his father's effects. Have him stay at the Inverlochy alehouse, and we'll meet him there three to four days hence."

"Three to four?" asked Livingstone.

"Come dark, I aim to set a course for Dunbarton."

"Are you certain?" Emma asked. "I would think the testament of two would be enough to convict the third."

Ciar snatched his cup from the table. "I'm not taking any chances."

* * *

Emma had already wrapped the last of the oatcakes in a cloth and filled an empty wine barrel with spring water when Ciar returned from asking Archie to find Mr. Kelly.

She brushed off her hands. "I think we ought to take plenty of food. And I found an empty cask that I filled at the spring. How long does it take to sail to Dunbarton?"

"A day with a favorable wind. Though if the weather doesn't cooperate, it could take a week." Ciar grasped her hands. "Nonetheless, I want you to stay here."

Her back tensed. "Here? Without you?"

"Nay, sorry, you'll stay with Nettie and Archie in their cottage."

A new place? No, Emma hated new places. And she'd only met the crofters but once. "I-I hardly know them. And I'm not familiar with their cottage at all. I planned to go with you."

"I ken the situation isn't ideal." He groaned, releasing her hands. "It is too dangerous to take you with me."

"But what about confronting Wilcox? I am an outlaw as well. I must be there to clear my name, too."

"Agreed. My men and I will have to sail through the Firth of Lorn on our way to Fort William. I'll stop for you then."

"But wouldn't it be easier if I were in the galley with you?"

"I cannot allow you to go. Make no bones about it, we

are heading into a lion's den where danger lurks at every turn." He cupped her cheek softly. "Stay with Nettie for a few days. I'm certain it shouldn't be any longer than that. A sennight at most."

Emma jerked away from his touch. "If you are insistent on leaving me behind, I will stay right here where I am familiar. There is plenty of food to last a fortnight if need be. And Nettie can check on me once or twice a day if it would make you feel more at ease."

"But—"

She slapped his arm. "Allow me this one concession. I am the one being asked to stay. I should have a say in where I shall sleep."

He said nothing for a moment before he released a pent-up breath. "Very well, but if you feel uncomfortable being alone, I do not want you to hesitate and go to Nettie's. They'd love to have you."

"Oh, aye, everyone would love to have a blind woman bumbling about their cottage, knocking over the lamps and vases and whatnot."

"You are awfully hard on yourself."

"I am honest."

Blast, blast, blast. Emma knew she would only be in the way if she set sail in the galley. But why couldn't Ciar send his men to trap this Riley person? Why did he insist on sailing down to Dumbarton with them?

Emma didn't ask. She knew the answer to her question as well.

Ciar needed to face all three culprits and let them know he would not tolerate being played a fool. Nor was he a coward. Any Highlander worth his salt confronted his foe and called them out.

She stopped in the middle of the chamber and buried

her face in her hands. "Things have been utterly perfect, so blissfully wonderful. I don't want it to end."

Wrapping her in an embrace, Ciar pressed his lips to her forehead. "I ken, *mo leannan*. You are so dear to me I cannot bear to see you upset."

"Must you go?" she asked, knowing she shouldn't. "Braemar could fetch him."

"Nay, lass. I have to face him myself."

"What about the other two?"

"We'll bring them to justice once we gain an audience with Wilcox."

She pushed him away. "But what if the governor doesn't believe us? We will both be captured and sent to the gallows."

"Better off to the gallows than hiding for the rest of our days."

"Nay!"

"Forgive me." He brushed a wisp of hair from her forehead then pulled her into his arms. "I spoke out of turn."

"You certainly did," she said, resting her head on his chest. Oh, how she loved the thrum of his heart. "We will clear our names and set everything to rights."

"Aye, lass." He used the crook of his finger to tilt her face up, then kissed her. "I must go."

"Promise to think of me every moment?"

"Thinking of you will be my driving light."

She reached back and unclasped the silver medal she wore around her neck. "Bend down." Securing it around his neck, she said, "Then I shall give you this for protection. Saint Lucia has watched over me since I was two years of age, and now she will bring you safely back."

"Thank you." He hugged her once again. "Be careful not to venture outside where you can be seen. Only walk from the passageway to the cove with Albert. You're familiar with that path, and any passing ships won't be able to spot you."

"I will."

"That's my lass." He kissed her cheek one last time. "We'll be sailing for Fort William before you know it."

And then he was gone.

Emma stood for a moment while Albert paced by the door. The hollow, belowground cellar suddenly felt cold, silent, and lonely. What if something bad happened to Ciar? What if he didn't return?

"Dear God, watch over him."

Chapter Twenty-One

*T*he sun's rays shone through gaps in the cloudy western sky when Ciar ordered the galley's sails furled at the confluence of the rivers Leven and Clyde. Ahead, Dunbarton Castle dominated, her fortress walls extending high up the promontory.

"Word is the soldiers take their respite at the Clipper Alehouse near the bend of the Leven," said Livingstone, holding the tiller firm.

Ciar raised his spyglass. "Man the oars. We'll cruise past."

"You heard him, men!" bellowed the man-at-arms. "To your stations."

Dunbarton was similar to many Scottish burghs, with a town square not far from the riverfront. Boats were moored on either side of the river, where they had easy access to the sea. "It will be easy to slip in without drawing notice."

"Aye, and I hardly recognized you with a full beard. A man would have to look twice before he'd ken your face."

"Crooked nose and all?" Ciar snorted. "Nonetheless, I'll be calling into the tailor's shop first."

Tired and irritable from a night of hard sailing, they left the Dunollie men to watch the galley while they headed for the square.

Once he was outfitted in a pair of breeches, a buckskin coat, and a tricorn hat low on his brow, Ciar followed Livingstone into the Clipper. He ordered two pints and pushed one across the bar for his friend while panning his gaze across the alehouse patrons' faces. There were only a dozen or so dragoons in the crowd. "He's not here."

"Want me to ask questions?" asked his man-at-arms.

Ciar inclined his head toward an empty table in the shadows, well away from the light of the window. "After we've settled in. Nothing draws attention faster than a man who's too eager."

He hadn't missed the sideways glances when they'd arrived or the whispers now. Clearly, everyone was wondering who they were and if they'd cause a stir. He slid into the seat against the wall, where his back was protected. "Drink slow, my friend."

A barmaid stopped by and bent over the table, until her wares nearly burst from her bodice. "Come in from fishing the Clyde, have you?"

"Something like that."

She waggled her shoulders. "Would ye like some company?"

After spending so much time with Emma, this woman tempted him about as much as a hog. "Perhaps a bit of information."

"What kind of information?"

"A friend of mine was just transferred to a regiment at Dunbarton—have you met anyone new as of late?"

"Possibly." She held out her hand. "But it'll cost ye a penny."

Ciar nodded to Livingstone, who dropped a coin in her hand.

She slid it into the folds of her skirts. "What is your friend's name?"

"Riley—was sent down from Fort William."

The wench's eyes flashed wide before she wiped a hand over her mouth and glanced away. "Riley? Aye, I've met him."

"Does he come here often?" asked Livingstone.

"As often as the next soldier, I suppose." She twirled her bodice laces around her finger. "Plays cards. Likes to tup as well."

Ciar nudged Livingstone with his elbow and gave a nod. "The second penny is for your silence."

She took the second coin and rubbed it between her fingers before it disappeared just like the first. "He don't mean nothing to me, but you're not planning to hurt him, are ye?"

"Nay, lassie. After all, he is an old friend."

The woman tipped up her chin, her eyes narrowing. "What is your name?"

"Manfred." Ciar stared the woman in the eye and drank. "If anyone asks, his old friend from Fort William, Manfred, has a wee bit o' treasure for him."

* * *

If Riley was out riding sorties, he wouldn't find his way to the Clipper Alehouse until after dark—if he came at all.

At least it gave Ciar and his men time to set a trap. He had three of his crew take a table near the door. The other three stood at the bar while he and Livingstone ate a meal of lamb stew and bread at the same table where they'd met the barmaid.

She must have found a customer for the night because she was nowhere to be seen. At least that's what Ciar thought until Riley walked through the bloody door.

As soon as he stepped inside, the vixen ran from the back. "These men are waiting for you!"

"Ballocks!" Ciar growled, pushing to his feet.

Riley's jaw dropped with stunned recognition, and then pure terror flashed through his eyes.

As the weasel turned, the Dunollie men blocked the front door. Whipping around, the bastard pushed over a table and ran to the back. Ciar followed as he shoved chairs aside.

A dragoon caught his arm, yanking him to a halt. "Not so fast."

Instinctively, Ciar gripped the man's throat and stared him in the eye while Riley banged through the rear door. "This isn't your fight."

Gurgling, the soldier went limp. With a shove, Ciar released him and sped outside while the slap of footsteps followed. He stole a glance behind. *Livingstone.*

A dark shadow disappearing around the front of the building caught his eye, and he sprinted toward it, leaping over barrels and old crates.

Skidding, Ciar rounded the corner.

Ahead, Riley headed for the wynd across the road while shouts came from the alehouse. The wee street twisted toward the river, but there was no other way out but to double back.

"There he is!" yelled Livingstone, with MacDougall men in his wake.

"Cut him off around the bend. I'll follow." Ciar glanced back. "We cannot lose him!"

Trusting his men, he darted straight for the water. It was a risk, but dividing forces was the best chance to nab the scoundrel.

Sprinting along the river, Ciar sucked in deep breaths, ignoring the burn of his thighs. He slowed a tad, scanning the river's edge, peering into building doorways, squinting to discern objects in the shadows. With a sudden burst, a barrow clattered to its side as Riley darted out of the wynd. Over his shoulder, the dragoon spotted Ciar and sharply swerved east.

Anticipating the change of direction, Ciar ran after him. He reached out, stretching as far as possible, his fingers almost skimming the sentinel's coat while mud from Riley's shoes splattered his face.

The brigand swung back with a fist. "You'll hang!" he screamed, his voice high-pitched and breathless.

Ciar ducked and dove, wrapping his arms around Riley's legs and tackling him to the road. "There will be a hanging, but it will not be mine."

"Move your beastly arse off me!" Riley shrieked, kicking his feet, his fists thudding against Ciar's back. "I am a soldier of the crown."

Rising to his knees, Ciar threw a hook across the man's jaw. "You are a murdering deceiver, and I aim to make you pay for the misery you've caused me and Tommy MacIntyre's kin."

But Riley didn't hear a word. He dropped to the dirt, out cold from Ciar's punch.

Wheezing, Livingstone came running. "Haste. Half the dragoons from the alehouse are headed this way."

"Where are the men?" Ciar asked.

Livingstone crouched with his hands braced on his knees as one named Willy approached. "I ordered the rest of them back to the ship," he panted. "They're preparing to set sail."

Ciar stood and hefted Riley over his shoulder. "Keep

an eye out. The last thing we need now is an escort to Dunbarton's dungeon."

Together they slipped through the shadows, listening for troops, ready for an attack. Just as Ciar thought they'd make it without a fight, a dragoon leaped from behind a fence, swinging his saber. Ciar tightened his grip on Riley and bobbed away from the hiss of the blade. With the lout's recoil, he darted with the speed of a falcon, jabbing an elbow to his opponent's nose, dropping the dragoon to his face.

"Must ye knock everyone unconscious?" asked Livingstone.

"Better them than me." His muscles burning with fatigue, Ciar lumbered down the steps to the wharf. Riley had to weigh fifteen stone at least.

"Halt!" someone yelled from above.

"Faster," Ciar growled, willing his legs to pump harder, grunting with the agony of the weight across his back.

Livingstone took the lead, signaling for the men to cast off.

Just as the galley drifted away from the pier, Ciar hoisted Riley from his shoulder. "A bit o' help here!"

A musket fired as two men grabbed the redcoat and dragged him into the boat. Ciar covered his head as he leaped for the hull. Rolling to his back, he looked upward.

The sail hadn't yet picked up wind. He hopped up and grabbed an open oar, pulling with all his strength. "Keep your heads down, and row as if the devil is blowing hellfire up your arse!"

* * *

Humming a Celtic ballad, Emma stirred the pottage Nettie had brought and tapped the wooden spoon on the edge of the kettle, the sound ringing throughout the chamber. "I think we'll both like this, Albert." After all, every morsel Nettie had delivered to the Gylen cellars had been exceedingly delicious compared to the bland fare they had been eating.

The dog moved beside her and growled—not exactly the response she expected.

"What is it?" she whispered, listening while the hairs on her nape stood on end.

The echo of muffled footsteps came from the passageway, but it wasn't Ciar's bold stride. This gait was slower and precise, as if each step was being placed with careful calculation.

Her stomach turned over. *Dear God, please don't let him be hurt.*

She clasped the spoon in front of her chest. "Hello?"

No answer came, but a hushed whisper curled through the air.

Emma gasped, certain she'd heard someone say, "She's in there."

Barking, Albert bolted forward while Emma dropped to her knees and crawled under the table between the chairs, her heart beating so fast it thundered in her ears.

The door swung open to Albert's vicious snarls. A riding crop hissed through the air, followed by a yelp.

"No!" Emma shouted, stretching her hand out for her dog.

Albert skittered beside her, shaking with fear while heeled shoes tapped the floor. "Well, well, we've found the rabbit but not the fox."

As Emma recognized the man's voice, ice shot through her veins.

A chair grazed the flagstone as Governor Wilcox pulled it away. "Hello, Miss Emma. We meet again."

Either she was shaking as violently as Albert or the dog was trembling so badly he was quavering her. Nonetheless, she refused to stand and curtsy before the man. Not after all the pain he'd caused.

"Swallowed your tongue, did you?"

She said nothing.

"I'll make it easy. I require only one tidbit of information. Where is Dunollie?"

"How did you find me?"

He chuckled. "It was just a matter of time. I have spies everywhere. Clever, though, it wasn't until his men sailed into the hidden cove that I received a report." He grabbed her elbow and dragged her from under the table. "Tell me where MacDougall is now, and I'll forgive your crimes."

She jerked her arm away. "He's innocent, and you'll never find him."

"Everyone slips sooner or later."

"Not Dunollie."

"Hmm. What I cannot understand is why he would leave a blind woman stranded on an island alone." Wilcox pulled her toward the hearth while Albert growled. "One who cooks, it seems."

Emma clamped her lips together.

"My guess is wherever he went, he won't be gone for long."

"You're wrong. He's…he's…" She wrapped her fingers around Albert's collar and drew him to her side.

"He's what?"

Wilcox emitted a hint of amusement in his tone, enough to make Emma gulp. What should she say? If she mentioned Dunbarton, the governor might send warships to intercept him.

She did her best to appear undaunted, though her heart raced so fast she could hardly think. "He will not return until he has proved to you that he had no part in Tommy MacIntyre's murder."

Albert pulled against her grip, barking and snarling. But Emma held tight; if she let him go, he might end up hurt.

The man's chuckle was as ugly as it was cynical. "Why do I not believe you?" He grabbed her wrist, but the dog snarled and pushed between them. "Lock her in irons and shoot the mongrel."

"No!" She dropped to her knees and threw her arms around Albert's neck. "I'll go with you willingly if you promise to leave him be."

Wilcox snorted loudly. "You are in no position to make demands of any sort."

"Please." She ran a steady hand over Albert's coat. "There's no reason to harm him. He's only trying to protect me."

"You said you'd freely surrender?"

"Aye."

"Tell the dog to stand down," said Wilcox.

Emma sliced her palm in front of Albert's face. "Stay." Once he quietened and sat, she squared her shoulders and held out her wrists.

"Slap a pair of manacles on her. Leave the mangy hound." Wilcox started for the door. "Dunollie will return, mark me. And when he does, we'll trap him in his own sinister game."

Chapter Twenty-Two

*E*mma shivered with the cold, adding to the intensity of her trembles. Huddled in the bow of the boat, she had never been so terrified in her life. They hadn't even given her a chance to don her cloak. And now Wilcox and his men were taking her back to Fort William in irons. The cold manacles around her wrists hung heavily, the chain between them resting on the floor at her feet.

The men around her went about their duties, sailing the ship northward into Loch Linnhe, not one uttering a word to her. At the governor's orders, they tacked east until they tossed the sea galley's ropes to the sentries on the shore.

As they worked to tie the boat to the pier, Wilcox stepped beside her, his stench of sickly perfume now unmistakable. "This ought to be familiar. You are the one who picked the lock on my sally port, are you not?"

Emma would never admit guilt to this man. "If only I were able to accomplish such a feat," she managed to say, masking the fear from her voice.

"It matters not. Regardless, you will be my bait. Once I have made a public spectacle of you, Dunollie will not be able to stay away."

She instantly tensed. *No!* "If you believe a man as important as Ciar MacDougall will come for a blind woman, you have greatly overestimated his affection for me. I am merely a friend, the sister of his closest ally, and that is all."

"Hmm. I think not. Take the woman to the officers' hold." Wilcox clapped his hands. "On the morrow you will be locked in the pillory and disgraced. Let us see how long it will take for MacDougall to rescue you. After all, isn't that what Highlanders pride themselves on—honor, duty, loyalty? Those virtues are commendable, though the only problem is that their meaning is displaced among you Scottish folk."

Emma balled her fists, her face hot, as two dragoons grasped her elbows and escorted her off the galley. The iron gate screeched as they led her through. She counted seven steps, reminiscent of the night she'd stolen inside and rescued Ciar. Oh, the irony of returning with her wrists bound and facing utter humiliation come dawn.

The sweet scent of horses and hay wafted from the barn as they crossed the grounds to the same cell where Ciar had been held.

One of the dragoons shoved her inside. "I'd try to sleep if I were you, 'cause tomorrow you will have no rest at all."

Emma held out her hands. "Will you not take these off?"

"Orders are you must be restrained at all times, else you might escape like an evil sprite."

After the door slammed shut, Emma's eyes stung as she slid down the wall. Whatever was she to do? What had happened to Ciar? Why hadn't he come? And Albert. *Good heavens, Nettie, please take care of Albert.*

Collapsing into a heap, she let the tears come. If only

Ciar had taken her to Dunbarton. Why in God's name had he left her alone?

The mere thought made her chest heavy, her throat close. Emma's capture was her own fault. She'd refused to go stay with Archie and Nettie.

Curses, I'm as stubborn as my brother!

She should have listened. But she'd been so happy, she'd falsely believed the illusion that no one could touch her while she hid in the cellars of the ruined castle. Oh, how wrong she was. And now if Ciar received word about her abduction, no doubt he would try to rescue her.

Lord, no! Please, Ciar, please. Stay away.

At some stage, Emma cried herself to sleep, and she didn't awaken until the guard opened the door. "Up with you, wench. You have a big day ahead."

"Is there not anything to eat?"

"Prisoners are fed once a day. You'll receive yours after sundown."

Good heavens, she was hungry and thirsty. "A cup of water then, please."

Liquid sloshed. "Did you not see the bucket and ladle?"

When the guard raised a full ladle to her mouth, Emma drank, then wiped her lips. "Forgive me, I have not seen anything in two and twenty years."

"Just as well," he said. "'Cause you wouldn't like what you'll see today."

The water in her stomach churned with a sickly, simmering swirl. Though she might be afraid, she did not care what the crowd might say or do, as long as Ciar stayed safe and kept away until he had the evidence he needed to clear his name.

Soldiers marshaled her out the gates and up the rickety wooden steps to the pillory.

"Good morning, Miss Grant," said Governor Wilcox, his tone sardonically displeasing. "I hope you slept well."

Emma rubbed a kink in her neck but kept her lips tightly closed.

"I am here to offer you one last chance," he bellowed loudly enough for all to hear. "Tell me where the scoundrel Ciar MacDougall is hiding, and I will remove your irons and release you this very day."

She scoffed. "I cannot tell you where he is because I do not know."

At least she told the truth on that count. Though Ciar had gone to Dunbarton to find Riley, Emma doubted he was still there. Perhaps Riley hadn't been at the fort. Perhaps the sentinel had been transferred to another post. Whatever the reason, Emma refused to believe that Ciar was in trouble. And if she knew anything about the man, he would never give up until he proved the truth.

With luck, she prayed, he was far away from Fort William and would never learn of her capture.

"Very well, then, enjoy my hospitality," Wilcox said.

Emma held her head high, standing regally as a dragoon removed her manacles.

"She's blind," came a whisper from the crowd.

"'Tis true what they say, that God has condemned her for her sins and delivered his wrath. She is the devil's own."

Emma clenched her teeth. Robert had sheltered her from the evils of society, but she knew well enough the fears and superstitions about the blind. She wanted to shout that she was a good person. She wanted to tell them about Ciar's innocence, but they wouldn't listen, not when they thought her a demon.

The soldier forced her to bend forward and lowered the bar over her head, trapping her wrists and neck. Panic surged through her blood. She fought against the rigid pillory while taunts from the crowd grew louder. Something vile smelling smacked the side of her head and streamed toward the corner of her mouth. She spat, but the acrid taste of mold made her gag.

"Stop!" she shouted, but her claim only made the crowd badger her more.

"You are a disgrace!"

"Take her to the gallows!"

"The woman's a witch. She will cast spells on us all unless she's drowned!"

Emma winced, shaking her head. She refused to listen. She would not let their hateful words hurt her. No matter what, she must remain strong. One day this misery would be over. Ciar was out there somewhere. She had to put her trust in him. He would clear his name and come for her.

Closing her eyes, she sent her mind back to Gylen, to the cozy cellar, the quiet cove, to Ciar's loving arms protecting her…

* * *

The return trip to Kerrera should have taken a day, two tops. But it seemed the luck from Emma's medal of Saint Lucia had run its course. Once Ciar and his men sailed out of the Firth of Clyde, there was no wind to be found and, when a gale finally hit, it came from the north like a rogue. They were pummeled by torrential rain while they tacked from east to west, barely making progress. Now it had been over a sennight since they'd set sail for Dunbarton.

Rain still came down in sheets when the men pulled the galley ashore at Kerrera.

"Do you intend for us to stay the night?" asked Livingstone.

Ciar wiped the droplets out of his eyes. "MacIntyre will think we're not coming."

"Surely he'll wait, given the storm." Livingstone hopped over the side, and Ciar followed. "There's room in the cellars for the men to camp. And Riley isn't going anywhere."

Ciar glanced back to the mast where the dragoon was tied, his chin dropped to his chest. The man was conscious, though he had a mouth filled with bile.

"Lock him in the rear cellar," said Ciar. "Bail out the water from the hull, then let the men take their rest."

Good God, he was bone weary. It was late, and one more night shouldn't make a difference at this stage. If MacIntyre had returned to Spean Bridge, Ciar would just have to send someone to fetch him.

As he entered the passageway, a musket fired down near the cove. He stopped for a moment. Before he could consider whether to go out and see what the men were up to, Albert dashed through the passageway, tail wagging as if he'd missed Ciar immensely.

He scratched behind the dog's ears, noting the laddie's coat wasn't as well-groomed as Emma usually kept it. "Did you miss me?"

Albert yowled and started for the exit.

Ciar pulled his collar. "We need to pay a visit to Emma first."

Albert yowled again, hopping on his rear paws and snorting as if he desperately needed to go outside.

"Go on then." Ciar waved him away with a flick of his hand. "But stay out of trouble."

Another musket fired. Strange. But he was too eager to see to Emma to think much of it.

Albert stayed on Ciar's heels. "I thought you needed to go out, laddie." Water sloshed from his shoes while he plodded down the passageway. As he neared the door, a sinking feeling gripped his stomach. *Oh, God, the dog was trying to tell me something has happened to her.*

Ciar's breath stopped dead in his chest as he ran into the vault. "Emma!"

When she didn't answer, he spun toward the hearth.

"Em—?"

The last thing he heard was a sickly thud swelling through the cavern.

* * *

Robert Grant dug in his spurs as he demanded a gallop from his horse. Never in his life had he been so angry. As soon as he'd received word from Janet, he'd raced for Achnacarry, praying his sister had returned. Over a fortnight had already been wasted. Worse, it had taken a week of hard riding to reach his wife, where he learned Emma had not only spirited to Fort William with the son of Lochiel's coachman, she'd picked the locks to the fortress and aided in Dunollie's escape after the man had been incarcerated for murder.

The man Robert had considered his greatest ally had the gall to send the stable boy home, but the MacDougall scoundrel had gone into hiding with Emma. What the blazes was he thinking?

And things only grew more precarious by the moment. Not only was Robert's sister ruined, she had been captured on the Isle of Kerrera, taken back to Fort William, and locked in the public pillory for all to torment and ridicule.

Robert had only discovered the bulk of this information after he'd paid a visit to Achnacarry. He'd been riding for a sennight with little sleep and had barely had a chance to greet his pregnant wife when he had no option but to change horses and make haste for Fort William.

I'll never forgive Ciar for this!

Had the man completely lost his mind? Why in God's name had he gone into hiding and taken Emma with him? A blind woman, for heaven's sake. As Robert rode, the burning ball of fire in his chest raged.

He crossed the bridge at Inverlochy and demanded more speed, the horse snorting with exertion. When High Street came into view, the sight of his sister, wrists and head locked in the bars of a pillory, made the bile in his stomach churn.

A crowd stood around the platform, their jeers echoing down the cobbled road as Robert rode forward, his horse spent.

"You're the devil's own!" spewed a woman.

"You should have been drowned at birth. You are a scourge that should be snuffed in flames."

"No!" Emma cried, her voice hoarse and grating.

Her hair was matted. As Robert dismounted, he couldn't see her face. "Go on, the lot of ye!" he bellowed. "You're fiendish troublemakers!"

He dashed up the steps, but was met by a dragoon pointing a bayonet between his eyeballs.

Robert could have ripped the weapon from the blighter's hands and bludgeoned him with it. "Release her," he growled.

"Brother!" Emma croaked.

The man threatened him with the bayonet again. "You, sir, are interfering with justice."

Losing his patience, Robert grabbed the musket's barrel, yanked it from the soldier's hands, and jabbed him in the shoulder with the butt. "Do you find torturing and humiliating blind women amusing?"

"Stand down, you insolent cur!"

"Release her now," Robert seethed through his teeth. "And I will take her directly to Wilcox and castigate the cowardly governor for the abhorrent treatment of the sister of the Clan Grant chief."

The man stood dumbfounded.

Sauntering forward, Robert grasped the weasel by the cravat. "If you do not unlock the pillory immediately, I will impale your arse with this worthless bayonet."

A bead of sweat streamed from the soldier's temple. "M-my superiors will hear of this."

He pushed the man toward the lock. "They will, and I'll be the first to tell them."

As the dragoon opened the padlock and lifted the bar, Emma dropped to her knees.

"Good God, you're too weak to stand," Robert barked, scooping her into his arms. "Have they not been feeding you?"

She weakly brushed her fingers across her dirty mouth. "A slice of bread and a cup of water."

He dashed down the platform. "How long have you been here?"

"Three days, I-I think."

Robert's jaw twitched as he marched through Fort William's gates and headed straight for the governor's office. "Hold fast, dearest. I'll have you safely at Achnacarry in no time."

"But—"

Before she uttered another word, Robert kicked open Wilcox's door. "What in God's name were you thinking, making a public display of the blind sister of one of the most powerful clans in the Highlands?"

The sour-faced governor looked up from his writing

table. "Grant? Devil take it, you're not the Scot I was hoping to see."

"I would have arrived sooner had I not been north of Inverness when I received word."

The man placed his quill in its holder. "Your sister aided a murderer to escape this very fort. She's dangerous and cunning."

Robert looked down at the half-starved woman in his arms. "You mean to tell me you're afraid of this wee lassie?" He looked Wilcox in the eye. "Furthermore, you're saying that she, a blind woman, broke into this fortified establishment, slipped past innumerable guards, and freed *your* prisoner?"

Feigning disbelief, Robert stepped forward. "You saw my sister break into your prison?"

Wilcox's gaze shifted as he licked his lips. "She was here—visited me the morning before Dunollie escaped. Furthermore, her dog barked, and a woman was seen fleeing with him."

"A woman?" Robert snorted. "This woman? Hardly. How can a sightless lass elude your *highly* trained soldiers? That she might have is unconscionable, unless you are completely incompetent in the exercise of your duties."

Wilcox rubbed the back of his neck.

"I am taking my sister home."

"She is my prisoner and an accessory."

"She is a victim." Robert eyed him. "And you are abusing your station in making a public spectacle with her."

The governor let out a long sigh, looked to the window and back. "I had thought to use her as bait, but after three days, the bastard still hasn't shown his ugly face."

"What happened...to Ciar?" Emma mumbled.

Robert tightened his grip around her. "See? She has no

idea as to Dunollie's whereabouts. For all you know he's
fled to Ireland or worse."

Emma shook her head. "No, no."

"Calm yourself, sister. You are delirious with exhaustion
and hunger." Robert eyed the governor. "She has paid far too
high a price for your incompetence."

"I disagree. Her punishment thus far has been lenient. We
discovered her in a hidden cellar on the Isle of Kerrera—
Dunollie's lands, mind you."

Robert backed toward the door. "That still does not make
her guilty."

"Go on." Wilcox flicked his hand. "Get out. She is of no
use to me now. You ought to keep a tight rein on the chit—
lock her away for good."

Without another word, Robert headed for his mount. "I
will see you safely home, lass," he whispered as he set her
on the horse and mounted behind her.

Steadying Emma in his arms, Robert shook his head. "I
once considered Dunollie my greatest friend. But I swear on
our father's grave, he will never come near you again."

"No!" Emma shrieked, throwing an elbow and smacking
him in the arm.

Good God, the lass had endured unconscionable trauma,
driving her to complete madness. She mustn't have any idea
what she was saying. "Shhh, girl, and calm yourself. You
are safe now."

Chapter Twenty-Three

Something warm and slavering swiped across Ciar's face. The warmth was pleasant but the lingering moisture made his eyes flicker open for the briefest of moments. Groaning, he rolled his head aside while a hammer in his head punished him for moving.

"No, ye beasty," demanded a young voice. Female, but too high-pitched to be Emma.

When someone applied a cool cloth to his forehead, Ciar forced himself to open his eyes.

He didn't recognize the bedchamber. It was relatively small, and rain tapped the roof. Above were exposed beams, as if he were in a windowless attic room. His body was covered by a quilt, his head resting on a feather pillow. Beside him stood a serving maid wearing a white apron over a plaid kirtle.

Ciar looked from her hands to her head. Her brown tresses were covered by a mobcap, and as she leaned over him, wisps of her hair swayed with the motion. "Ye're awake."

"Where am I?" he asked, his throat dry.

"Glencoe. A guest of His Lairdship, Hugh MacIain."

Pressing the heels of his palms against his throbbing temples, Ciar winced, trying to remember. "How the blazes did I end up here?"

The sound of boots pounding the floorboards made the pain grow worse. "I brought you to MacIain after the redcoat bastards bludgeoned you," Livingstone said. "It was the only place I kent you would be safe."

Ciar tried to move, only to make the throbbing worse. "But MacIain? Glencoe?"

"He's the staunchest Jacobite in Scotland."

"I need to find Emma."

Livingstone gave the maid a dismissive wave of his hand. "Leave us and take the dog with you." As the door clicked behind her, the man-at-arms pulled a wooden chair beside the bed. "How much do you remember?"

"Musket shots. Aye, I went into the cellars to find Emma, but she wasn't there. And I heard muskets."

"We were ambushed by redcoats. One of them was waiting for you inside—hit you on the head with an ax handle."

Ciar groaned. "Another bloody knock in the head?"

"Aye. I reckon I need to fasten an iron helmet on ye."

"But you said they ambushed? Was Emma harmed?"

"They took her to Fort William about a sennight ago."

The cloth dropped to his chest as Ciar tried to sit up, blinking his eyes against the pain. "God no."

He tried to swing his legs over the side of the bed, only to be pushed back by Livingstone. "You need to listen to it all afore ye charge out of here like a wounded bull.

Ciar dropped to the pillow, weak as a bairn. "I'll not sit idle whilst she suffers."

"Didn't think you would." Livingstone picked up the cloth

and tossed it into the washbasin. "As I was saying, dragoons were lying in wait—Wilcox's men they were and thank God they were bad shots. Willy was hit with a glancing blow to his shoulder, but he'll survive. Moreover, there were only three of the bastards. It didn't take long to overcome them."

"Where are they now?"

"Locked in the back vault beneath Gylen Castle—I left a pair of men there to guard them until 'tis safe to release the maggots—else they'll go cryin' to Wilcox."

Ciar ran a hand over his whiskers. "Who else kens we were there?"

"No one as far as I'm aware. Their orders were to wait until you returned and to stay out of sight. After you arrived they were supposed to return to Fort William and summon the governor."

"They told you this?"

"With a wee bit o' encouragement."

Livingstone held a cup of water to Ciar's lips. As soon as it touched his mouth, Ciar guzzled greedily. "How long have I been here?"

"Two days."

"But the Coe is nearly a stone's throw from Fort William."

"Brilliant, aye? Keeping you in the devil's back garden." Livingstone set the cup on the washstand. "'Tis the only place I could think of they wouldn't look. After his da's house was burned to the ground, MacIain built another with a false ceiling. No one kens you're up here."

"Aside from the serving wench."

"She's loyal to the *cause*."

"What of Riley?"

"He's here—under guard. After you were knocked unconscious, I sent word to Kelly. He and Tommy Jr. nabbed Brown and Manfred. They're holding them in Inverlochy."

"Then there's no time to spare." Ciar pushed himself up and swung his feet over the side of the bed, grabbing the post to steady himself. "Do the captives ken why they're being held?"

"I told Kelly not to say anything to tie him to you. They have no idea Dunollie is involved." Livingstone patted Ciar's shoulder. "Your face is as white as bed linens. It might serve you well to stay abed for another day."

"I'll rest when this is ended and nay before."

"Thought you'd say that."

Ciar stood, his legs shaking beneath him.

Livingstone caught his arm. "You're in no shape to be going anywhere, let alone the dragon's lair."

"Give me a slab of bacon, a half-dozen eggs and a shot of whisky, and I'll be set to rights."

"Aye. Or face down in your plate."

"Shut it," Ciar growled—right before his knees buckled beneath him and everything faded into blackness.

* * *

Only a fortnight had passed since Emma bid farewell to Ciar on the Isle of Kerrera. But it seemed like an eternity.

"I'm sorry Robert is so anxious to take you home," said Janet sitting across the coach. "He should have given you more time to recover."

"Aye," Betty agreed, swaying into Emma's arm as a wheel rolled through a hole in the road. "You're in no state to be traveling."

After Robert had rescued her from the pillory, he'd taken her to Achnacarry, where she was fed and sent straight to bed, though they only stayed one night there. First thing this morning, her brother had insisted the only place he could keep a proper eye on her was Glenmoriston, where they now headed directly.

"It doesn't matter," Emma mumbled.

Janet's fan zipped open, the breeze from its flapping strong enough to cool Emma's face. "It most certainly does. You have had a terrible ordeal. Whatever prompted you to slip away from Achnacarry in the first place, I cannot understand."

"I must concur, miss," said Betty, the traitor. "You could have ended up in grave danger. Och, in fact ye fell straight into unimaginable peril."

Emma folded her hands. How could she ever make them appreciate what she'd accomplished? "I did that which needed to be done, and that is all."

"Good heavens," said Janet, her voice scornful. "I can name dozens of Highlanders who would have rushed to Dunollie's aid."

Emma sat forward and pounded her fist on the bench. "But they were all out organizing a rising to thwart the Hanoverian king."

"Grant and Cameron would have come around to help His Lairdship," said Betty.

"Neither of you understand." The walls of the coach felt as if they were closing in around her. "Ciar was accused of murder. Governor Wilcox was planning to send him to the gallows."

"Oh, I think we understand very well," said Janet, the slats of her fan hitting in rapid repetition as she closed it.

Taking a deep breath to calm the ire boiling beneath her skin, Emma pressed her back against the seat. "Dunollie is the only man besides my brother who has ever shown me kindness. I would die for him."

"Heaven forbid," Betty mumbled under her breath.

Emma scooted away from her lady's maid. The pair of them thought they knew how she felt about Ciar, but they *never* would. They could only see her as an invalid—someone who would always tag along, who would always be there in the background but never have a home or life of her own. Until she'd gone to Achnacarry, Emma believed it herself. She never dreamed that she'd want to leave Glenmoriston and marry. But with Ciar she could do anything. Truly, he understood her better than her own kin.

She needed to find out what had happened to him straightaway.

The fact that he hadn't come for her made her fear the worst. Had something horrible transpired at Dunbarton? Would she ever see him again? And what about her beloved Albert? Was he still on Kerrera? Had Nettie taken the dog in? Surely she would have fed him once she realized Emma was gone.

Emma spent the rest of the journey pressed against the side wall of the coach, refusing to engage Betty and Janet in conversation. If they believed she was incapable of helping Ciar and unmitigatedly daft for slipping away in the middle of the night, then they could go hang.

Miserable hours passed before the familiar rush of Moriston Falls announced they'd arrived on Grant lands. Not long after, the wheels of the coach rolled over gravelly stones down the sycamore-lined drive, the leaves rustling outside the window.

As soon as they rolled to a stop, Robert's voice boomed across the courtyard. "Lewis, carry my sister to her bed. Betty, see to drawing her a bath."

"I am not feeble in body or in mind. I will walk to my

chamber on my own," Emma shouted, reaching over Betty and finding the coach's latch. She opened the door, though she wasn't stubborn enough to leap out before a footman grasped her hand. The last thing she needed was for her obstinance to trump her common sense and send her face-first to the cobblestones.

"'Tis lovely to see you, miss," said Hubert, the footman. He'd been in service at Glenmoriston since he was a lad of sixteen, and Emma would recognize his voice anywhere.

"Thank you. I wish I were happy to be here."

She held her head high and made her way through the front door, crossed the entry, and whisked up the stairs of the house that she knew so well, she anticipated the creak of the ninth step and the way the banister ended in a smooth curve at the top.

"Whatever is wrong with Miss Emma?" asked Mrs. Tweedie from below. Emma had always adored the housekeeper, but once the woman learned of her escapades, she'd side with Robert for certain.

"She's had an ordeal," Janet explained. Good heavens, they all seemed to expect Emma to recover and go about her affairs as if she hadn't fallen in love with Ciar. As if he hadn't opened a new window of possibilities for her.

When she finally made it to her bedchamber, she strode inside, locked the door, and flung herself onto the bed.

For the second time since Wilcox had captured her on Kerrera, she allowed herself to weep. Burying her face in a pillow, she wept for Ciar. She knew something dreadful had happened and yet Robert bore him no remorse, insisting Dunollie had crossed the line. Robert swore Ciar should have refused Emma's help and the fact that he had not done so had made him a lesser man in his eyes.

A lesser man?

"Ciar is a greater man than any other!" she screamed into the pillow. "He was framed for murder and wronged. You discredited him too, brother. When he needed his allies you forsook your dearest friend!"

Chapter Twenty-Four

*H*ugh MacIain shook Ciar's hand. "Would you like some added muscle? I'd be happy to ride with you and your men."

"You've taken enough of a risk by hiding me in your attic. I'm grateful, friend, but I'd hate to have you and your kin pulled into this mess."

"I'd gladly ride alongside you any time. One never kens, someday I might be knocking on your keep's door."

"You'll be welcome. Day or night."

Regardless of the niceties, Ciar could have murdered Livingstone for letting him sleep another day. He accepted the reins of a horse from a stable hand, mounted, and signaled for his men to follow.

Leading them across the shallows of the River Coe, Ciar beckoned his lieutenant to ride beside him. "What the blazes were you thinking?"

Livingstone's eyes widened beneath his feathered bonnet. "Berate me if ye like, but you were in no shape to ride yesterday. And I'd wager today is questionable as well."

Ciar ground his molars, making the ache in his head throb. Pain didn't matter. He'd spent far too much time abed. "We ride."

"Agreed." Livingstone wrapped the lead rope around his hand, pulling along the horse carrying Riley bound and gagged. "Besides, I've arranged for Kelly to meet us at the abandoned barn on the outskirts of town."

A bit of tension released at the back of Ciar's neck. "You did?"

"He *was* waiting for us in Inverlochy north of Fort William. You didn't plan to ride right past the fort undetected, did ye? Mark me, every red-coated bastard this side of the great divide has a musket ball with your initial carved in it."

Ciar cued his horse for a trot while his ire fizzed all the more. Of course he hadn't thought of all the details. He'd been unconscious. "Kelly has Manfred and Brown, you say?"

"MacIntyre is with him as well."

Damnation. Ciar wouldn't have done any better himself. "Very well, let us skirt around Loch Leven and approach from the foothills of Ben Nevis."

Livingstone's grin stretched his whiskers. "Now I ken you're on the mend."

Ciar clenched his fists around the reins and settled his seat in the saddle. He'd be a great deal happier once his name was cleared and he'd rescued Emma from Wilcox's clutches. The route he'd just planned would take them a good three hours longer—three hours more Emma would be forced to suffer. But, damn it all, if anything went awry, her suffering might endure for sennights.

Of course, it was on the cards that they'd be pelted with rain throughout the journey. By the time they arrived at the old barn, Ciar's clothes were soaked clean through. He clenched his teeth against the chattering, dismounted, and led the way inside.

Hell, the rain dripped through the rotting roof, making the moss-encrusted ground slosh. At one side the ceiling had completely caved in, leaving a pile of jagged planks with mangled nails sticking out like elongated briar thorns.

"I thought you might have been a bloody myth," said Kelly, stepping forward with an extended hand. "One more night in this shitehole, and I would have chartered a boat back to Ireland."

Ciar gave a firm handshake, grinning without unclenching his teeth. "Thank you for bearing with me. It seems the red-coated blighters nearly did me in."

"Not to worry. I'm certain your generosity will make it worth my while."

"Indeed it will, Mr. Kelly."

"Agreed," said MacIntyre, also shaking Ciar's hand. "My father's spirit will not be at peace until these murderers receive their due."

"Then let us not delay."

Ciar studied the two dragoons, their uniforms filthy and moth-eaten. He recognized Manfred, but one glance at Brown and he wanted to kick in the cur's teeth in. He was a beefy, thick-featured ox, as if the mason who chiseled his face hadn't finished the job. He had a puckered scar extending from his eye to his chin, and his nose looked as if it had been broken more often than Ciar's.

He sauntered toward the man. "On your feet, soldier."

Brown's eyes shifted as he stood, his hands bound in front of him, his feet tied with a length of rope. "I should 'ave bashed your 'ead clear in."

Ciar fingered the hilt of the dirk in his belt. Never in his life had he wanted to thrash a man as much as he did now. "Hindsight is a great teacher, is she not?"

He would not allow Brown to bait him further. Turning, he started for his horse when the maggot barreled into him from behind. Hit in the middle of his spine, Ciar flung out his hands as he crashed into the pile of rotting roof planks. A sharp pain shot through his cheek. As he threw an elbow at Brown's temple, the nail that had ripped through his flesh flashed in the corner of his eye.

Brown's head snapped sideways as he reeled from the strike. Rolling to his feet, Ciar gripped the board and swung it back to deliver a killing strike. Terror flashed through the dragoon's eyes as he raised his bound wrists to protect his head.

Ciar bared his teeth, bellowing like a madman. The board smashed through Brown's guard, but just before the nail struck his skull, Livingstone tackled Ciar from the side.

Again, he fell on top of the rotting timbers, nails lacerating his thigh and arm. "Get off me!"

"Gladly, but nay until you've faced Wilcox. Ye kill this bastard now, and you may as well set sail for the continent, 'cause you'll never rest another day in Scotland."

Ciar pushed up, sending Livingstone crashing onto his arse. The man was bloody right, and that made him want to tear every piece of remaining timber from the barn with his bare hands. "We ride," he growled, heading for the horses.

Outside, Riley smirked beneath the rim of his dripping tricorn hat. "'Tis still our word against yours, Dunollie. The governor will never believe your story—not after you kidnapped three of the king's dragoons."

Ciar scowled all the more. Riley was the next scoundrel who deserved a thrashing.

He mounted and wiped the blood off his cheek with his sleeve. He most likely looked as bedraggled as his prisoners.

* * *

When Ciar muscled his way into the governor's offices, a slight secretary moved in front of the door, his monocle dropping from his eye. "You cannot go in there. Guards, stop him!"

Ciar grabbed the man's shoulder and brusquely ushered him out of the way. He'd managed to talk his way through the gates, and he wasn't about to let this runt of a man stand in his way now. "I'm going in, and no one will block my path, especially you."

MacIntyre and his men followed with the prisoners while Ciar yanked on the latch and burst into the chamber.

Three officers looked up from a table with Wilcox at the head. "Dunollie?" He thrust his finger at the lieutenant. "Seize him."

"Not today!" Ciar boomed, drawing his sword from its scabbard. He panned the blade across the room. "No one will lay a finger on me until I've had my say."

Wilcox tipped up his chin, resting his hand on the hilt of his silver-handled pistol. "I would be within my rights to shoot you dead where you stand."

Ciar didn't lower his weapon. "Perhaps not after you've been presented with the evidence. Livingstone, MacIntyre, Kelly, bring in my prisoners."

He glanced over his shoulder as the men filed in, crowding the governor's rooms.

"You dare to arrest soldiers of the crown?" demanded the lieutenant.

"May I introduce…" Ciar gestured with his sword. "Tommy MacIntyre's heir. He has identified certain effects belonging to his father. Things found in the possession of these three miscreants."

Riley gripped his bound fists over his chest. "You'd do anything to keep your neck out of a noose, MacDougall."

"Do not try to hide your finger, sentinel," said MacIntyre. "Me da's ring was the first thing I spotted when you were sitting that nag."

Ciar threw a questioning glance at Kelly while the Irishman shrugged. Evidently Tommy Jr. had been saving for this moment to reveal yet another bit of evidence.

"Riley cannot deny it, 'cause there's proof—'tis engraved with TM."

Wilcox nodded to the lieutenant, who sauntered up to Riley and held out his palm. "Let me see it."

Riley made a show of struggling to take off the ring while Ciar's blood boiled. "Stop with the theatrics."

When the band finally slipped off, the lieutenant held it to the candlelight. "Looks like the letters have been filed."

MacIntyre leaned in and shifted the ring. "I can still see the T. Look there."

"It proves nothing," Riley said, smirking.

If only I could slap the grin from his vainglorious face.

With a tilt of his chin, Ciar motioned Kelly forward, who produced a leather-wrapped parcel. "More evidence, if I may."

Wilcox leaned across the board. "Make it fast. You men are filling my rooms with the stench of wet wool and interrupting the king's business."

"This won't take long." Kelly placed the bundle on the table, opened it, then held up a pocket watch. "We found this on Manfred."

Tommy Jr. pointed. "It belonged to my father and has *T. MacIntyre* etched on the back, and the engraving hasn't been filed."

The lieutenant concurred, the ring still in his pincers.

"I'll take that." Tommy Jr. snatched the ring, slipped it into his sporran, then pointed to the second item in the parcel, a knife. "And that's me da's sgian dubh. You'll have to take my word on it, but it has a nick about a third of the way up where it hit a wee stone."

The lieutenant unsheathed the blade and examined it. "There's a nick, but Dunollie could have given these things to you just to pin the murder on these men—the very three who witnessed his barbarity."

"Mayhap," said Kelly. "But the proof came when Brown showed me the sgian dubh at the Inverlochy tavern. He boasted about the whole thing, swung the piece by the chain, and told me all about his knife-throwing abilities."

"Lies, ye maggot!" Brown bellowed.

"Enough." Wilcox sliced his hand through the air. "The lieutenant is right. This evidence proves nothing."

Riley chuckled. "Exactly what I said."

Wilcox pointed. "And you had best keep your mouth shut, sentinel. These effects should have been returned to the next of kin, not pilfered by you and your fellow soldiers."

MacIntyre scooped up the parcel and twisted it between his fists. "You cannot be serious. Their guilt is as clear as the nose on my face. You haven't considered at all the reputation and nature of a respected laird from a family that has ruled in the Highlands since the Lords of the Isles."

The lieutenant strolled back around the table. "That doesn't make him innocent."

Tommy Jr. gestured to Ciar. "I believe his word over that

of these sorry louts for certain. Surely my testament to his character bears some weight. After all, it was me father who was murdered—stabbed in the back by a coward."

"One might think ye had a hand in it as well," said Riley.

Before did something he'd regret, Ciar sheathed his sword. "I came upon these dragoons on the road to Spean Bridge. They had killed an innocent man, and I caught them in the midst of stealing his belongings." He thrust his finger at Brown. "And this buffoon had the audacity to boast about it to Mr. Kelly."

"Your underhanded spy will say anything to earn his coin," said Brown.

Ciar placed his palms on the table and looked Wilcox in the eye. They had presented irrefutable evidence. It was time to call an end to this madness. "I did not kill Tommy MacIntyre. I will swear to it on my life." He threw an up-turned palm toward his prisoners. "Before you stand three corrupt men, two of whom boasted about their crimes. And I—"

"Move aside," boomed a deep voice from the doorway.

Ciar straightened as an officer marched in carrying a saddle.

"I'm Captain MacLeod from Dunbarton."

Swallowing his groan, Ciar looked to the ceiling. He'd never met a MacLeod with whom he'd seen eye to eye.

"I'd heard a rumor Ciar MacDougall was trying to clear his name. And I'll tell you true that news didn't surprise me." MacLeod arched a thick eyebrow, eyeing Dunollie. "No matter how much I dislike MacDougalls, the charge of murder didn't fit."

Ciar offered a curt bow of his head. "My thanks."

"After it was reported that Mr. Riley was abducted from an alehouse by Dunollie, I did some investigating of my own." The captain tossed the saddle on the table. "This belonged to Tom MacIntyre."

"Another of the decedent's possessions?" asked Wilcox.

Riley's eyes bugged wide, his face growing redder by the moment. "It still doesn't prove I killed the man."

"But it proves you're a thief," said the captain. "Furthermore—"

"I didn't throw the knife," said Brown, sweat streaming from his brow. "Isn't that right, Manfred? You tell them."

Manfred stood frozen like a frightened deer. "Shhh."

Ciar rubbed his hands. Aye, he knew the truth, but having it uttered by his accusers would be all the more pleasing. "What was that, Mr. Brown? If you did not, who wielded the knife?"

"Mr. Riley," said Captain MacLeod. "Sentinel Warburton, step forward!"

A soldier wearing a grenadier hat marched inside and saluted. "Sir."

"Let us set this issue to rights once and for all."

"Please do," said Wilcox.

"Go on," MacLeod urged.

"Well, I nay care to speak out against no one, but the captain said 'twas me duty to report the truth."

Wilcox impatiently rolled his hand through the air. "Which is?"

Warburton shot a nervous look to Riley. "He showed me the name carved under the seat of the saddle then told me he was aiming to leave the service a rich man."

"And how does he plan to do that?" asked the captain.

"Told me he's a highwayman. Said I could get a slice of the spoils if I joined ranks with him—and he'd never be caught on account of his good standing with the queen's— *er*—thc king's dragoons."

Riley struggled against his bindings. "Lies!" He spat in Ciar's direction. "Dunollie did it. I seen him with me own eyes. The lot of you are scheming against me."

"It was 'im all along," shouted Brown, thrusting bound arms toward Riley.

"Too right. Both of 'em forced me to go along with it." Manfred finally found his voice.

"Silence." Wilcox stepped from around the table. "I thank you, Captain, for your quick work in bringing the truth forward."

"I am the one who is grateful that a member of the army sought to uncover the truth." Ciar shook MacLeod's hand. "I am in your debt, sir."

The man's handshake was firm. "My duty is to maintain the peace. I hate to see an innocent man suffer for a crime he did not commit, even a MacDougall."

"Dunollie, you are free to go," said Wilcox.

Ciar held up his palms. "Not so fast. I understand you have taken Miss Emma Grant into custody. I will not take another step without her."

Wilcox frowned. "I'm afraid you will lose on that count."

"But she is innocent."

"I daresay she is a pest. But, alas, she is not here. I'd hoped to lure you sooner by making a public display. When that didn't work, her brother took the hapless girl home."

"To Glenmoriston?" Ciar asked, his voice shooting up.

"I assume so."

"When was this?"

Wilcox looked between his officers. "Has it been four days now?"

Shite.

Not that Ciar didn't want Emma to be safe, but Robert wasn't a man to cross even if they were allies.

"Now if you would all vacate my offices, I have a meeting to continue." Wilcox's eyebrows disappeared beneath his periwig. "And, Dunollie, I suggest you forget about the Grant woman and take a long rest in your medieval castle. You Highlanders are giving me ulcers."

Clenching his teeth and bowing his head, Ciar backed toward the door.

Chapter Twenty-Five

*T*he pungent smell of the bacon Mrs. Tweedie had brought in with the breakfast tray turned Emma's stomach. She rolled over, hugging a pillow to her chest. Robert had visited her chamber once since they'd arrived home. Their discussion had been rather short. He'd insisted she was behaving like a spoiled child and forbade her from uttering Ciar MacDougall's name ever again.

He never asked how she felt or allowed her to complete a sentence in defense of the Highlander she knew only to be kind and good and honorable. In her brother's eyes, Ciar had become a scoundrel of the worst sort, Emma was ruined, and she had naught but to resume her role as the dutiful sister, fated to live in spinsterhood for the rest of her days.

When a knock came at the door, Emma drew the quilt over her head. "Leave me be."

"I may not be able to pick locks, but I do have a key to this door." The timbers muffled Janet's voice, though she was clear enough. "And I will stay away no longer."

Emma groaned and pulled herself up, fluffing the pillows behind her back. Her brother's wife took his side, of course. She had to. They were married, after all.

The key scraped in the lock, and the door's hinges creaked. "Good heavens, you haven't eaten in days."

"I'm not hungry."

The wooden chair beside the bed groaned as Janet sat. "I ken how much you must be hurting."

"Do you?" Emma couldn't hide the sarcasm from her tone.

"I believe so."

"'Tis easy for you to say. You are a happily wedded woman."

"But my happiness didn't come without paying a price. You ought to ken as well as anyone. You were there the day my father came and accused Robert of . . ." Janet cleared her throat. ". . . destroying my virtue."

Oh, yes, Emma remembered all too well, though someone in the household appeared to have double standards. "And yet my brother sees fit to say the same about me."

"You haven't spoken much of your ordeal, aside from fiercely supporting Dunollie, which makes no sense at all. What happened all that time you were away? And why did he leave you *alone* on a barren isle?"

Emma clasped and unclasped her hands. "I'd prefer not to say."

"Why? We have never harbored secrets between us. Why now?"

"Because if you misunderstand anything I say, you'll go straight to Robert. He's already forbidden me to speak of Ciar. I simply don't feel as if I'll be taken seriously by you or anyone in this household."

"I see." Janet sniffed, the chair creaking as she paused. "I also can confidently say I understand. If you recall, after I left Glenmoriston with my father, I was ruined. Moreover, it was nearly a year before I saw Robert again, and it took all but an act of God to prove to Da that Robert's actions had been in consideration of my well-being."

Emma smoothed her fingers over the quilt. What she wouldn't give if her cloud had a silver lining like Janet's. Things seemed so hopeless. She didn't even know where Ciar was, or if he'd been hurt. Or...

"I'll say this," Janet continued. "Explain your story, and I give you my oath nothing you say will go beyond these walls unless you grant me permission to discuss anything in particular with Robert."

The bacon wafted. "May I have a cup of tea?"

"It is most likely cold."

"That's all right."

A china cup tinked as Janet poured and then passed along the cup and saucer. "There's still a bit of warmth in it."

Emma took a long drink and rested it on her lap. "So many things happened at Achnacarry, all to which you were witness. Ye ken, Ciar gave me Albert—such a dear and thoughtful gift. Lord, I miss that dog."

"Where is he now?"

"The soldiers left him on Kerrera. I pray Nettie is feeding him."

"I'm sure she is." Janet patted Emma's arm. "So...as I observed, Dunollie paid you a great deal of attention at Achnacarry."

"He did."

"And you enjoyed his kindness."

May as well have out with the shocking details. "I kissed him—or he kissed me. In the passageway."

"Whilst we were there?"

"Aye." Emma finished drinking the contents of her cup

and handed it and the saucer to her sister-in-law. "The kiss was rather improvised, and I wasn't expecting him to, but when he did, my entire body felt like it was floating on a puffy cloud."

Janet hummed a wee chuckle. "I ken that feeling all too well. But Dunollie should not have taken liberties."

How could Janet say such a thing? Emma knew something of the liberties Robert had taken when Her Ladyship was but a guest at Glenmoriston, especially kissing—kissing and moaning that could be heard throughout the house. And after Emma's adventure with Ciar, she now knew why.

"Ciar said the same," she explained. "He apologized over and over."

"Is that why he gave you the dog?"

"I don't think so. He gave me Albert because we bonded instantly, and Dunollie thought he might help me."

"And thus your affection for the big laird grew."

"It did."

"But even then, what prompted you to go alone to Fort William?"

"I wasn't alone," Emma hedged. "I was with Sam."

"A mere lad of sixteen, mind you."

"He was the only person at Achnacarry who I thought might agree to help me."

Janet's chair again groaned with movement. "*I* would have helped you."

Emma dragged a pillow across her midriff and hugged it. "I think not. You would have told me to let the men handle it. You even wrote missives to Robert and your da, remember?"

Since Janet hadn't reacted too overbearingly to the kiss, Emma explained the rest, from meeting with the governor and figuring out the number of steps to the sally port, to the night of the breakout and how they managed to slip away from the dragoons. She even went so far as to explain about Ciar's hiding place in the cellars of Gylen Castle and how he'd slept on the floor.

At first.

Nonetheless, Emma would carry every intimate and precious detail of their romance with her to the grave. She'd atone for her sins on Judgment Day if she must, though she couldn't fathom how loving Ciar was a sin.

Those fleeting moments with him were the happiest days of her life. She would treasure them and never allow a soul to utter a word of condemnation about the feelings they shared.

"I cannot believe how strong you are," Janet said, her voice sincere. "Your tenacity never ceases to surprise me."

"Before we went to Achnacarry for Kennan and Divana's wedding, I never thought I'd fall in love. Ye ken I never wanted to leave Glenmoriston because it is so familiar to me. But now I want to run from this place and never return."

"Oh, dear," Janet whispered. "We certainly do not want that. You are our sister, and we love you no matter what. You know that, do you not?"

Emma squeezed the pillow. "Love me though I am ruined?"

"Of course. Nothing has changed."

"Everything has changed." She flung the pillow aside. They still thought of her as a fragile waif—an incomplete person to be hidden away and only whispered about. Emma clenched her fists. "After all I have said, do you not understand? I *love* him."

Janet heaved a long sigh, one expressing frustration. "Perhaps I ought to write to Dunollie."

"What good would that do? Unless we've received word of his pardon, he will not be home to intercept a letter."

"You said he'd gone to Dunbarton to find one of the guilty sentinels?"

"Aye, and I've not heard from him since."

"I have an uncle nearby in Glasgow. Perhaps I'll start by writing him. Will you allow me that?"

"If you think it might help, I'd thank you."

"This is a precarious path you've chosen, but believe me when I say I want to help you. More than anything I want you to be happy." Janet clutched Emma's hands. "We first need to figure out where we can find Dunollie. In the meantime, I'll work on softening Robert's anger."

A heavy weight began to shift from Emma's shoulders. Was there hope? "I would give the world to make him understand."

"Time has a way of helping men forget."

As long as Ciar doesn't forget me.

"I'll send Betty in and ask her to draw you a bath. That ought to make you feel a bit better, dearest."

Though Emma nodded, she doubted anything except receiving news that Ciar had cleared his name would make the melancholy pass.

* * *

The two-day journey to Glenmoriston was pure torture. Ciar didn't give fig about his nagging headache. The agony was the endless time it took to ride through the glens and over craggy mountains.

If the horses had been able to keep going, he would have ridden all night, but Ciar and his men had been forced to stop at the tavern in Laggan last eve. Though he hadn't slept overmuch, the respite did afford him time for a bath and a shave, which would help him pass muster where Grant was concerned.

Now, as they started up the north shore of Loch Ness, he could hold back no longer. He beckoned the men with an arcing wave of his hand and cued his horse for a gallop. He rode as if chased by the devil, leaning over his mount's withers, keeping his elbows tight to reduce the drag.

The wind howled from behind, making the loch's waves crest with whitecaps. Above, the clouds hung low, threatening to release their ire. And to his left, the birch and sycamore trees fought with the gale, popping and rustling, agitated in restless fury. Leaves scattered through the air, hinting at the change of seasons. Even as rain spat from the skies, Ciar refused to slow the pace.

His heart hammered at the signpost to Invermoriston and he turned northward, riding along the River Moriston. The gelding slowed to a trot as his iron shoes thundered across the timbers of the bridge spanning Moriston Falls—the very place Emma had spoken so fondly of. The bower her grandfather had built was clear now. Funny, after all the times Ciar had traveled this route, he'd never noticed how the rush of the water boomed around him, nor had he seen the bower tucked among the trees.

And now he was so close to her, his heart twisted into a hundred knots, making his chest ache. Up the hill he rode until Grant's expansive manse came into view. Ciar reined his laboring horse to a stop, scanning the numerous windows above the ground floor. Did one of them look out from Emma's bedchamber or was her room rear facing?

Livingstone rode in beside him. "What's the plan?"

Ciar's gaze slipped to the brass knocker. "I suppose I'll rap on the door and see who answers."

"Do you ever answer your own door?"

"Nay."

"So will you speak to the lass first, then?"

"I'll try to."

But his plans were thwarted when Grant stepped outside with a healthy contingent of men at his flanks. By the scowl on his friend's face, this wasn't going to be easy.

Ciar dismounted. "Were you expecting a battle?"

Robert's eyes grew dark as he swirled the palm of his hand over his dirk's pommel. "Perhaps. I wasn't expecting you to show your face on my lands, for certain."

A tic twitched at the back of Ciar's jaw. "No? Is there a rift between us of which I've not yet been informed?"

May as well make him spell it out.

"Bloody oath there is." Thrusting his hand toward an upper window, Grant continued, "I've a sister inside who hasn't come out of her chamber in days. Moreover, she's ruined on account of you and your carelessness."

A shadow moved behind the curtains. Was it Emma? Dear God, she must be at her wit's end after her ordeal. If only the wind had been with him on the voyage from Dunbarton, he might have arrived before the dragoons took her.

"I was delayed."

"You left her alone on an island. Do you have any idea how fragile my sister is?"

"She insisted, but—"

"Insisted? And where were you at the time? Or was your mind addled because you took advantage of an innocent maid?"

A lead weight dropped to the pit of Ciar's stomach. Had he taken advantage?

Nay.

He'd fallen in love. Emma had shown him so much about what it meant to be alive. How could he explain it all in a few words?

He spread his palms at his sides. "I love her."

"You?" Grant guffawed. "A condemned man?"

Livingstone hopped off his horse. "Wilcox granted a pardon."

"I should have guessed since you've returned from the dead. Nonetheless, that still does not allay the carelessness in the way you treated my sister."

"Carelessness? I did nothing but treat her with respect."

"Aye? Then why in God's name did you not send her back to Achnacarry with the stable boy?"

"Because she was seen with her dog. She picked the locks both to the sea gate and to my cell. Had she returned with the lad I feared there would be retribution."

"Except Wilcox showed up here. Not at my father-in-law's keep."

Ciar raked his fingers through his hair. Damnation, he hadn't considered that. Mayhap he *should* have sent Emma back with Sam. "My actions were only in your sister's interests, you must know that."

"I know nothing except that I found my sister starved and locked in a pillory. A disgrace no gentlewoman should ever experience." Grant thrust his finger toward the drive. "Now take your men and leave my lands afore I lose my temper and end this in a duel."

"Ye must ken I do not want to fight you." Ciar flicked his scabbard's leather strap, releasing the hilt of his sword. "But I cannot tuck my tail and run. Not until I've seen Miss Emma."

Grant was a formidable swordsman, but Ciar was bigger and had the stronger arm. They'd sparred many times before, and either Grant was willing to die for his sister's virtue or he was bluffing.

Taking a step forward, Ciar darcd to hope. "I'd marry her today if it would change your mind."

But Grant's expression grew darker as he thrust out his chin. "How can I allow my dear, frail sister to marry a man who has no concern for her well-being? Must I say again that you ought to have sent her back to Achnacarry." Robert's sword whooshed through its scabbard as he drew it. "But no, you opted to take her to a ruined castle on a barren isle where you then abandoned her. How many times must I repeat your offenses?"

His gut clenching, Ciar readied his weapon. "You were not there to judge. As I said before, every decision I made was to uphold your sister's welfare and protection. If I had known she would have been safe on Lochiel's lands, I would not have hesitated to send her back with Sam." Crouching, Ciar circled to the right. "However, at the time I believed her life was in danger, and the only way I could assure her safety and clear her name was to take her into hiding with me."

Grant countered, sidestepping. "But you failed miserably."

Bellowing like a mad bull, Robert attacked with a thrust to the heart.

Lunging, Ciar defended with an outward parry as he drew his dirk with his left hand.

In the blink of an eye, the bull-headed oaf bared his teeth and swung back, aiming a deadly strike.

Ciar jumped away from the hissing blade. "Stop this madness! What is it you want? Lands? Wealth?"

Grant sidestepped and thrust again. "I want never to set eyes on your grisly face again."

Defending every strike, Ciar's sword clanged as Robert attacked in a fit of rage. The bastard hacked at every soft spot imaginable, making it impossible to shove him away long enough to reason with him. Their blades stalled, clashing in a struggle of one weapon against the other, the iron screeching until the swords met at the hilt. Refusing to injure his friend, Ciar pushed Grant aside and smacked his shoulder blade with the pommel of his hilt.

The bull of a man stumbled and whipped around.

"No!" Emma's voice rang out with the tenor of a bell.

Ciar's gut twisted as the sound of slippered footsteps approached. Albert barked.

Robert's blade flashed.

"Stoooooop!" Ciar yelled as time slowed. He booted Grant in the hip. As the man fell, his blade swept forward, slicing across Emma's arm. Down she went as her shrill scream prickled like tiny knives in his back.

With his next heartbeat, Ciar dropped to his knees, wrapping the only woman he'd ever loved in his arms.

Chapter Twenty-Six

*E*mma felt no pain. Ciar's arms enveloped her—warm, loving, protective. He was here, and that was all that mattered. After all the worry she'd endured, at last he had come for her.

He pressed his lips to her temple. "I'm so sorry, my love. We had no wind sailing up from the Firth of Clyde. The voyage took an entire sennight."

"I cannot believe you're here." The dog licked her face. "And you brought my precious Albert!"

"He missed you so very much. We both did." He wrapped a cloth around her arm, tying it snugly. "This is my cravat. It will stanch the bleeding for the now. Are you feeling faint?"

She smiled at him, brushing her fingers over his smooth, beardless cheek. "I'm so happy to see you a wee scratch cannot affect me in any way."

"I'm afraid 'tis more than a scratch, *mo leannan*."

She closed her eyes, relishing the deep tenor of Ciar's voice. Masculine, yet gentle.

"Release my sister," Robert growled like a belligerent boar.

"No!" Emma cried, clinging to her Highland hero.

"You're bleeding," said Robert. "Fetch the healer at once," he ordered one of his men.

Ciar rose to his feet, cradling Emma in his arms. "She needs rest," he said. "Have you bandages?"

"You will put my sister down this instant," Robert demanded.

Emma flung her hand toward her brother, found his tartan sash and grabbed it. "If you truly love me you will cease this mindlessness."

"I agree!" called Janet, over the patter of her feet running from the house. "You are being overbearingly rude to our guest."

"Thank you, Janet." Emma smiled in Janet's direction. Bless it, she would stand up to her brother and bear the consequences. "I will only return to my chamber if the chieftain of Dunollie takes me above stairs. And if you deny him, I will insist that he take me elsewhere."

"I adore your fortitude, lass, but you need to have your arm tended before we can go anywhere." Ciar started for the house. "We'll finish our conversation later, shall we, Grant? And mind you, it hasn't escaped me that your sword was the one which struck Miss Emma. Furthermore, I did nothing but defend your attack. Prepare to accept my offer of marriage forthwith. I shall not be denied."

Janet kept pace, the tap-tap of her slippers moving swiftly. "Are you suffering, my dear?"

"I've never been happier." Emma brushed her fingers along Ciar's chin. "You've shaved."

"A man must put his best foot forward when wooing

a wife," he whispered, marching inside. "Now try to keep quiet until I have a look at your arm."

Emma's stomach fluttered. In fact her entire body was aflutter. Wife? Did he truly say "wife"?

"I'll bring up some willow bark tea," said Janet. "You mightn't feel pain now, but I guarantee it will hurt a great deal more once the excitement abates."

"Thank you." Ciar hastened the pace. "Which way, my love?"

"First landing. Fourth door on the left."

The ninth step creaked as they climbed just as it always did. "I would have been here sooner, but when we returned to Gylen, I was bludgeoned by one of Wilcox's men—was in and out of consciousness three days. But I must tell you every time I opened my eyes I longed to hold you in my arms again."

"I kent something horrible had happened."

"But it was worse for you. I am so sorry I wasn't there when Wilcox arrived."

She curled into him, never so thrilled to be alive. "'Tis all forgotten now I'm in your arms."

"Arf!" Albert yipped as Ciar strode through the corridor.

"There's my dog, come, laddie!"

"Fourth on the left?" Ciar asked.

"Aye."

He strode inside along with Albert. "He's excited to see you."

"Truly? I was afraid I'd never see him again."

Ciar rested her on the bed. "You've bled through my makeshift bandage. Where can I find cloths?"

"There ought to be a stack of clean ones beneath the washstand." Emma patted the mattress beside her. "Come, laddie."

Albert jumped up, wriggling and rubbing his head in her lap.

She wrapped her arms around him and ran her fingers through his fur, laughing even though her arm throbbed with her effort. "I've never been so happy to be injured."

"I hope Robert didn't cut you too deeply." Ciar returned to her bedside. "Albert, down."

"Nay." She held tight. "I want him here."

"Then you shall have him." He chuckled and slid a cloth beneath her arm. "Can you open and close your fingers?"

As she did, Emma hissed with a sharp pain.

He brushed his knuckle across her cheek. "I'm so sorry, *mo leannan*. I should have reacted faster."

"It wasn't your fault. Robert doesn't understand. He thinks you took advantage of me."

He kissed the place where his knuckle had been. "Did I not?"

Emma closed her eyes and sighed. "Never in all your days diminish what we shared. It was magnificent and pure."

"Nothing short of miraculous," he said, his breath whispering along her nape.

She scraped her teeth over her bottom lip, dying to ask about what he'd meant when he carried her into the house. "Um...would you mind repeating what you said after I noticed you'd shaved?"

"I beg your pardon?"

"Ye ken...what was it you said about wooing a wi—"

"Good heavens, Miss Emma." Betty burst through the door. "You must forgive me. I was in the kitchens when the accident happened."

"Step away from my sister's bed," boomed Robert in a most unpleasant tone. "Mary Catherine, the family's healer, has arrived."

As Ciar's warmth moved away, the chamber filled with excitable people all yammering at once.

"I've brought a tincture of willow bark tea," said Janet, moving close. "This ought to take the edge off the pain."

Albert moaned.

Emma reached up. "Ciar!"

"I'm here." His voice came from the foot of the bed. "You'd best drink Her Ladyship's tea."

"How are you feeling, Miss Emma?" asked Mary Catherine, taking her hand.

She glowered, hopefully directing her ire at her brother. "I was much better when Dunollie was tending me."

"Well, he's not a healer." The woman examined Emma's arm and removed the bandage. "Oh, dear, this needs compression. Betty, apply a cloth, quickly."

"I'll do it," said Ciar.

"No," Robert groused. "I must speak with you in my library."

"But Emma needs—"

"I concur with Grant," said Mary Catherine quite tersely, as if she'd entertain no argument. "Everyone out aside from Betty and Lady Janet—that is, if you have the stomach for it, given your condition, m'lady."

"I would prefer to be no place other than at my dearest sister's side." Janet placed the mug in Emma's free hand. "Heed me and drink this down before she starts."

"Robert!" Emma howled, ignoring everyone else. "You be nice to Dunollie or I will never speak to you again!"

"I'll hear him out. Then I shall decide what is to be done."

The door clicked shut, and the men were gone.

Emma relented and drank the bitter tea. If only she hadn't been injured, she would stand between her brother and the Highlander who'd stolen her heart and refuse to budge until Robert relented.

She placed the cup on the side table. "I cannot remain here while my brother acts like an angry bull."

"I think he kens how you feel about Dunollie." Janet brushed the hair away from Emma's forehead. "I made certain of it."

"Oh?" she asked. "Tell me."

"Let us just say the laird of this house kens his wife and sister will be moving to Achnacarry if he doesn't pull his stubborn head out of his backside."

* * *

Grant slumped into the chair behind his writing desk, a dark scowl fixed on his face, making the knife scar he'd received in a duel with Kennan Cameron puckered and red. Kennan was Janet's brother, but the two men had been sworn enemies at the time. Ciar remembered the incident as if it were yesterday—in fact, the ordeal was most likely what had started Grant's love affair with his wife.

"Sit." The curmudgeon gestured to the chair across the board. "You look like shite."

"Was just thinking the same about you." Ciar glanced to the sideboard. "Mind if I pour?"

"My thanks," Grant responded.

Ciar sauntered over and pulled the stopper out of the decanter, pouring two drams. "Ye ken I'd rather be with Emma at the moment."

The mad bull scowled. "You're not going anywhere near her."

Ciar placed a glass in front of his *friend* and took a seat across. Saying nothing, he studied Robert and sipped. How many times had they sat in these very chairs and enjoyed a roll of the hazard dice or a game of cards? The library hadn't changed much in all that time. The walls were lined with hundreds of leather-bound books, the family bible sat on the table near the white marble hearth between two wing-backed chairs, the old globe rested in a stand near the window. How Ciar would like to be anywhere on that round map aside from here at the moment.

Robert turned the glass between his fingers and stared at the amber liquid. "Bless Janet. She's the reason I haven't ordered my men to tie you to a whipping post. Lord kens you deserve it."

"Perhaps I do." The old lead ball churned in Ciar's gut. In truth there were many things he would have done differently, though hindsight had a way of making men wise. "However, I'll tell ye true here and now, Emma was seen fleeing Fort William with me—mainly on account she brought her dog. They even shouted 'Grant' as we were fleeing. We headed for Corran, where Dicky MacIain took Sam across the loch. I swear to you on my life your sister would have been caught right there had she been on the ferry with the lad."

Robert sipped, his eyes wary. "How can you be so certain?"

"We hid beneath the pier whilst redcoats rode in. They searched for us—even waited for Dicky to return from crossing the narrows."

"Good God, 'tis a wonder you slipped away." Robert set his glass on the desk. "But you shouldn't have fled with her in the first place."

"Oh, I see." Ciar guffawed with a sardonic snort. "I should have tucked tail and run like a coward after she risked all to break into one of the Highland's most secured fortresses to help me escape."

Robert glowered, his scar even redder now.

Perhaps it was time to stir up the past. "As I recall, two years ago you fled into the mountains with Janet in the midst of a snowstorm, mind you."

"That was different."

"Was it? I think not overmuch. Allow me to remind you—the woman who would become your wife slapped a soldier at the Samhain gathering and all hell broke loose. I was there." Ciar leaned forward and drove his pointer finger into the table. "We rode out together and found Kennan beat half to death. *Remember?* Then we decided I would take him to a healer whilst you went after Janet."

Wiping a hand across his face, Ciar could have sworn Robert almost smiled—the impetus encouraging him to continue, "What if it had been the other way around, and I'd been the one to go after the lass?"

Robert's knuckles turned white as he gripped his glass. "Do not even think on it."

"All I am saying is my actions were to protect Emma, nay to harm her."

"Then why was she alone when Wilcox raided the Gylen ruins?"

Ciar shot another longing glance at the globe. Perhaps a jaunt to Spain would suit—as long as he took Emma with him. "I asked her to stay with Archie and Nettie, my tenants on the isle, but the lass refused. She said she was more comfortable in the..." He hated to say "cellar." The word made the place sound like a dungeon rather than a comfortable shelter. "In the labyrinth of secret chambers my father and I built should something like being wrongly accused of a crime happen—though we were both preparing for the advent of a political upheaval."

But the explanation only made Grant grow redder in the

face. "You agreed to her ridiculous request? Where was your mind? In your cock, I gather."

Mayhap it was. Ciar sipped his whisky. Damnation, the arse wasn't making it easy. "I planned to be away only three days, and Emma insisted she could care for herself. After all, she had plenty of food and Albert to guard her."

"Ah yes, the dog." Robert leaned forward and rapped his knuckles on the desk, making the ink pot and quill rattle. "I still believe you should have returned her to Achnacarry forthwith. Had you done so, her reputation might have been salvageable."

In truth, the moment she left for Fort William, she'd compromised herself, not that Ciar cared a lick about whether Emma's virtue was ruined or not. But what really needled him was Robert's bravado. The man seemed to let on as if he'd had a list of suitors lined up to marry the lass, which after every indication from Emma, was not the case.

Ciar squared his shoulders. "I offer for her hand in marriage. Right here and now. I am prepared to wed your sister today."

Grant drank, his color returning to its normal pale tone. "It gives me no great pleasure to admit I'll have to consider your suit."

Ciar regarded his friend across the desk. What was he hiding? What did he want? "Why are you battling me on this? We've been friends since we were bairns. Ye ken I'll give her a warm home where she'll be happy. She'll want for nothing."

"But what of you?"

"Me?"

"She thinks she's desperately in love with you."

Ciar's heart skipped a beat. "I hope she is. I love her more than anything on this earth."

Grant stood and grabbed the bottle from the sideboard. "Then why did you not declare your true feelings afore you offered for her hand? Must I repeat that Emma is fragile. She needs a husband who will be patient with her, a man who will be gentle and kind and understanding…"

"I'm all those things."

"Pardon me, but I've fought beside you. You're a beast."

"Aye, in the midst of battle, but when it comes to Emma, I'm naught but a lamb. I will challenge anyone who speaks against her."

"Perhaps, but after all that has transpired, I still believe you don't deserve her."

"I ken." Ciar stood, placed both his palms on the table, and gave Robert a dead-eyed stare. "But I give you my word I will spend the rest of my life proving that I do."

"Very well. I'm afraid you've left me with few other options. I will speak to the vicar, but heed me, if I *ever* hear a word of my sister's unhappiness, I will personally take it out of your hide."

An enormous grin split Ciar's face. "I'd think no less." Clapping his hands, he turned toward the door. "I cannot wait to tell her."

"It will not be you who gives her the news. In fact, I will not allow you to see her until the wedding."

The grin instantly fell. "You cannot be serious."

"I am, and that is one of my conditions."

"One?" There were more? Ciar's shoulders slumped.

"She has a sizeable dowry, you may be aware."

Quickly regaining his composure, he sliced his hand through the air. "I do not want a farthing."

"Good, because I insist the dower funds will be made available solely for Emma's use. She will exercise her discretion as to how the coin is invested and spent."

"Agreed," Ciar responded immediately, needing no time to consider the demand.

"Then leave me." Robert tossed back the remainder of his whisky. "I'd best see to her comfort. After all, as you categorically pointed out, it was my blade that cut her...even though had you not irked me beyond all reason, the accident never would have occurred."

Chapter Twenty-Seven

*E*mma cradled her arm across her midriff. The healer had closed the wound with five sutures, and it throbbed with pain. "When Ciar was here, it didn't hurt at all. Now it feels as if I've been prodded with a branding iron."

"It ought to heal nicely, given time," said Mary Catherine. "But you'll need to apply my honey poultice morning and night."

"I'll see to it," Betty replied from the other side of the bed.

A rap came at the door. "May I come in?"

Emma's heart squeezed. She would have much rather heard Ciar's voice echoing in the corridor than her brother's.

Her arm stung as she propped herself up against the pillows. "Only if you can swear to me you were civil to Dunollie."

The door creaked. "I believe once you've heard what I have to say, you will agree he received far better treatment than he deserved."

Emma doubted anything her brother said would be satisfactory.

"First of all, is the wound awfully bad?" he asked, his voice filled with concern, sounding more like the brother she loved.

"The cut didn't go too deep, though she'll be sore for a number of days." Mary Catherine wiped Emma's forehead with a linen cloth. "As long as Betty applies the poultice as I've directed, our lassie shouldn't suffer fever."

No longer able to sit while they discussed her health, Emma tossed back the bedclothes and started to swing her feet over the edge of the mattress. "Where is Ciar? I heard horses only moments ago. Did you send him away?"

Robert's hands clamped onto her shoulders. "Calm yourself."

Emma wriggled from his grasp. "How can I calm myself when my whole life is crumbling before me?"

"I'll show myself out," Mary Catherine said.

"I'll go with you," Janet echoed.

Betty's skirts brushed the side of the quilt. "I'll just take these soiled cloths down to the laundry."

Emma groaned. Were all her allies abandoning her?

The bed depressed as Robert sat. "First of all, I apologize profusely for hurting you. What made you dash into a swordfight like that? You could have been killed."

"I wouldn't have if you hadn't challenged Ciar. I love him, and I'll never again stand for you being belligerent toward him."

"Hmm." Her brother took in a long, very audible inhalation. "It appears he loves you as well."

Emma's stomach fluttered as if there were a swarm of hummingbirds inside. "Truly?"

"So much so, he asked for your hand in marriage."

Dear Lord in heaven, this had to be the best news

she'd ever received. She flung her uninjured arm around her brother's neck and covered his cheek with kisses. "Oh, Robert! Please say you're not telling tall tales. Promise me now before my heart bursts!"

He lightly brushed her cheek. "Marriage was his idea. He was rather emphatic about it."

Emma clasped her hands together. "No elixir could possibly take the pain away as much as the news you just gave me."

"I'm glad you are happy." He took her hand between his palms. "But I must say, if for any reason whatsoever you harbor doubts about Dunollie, I will put an end to—"

"Doubts? I've never been so certain about anything in all my days." She pulled her hand away, eager to leap out of bed. "Tell me, where is Ciar now? I must see him."

"I have asked him to stay away until the wedding can be arranged."

She sat straight as if a rod had just prodded her spine. "You did what?"

"He must prove to me his patience in this matter."

"But isn't it common for betrothed couples to visit with each other?"

"These circumstances are a wee bit different. After all, you stole away in the middle of the night. Risked your reputation to rush to his aid. Whilst a fugitive to the crown, he harbored you. No, you both need time to think this through."

"I ken my heart." She slammed her fist into the mattress. "I do not need time."

The bed bounced up as Robert stood. "In the interim, I shall contact the vicar, and you and Janet must commence wedding plans. There are guests to invite, gowns to make, meals to plan."

Guests? The only guest Emma wanted at the wedding

was Ciar himself. "Then tell the vicar I want to be wed in a sennight."

"A sennight?" Robert asked as if her request were preposterous. "I'll agree to no less than a fortnight."

Two weeks without Ciar? She'd die.

"And there will be no slipping out of this house in the middle of the night. I am putting the Grant guardsmen on alert. And mind you, your arm must heal. Acting irresponsibly might possibly put everything on hold."

"Oh, will it now? I recall you and Janet enjoyed a great deal of interesting activities when she broke her arm."

"Janet's broken arm has nothing to do with your present circumstances." Robert kissed her temple. "As your guardian, it is my duty to see to your health and happiness. Dunollie has agreed to these terms, and I expect you to do so as well."

She pushed him away—albeit gently. He had agreed to the wedding, after all. "Where will he stay for an entire fortnight?"

"That is up to him."

* * *

By the time Betty returned, Emma was up and pacing the floor of her bedchamber. "Oh, thank goodness you've come. I've been ready to jump out of my skin."

"What are you doing out of bed?" Betty grasped her elbow. "Come now, you need your rest. Mary Catherine left a sleeping tincture to relax you."

"I don't want to relax." Emma yanked her arm away. "But I need your help."

"Of course, miss." Betty chuckled. "Do you realize in a fortnight hence I'll be calling you 'my lady' . . . that is if you care for me to accompany you to Dunollie."

"Yes, yes, I want you to come with me." Emma led the maid to the settee. "But Robert is having me guarded, and I simply must see Ciar. We've barely had a chance to talk. And my dear brother sent him away before he could properly propose. I need to hear he wants to marry me from his own lips."

"Believe me, if you could have seen the look on that man's face when he was hovering over you like a mother hen, there would be no doubt in your mind."

"Please. I need you to go to town and tell Dunollie that I will meet him at the bower two days hence. And you mustn't tell a soul."

"If Robert is guarding the house, how do you expect to visit the bower unseen?"

Emma rubbed her hands. "I have it all planned. Dunollie will go to the bower around noon. After we've eaten, you and I will take a stroll, and lo and behold, who should we run into in Great Grandpapa's old bower but His Lairdship."

"Oh, dear," Betty sighed.

"Then you'll go to town?"

"I'll need a good reason. And 'tis too late to go today."

"Then you'll have to do it on the morrow. And aside from meeting with Dunollie, take a message to Master Tailor and tell him I want a yellow gown."

"But you wore yellow to the wedding at Achnacarry."

"Ciar said it made me outshine the bride. Not exactly out-shine, but he said the color was created for me. But this time I want plenty of lace and ribbons, and enormous sleeves."

"In taffeta. I think you will dazzle everyone in taffeta."

"Truly? Not silk?"

"Taffeta skirts with a silk bodice. You will be stunning."

"I hope Ciar will like it."

"Och, Dunollie would be head over heels in love with

you even if you arrived at your wedding wearing nothing
but a shift."

* * *

"Ye mean to tell me you're taking orders from Grant?"
Livingstone asked, slamming his tankard down on the bar
at the Invermoriston Alehouse. "He should be kissing your
backside for protecting his sister as long as you did."

"'Tis only for a fortnight. Once I've passed muster,
things will be set to rights again." Ciar didn't expect his
man to understand everything. "Go to Dunollie and fetch
my mother's ruby ring from the strongbox. Then I want you
to order thirteen galleys and my cutter to sail around John
O'Groats and into the Moray Firth. Wait for me at the mouth
of the River Ness."

"What the blue blazes? Are ye expecting a war?"

"I'm expecting to take the new lady of Dunollie home
in comfort."

"But what of the wool shipments?"

"They can bloody wait a few days. Now haud your
wheesht. Your complaining is making me cross."

"I'll never understand how men lose their heads over a
woman."

"Beg your pardon, Dunollie, sir."

Ciar turned, alerted by the sound of a woman's voice.
"Betty? I'm surprised to see you here."

She glanced from side to side, obviously uncomfortable
with being seen inside an alehouse. "Miss Emma sent me."

Gulping against the lump in his throat, he dismissed
Livingstone with a wave of his hand. "How is she? Is her
arm paining her overmuch?"

"Oh, no, the cut on her arm is the least of her woes."

Woes?

He slammed his fist into his palm. "I'll bury my knuckles in Grant's face if he has done anything to upset her."

"Heavens, no. I believe there has been quite enough masculine bravado, if I may be so bold." She leaned in and cupped her hand to her mouth. "Miss Emma wishes to meet you in the bower just after noon on the morrow."

"She—?" His stomach somersaulted...about five times. "Do you think that wise?"

"No one seems to care overmuch what I think. But she feels your meeting will remain a secret if you slip inside early. She intends to take a walk with me after her nooning."

He laughed from his belly. "She is brilliant, is she not?"

"Determined for certain." Betty shook her finger beneath Ciar's nose. "Mind you, I'll be watching. There'll be no *liaison* whatsoever."

Ciar gave the maid a wink. If only she knew.

Chapter Twenty-Eight

*S*ince his best suits of clothes were stowed away at Dunollie, Ciar spent the morning in the tailor's shop being pinned and prodded.

Finally able to lower his arms and breathe, Ciar used his brooch to refasten his plaid at the shoulder. "What are the damages?"

"Let's see here." The tailor slung his measuring ribbon around his neck and headed for his writing table, where he dipped his quill in the ink pot. "A shirt of first quality muslin, one pound fifty. A kilt in red-and-green tartan with white thread accents will be quite dear, I'm afraid." He dipped his quill. "Three pounds. Then you asked for matching flashes, hose, and a velvet doublet—"

"Dark green, mind you."

"Yes, of course—it will be a suit of clothes fit for a king."

Ciar chuckled. "A Scottish king."

The tailor jotted his notes on parchment along with prices, then summed the lot. "That will be seven pounds, thirty pence. Payable when the work is complete."

"My thanks." Ciar bowed. "I shall leave you to it."

"Very well. Good day, sir."

At last the time had come to make his way to the bower. Thank heavens Emma's lady's maid had visited him at the alehouse, else he might have had to lay siege to Moriston Hall to see his betrothed.

Curse it all.

In truth, Ciar would have liked to have finished the fight with Grant—to have taken him down a notch. They'd been friends since birth. Their fathers were fast allies, as were their grandfathers and on down through generations of ancestors. A typical Grant, Robert had always been quick-tempered. Though, in truth, his temper was the only fault Ciar found in the man.

He walked from town into the forest that skirted the river. In no way would he use the road and take a chance on being spotted by one of Grant's spies. Better yet, the sun was shining, making him step lightly.

He paused to pluck a few blushing pink foxgloves. Closer to the river, he found daisies in full bloom as well as corn marigolds. The only other time he'd ever picked wildflowers he'd been a wee lad trying to impress his mother. Until he'd met Emma he'd rarely paid much attention to flowers.

The sound of the falls began to rush as he neared the bridge. Staying hidden in the brush, he peered up and down the road. When he spotted no one, he dashed from his hiding place and sprinted across the bridge, through the scrub, and didn't stop until he was safely hidden by the stone bower walls.

Ciar laughed as he turned full circle. There he stood, a man of eight and twenty behaving like a lad of sixteen.

Fancy what a wisp of a woman had reduced him to. Yet there was no other place he wanted to be at the moment. His skin tingled with anticipation. He needed her in his arms. He absolutely had to know she was safe and happy and thoroughly, undeniably, utterly in love with him.

Ciar paced, checking his pocket watch every half minute. The bower was a round, medieval-looking shelter. An empty brazier stood in the middle, surrounded by wooden benches. If he had to guess, a great number of clan stories had been passed down in this place. He took a length of leather thong from his sporran and tied it around the flowers to make a posy.

It was half past noon. She ought to arrive any moment. Had she tripped and fallen? Did Robert prevent her from venturing outside? Was her wound causing too much pain?

When a twig snapped outside, he pressed himself against the wall and held his breath...until Emma stepped through the archway.

A ray of sunlight captured the coppery highlights of her hair. Standing in the threshold, she held her head high and remained very still, radiant in the light as if she were an angel. With a quick inhale, she turned her head his way. "You're here," she whispered.

"Aye, lass." Taking her hands, he pulled her behind the walls and into his arms. "Only you would have sensed my presence."

"I'd find you anywhere. You smell like cedar, spice, and a wee bit of magic." She rose on her toes as her arms wrapped around him. "Och, only you can make me swoon even when you're paces away."

"God, I've missed you."

Before she could reply, he covered her mouth with a kiss. As she melted against him, he ran his hands up her spine and allowed himself to devour her. Dear God, he'd craved to have her in his arms every moment since he'd found her missing at Gylen.

"Ciar," she sighed, dropping her head back while his mouth explored her neck, her delicate cheekbones, her eyelids, until he nuzzled her ear. "I'm so happy."

Forcing himself to calm his ravenous desire, he laced his fingers through hers and took a step away. "Why are you happy, *mo leannan*?

"Because you are here with me now. And because…"

Ciar grinned at her blush. "Because?"

"Of what Robert said."

How could he be so daft? He'd been so overcome by the sight of her, he'd forgotten the most important part of his duty. Lowering himself on one knee, he swept the posy from the bench and took one of her hands in his palm.

He cleared his throat, gazing at pure beauty. "Emma Grant, you have shown me things about the world around us that I never would have stopped to notice. And yet they are such important things. Like the heavenly scent of honeysuckle. You have enriched me mind, body, and soul. You, my love, have made me a better man, and I cannot imagine existing without you."

A tear splashed on her cheek, accompanied by her blissful laugh.

His chest swelled at the sound. "Will you do me the honor of agreeing to be my wife?"

She nodded before she managed to find the word. "Aye."

He took her palm and pressed it against his cheek, then kissed it reverently. "You have made me the happiest man in all of Christendom."

"And I am the happiest woman."

Remembering the posy, he stood and placed it in her hand. "I picked these flowers for you—a gift I thought would escape suspicion when you return to Moriston Hall."

She lightly brushed her fingers over the petals. "Exquisite."

"The first I found on my journey to the bower is a spray of foxglove. It reminds me of your cheerful nature, your kindness, of how you see the good in all that surrounds you."

She smiled, her finger lightly tracing the foxglove petals. Of course she distinguished them from the others.

"The corn marigold reminded me of how beautiful you look in yellow, for there is no other color that brings out your radiance."

Her eyebrows arched with her giggle. "Yellow," she whispered.

Oh, how he loved her expressions. "And the daisies are happy as are you, both inside and out, and their petals resemble the velvet of your skin."

She hid her nose in the bouquet. "Och, mayhap you've exaggerated a wee bit."

"Nay." He kissed her forehead. "For no flowers or words can express how deeply my love runs for you."

"Oh, Ciar, I've been praying you'd say those words."

"Every time they came to my lips, I bit them back. But now that I've cleared my name, I am free to shout how much I adore you from every peak in the Highlands."

Her fingers brushed his chest and meandered up to his lips, and he smiled broadly to show her the happiness in his heart. "I think just whispering in my ear will suffice."

Pulling her into his arms, he pressed his lips to the delicate appendage. "I love you, I love you, I love you."

"And I return your love with all my heart."

"I cannot believe I am banned from seeing you until the wedding."

"Robert is being unbearable. We're hardly speaking."

"I'm sorry for that." Ciar led Emma to a bench. "He cares for you. He's worried that I will not be a worthy husband."

Emma threw her shoulders back. "He's wrong."

"I ken. But I think brothers are even stubborner than parents when it comes to marrying off their sisters. I reckon that's why he has dragged his feet and you're not already wed." He took her hand and kissed her knuckles. "Which, might I say, is very good for me."

"And me." She drew his fingers to her lips and kissed him back. "And Albert."

Ciar glanced over his shoulder. "Speaking of the dog, where is he?"

"I left him in my chamber. I didn't want to risk having him bark or do something silly like go for a swim in the river and chase ducks. He'd alert everyone in the shire, much less Moriston Hall."

"And Betty?"

"She's waiting outside."

Ciar draped his arm across Emma's shoulders and nibbled her neck. "Then thank the stars I didn't act on my desires and ravish you as soon as you stepped inside the bower."

She arched her back with a quiet giggle. "I'm not certain I agree. After all, this is a place of magic."

"Is it now?" he teased, moving his kisses to her earlobe.

"So said my great grandmama. She insisted the water in the pool at the bottom of the falls made women fertile. And she ought to know, because she birthed eleven children."

"Eleven?"

"All healthy bairns, I might add."

"Well, I do not think you and I will need magical water. Once we are wed, we will make magic of our own."

"The vicar has agreed to our wedding date. Has anyone told you?"

"Me?" Ciar smoothed his fingers down her enchantingly

straight spine. Unbelievable. Robert hadn't managed to send word. "Who am I?"

She nudged him with her elbow. "The most important man, I'll say. At the Invermoriston church ten o'clock on Monday, October first."

"Must we wait that long?"

"We must if we want Robert to speak to us again. Otherwise, we can elope this very night."

He brushed aside the auburn tresses and kissed her in the tingly spot at her jawline. "The idea has its merits."

"Miss Emma," Betty called from the archway. "'Tis time we start heading back, else you will be missed."

Emma groaned. "Already?"

Ciar pulled her to her feet. "Time will pass quickly enough. Put your posy in water, and every time you see it, think of me."

Only she would understand what he meant. She visualized everything through touch and saw so much more than everyone else.

After kissing his love goodbye, Ciar waited for a time, though the bower turned hollow and lonely without her.

Until Grant stepped inside. "Sneaking around my back, are you, Dunollie?"

Ciar's gut clenched. He didn't want a fight, but if it came to blows, he'd bloody well ensure he'd be the victor no matter what. "It seems the date for my wedding has been set, though you did not see fit to send me word."

Robert relaxed his stance. "Ah, yes, my mistake. I should have sent a messenger this morn."

Ciar dropped his hands to his sides. Grant admitted an error? Perhaps they might call a truce. "Forgive me for breaking your rules, but when I receive a summons from the woman I love, it is not in my nature to ignore her."

Grant paced toward the brazier, clasping his hands behind his back. "My sister can be quite determined when she sets her mind on something."

It wasn't difficult to agree. "Perhaps that's why she's such a brilliant harpist."

"And lock picker."

"And dog trainer."

Grant crossed the floor and clapped him on the back. "She's quite accomplished at knitting as well."

Ciar threw back his head and laughed. "Good God, 'tis nice to see your sense of humor return."

Pulling a flask from his sporran, Robert handed it over. "You truly love her, do you not?"

"More than anything on this earth. I think I always have," Ciar said before he took a swig and gave the flask back to his friend. "What changed your mind?"

"Aside from a wallop up the side of the head from my wife, I overheard some of your conversation."

Thank God the pair of them hadn't gone down to the pool and tried to prove Great Grandmama's magic. "Some?"

"Most." Grant's shoulder ticked up. "I told Betty not to make my presence known."

"Did she inform you about the meeting?"

"Nay, my guardsmen saw you slip into the wood—not long before Emma rushed through her nooning and practically ran out of the house. It didn't take a bloodhound to figure out what the pair of you were up to."

Chapter Twenty-Nine

*J*anet took Emma's hands. "Oh, my! You are the most radiant bride I've ever seen in all my days."

"You're not just saying so to whisk away my jitters?"

Betty pushed in a hairpin. "Och, you were right about choosing yellow."

"Allow me to paint a picture." Janet smoothed the taffeta over Emma's palm. "First of all, your gown looks as warm as sunshine on a summer's day. The snug-fitting silk bodice topped by lace is lovelier than a daffodil. And I would be remiss if I didn't say the swells of creamy skin peeking above are enough to bring any rugged Highlander to his knees."

Emma clapped a hand atop her breasts. "Is it too much?"

"Just enough," said Betty. "And mind you, the corn marigolds and daisies I've woven into your hair make you look bonnier than a fairy."

Tapping her fingers about her tresses, Emma inclined her ear to her lady's maid. "You've seen many fairies, have you?"

"I've heard enough stories about them to ken what they look like."

On a sigh, Emma pressed her hands against her nervous stomach. "You are both very kind, but all I care about is whether Ciar likes it."

Janet hummed. "If I know men, he'll be so enraptured with you, he'll hardly notice the gown."

"After all our work?" asked Betty. "He'd best notice it."

"He will, especially the flowers." The posy was still in a vase on the mantle. "Ciar loves corn marigolds and daisies."

Janet laughed. "And foxglove, I hear."

"Ahem." Robert cleared his throat as he opened the door. "Your trunks are loaded and will be waiting. Dunollie has sent a coach as promised."

The hummingbirds in Emma's stomach multiplied by three. "Already?"

"Would you like more time?" he asked.

"Nay." She took Betty's hand and stood. "And you've packed my harps?"

"Just as you asked." Her brother's pocket watch clicked. "'Tis time."

"I only wish you were staying for a few days. I would have liked to have a grand feast," said Janet.

Robert's heels clicked the floor. "Aye, but Dunollie has something grander planned."

Janet had invited Ciar for the evening meal a few nights ago, where he'd announced that they must leave directly after the ceremony with haste. Emma had been brimming with excitement to find out what he had devised, but he would not reveal it even to her.

Once they were in the coach, Emma's nerves didn't ease. She was very familiar with the ride to the church, but today every bump in the road made it feel as if soap bubbles were levitating and popping inside her.

As the coach rolled to a stop, she gripped the bouquet of wildflowers she'd picked with Betty yesterday. "Is this really happening?"

From across the coach, Robert patted her hand. "Aye, lass. Are you anxious?"

"A little, but I shouldn't be."

Janet tweaked one of Emma's curls. "Every bride is nervous on her wedding day. But not to worry, I've known Ciar MacDougall all my life and, though he may be a bull of a man, he'll always be gentle with you."

"And if he's not, I'll bury him," Robert growled. It always took so little to rile him.

Emma brushed her finger over a daisy. "I have no doubts about the groom. I just hope I'm truly the woman for him."

Once they stepped into the vestibule, everything passed in a blur. Janet fussed over Emma's dress while Robert explained the process of giving her away, even though they'd practiced it with the minister last eve—though Ciar hadn't been present. Her brother didn't feel the groom ought to see his bride the day before the wedding. "I allowed my wife to invite him for a meal, and that was quite enough," he had insisted.

"Is he here?" Emma asked as they started down the aisle to the rolling notes from the organ.

"Aye," Robert whispered in her ear. "He's standing up front with a daft grin on his craggy face."

"How can you say such a thing about my betrothed?"

"Forgive me." Robert cleared his throat, patting her arm. "I've never seen him look happier."

"That's better."

When they stopped, Emma pictured everything in her

mind's eye. The vicar stood before them, and she felt Ciar's aura beside her. Bathed in a wash of his spicy scent, warmth radiated from him as he filled the nave with his powerful presence.

"Who gives this woman in holy matrimony?"

Emma held her breath, praying Robert wouldn't say anything rash.

But her brother took her hands and shifted them toward Ciar. "I do."

If the priest continued from there, Emma didn't hear him. She stood facing the man she loved. She slid her fingers up his velvet doublet and brushed them over the plaid and brooch at his shoulder. The fabric was crisp and new. His cravat was made of the finest linen and tied in a perfect knot with lace fringing the two ends.

Moving upward, she found his smile, smooth, freshly shaven cheeks, and thick hair curling down to his shoulders.

"You are beautiful," she whispered.

"Nay half as bonny as the bride." His breath lightly swept across her forehead. "Och, the wee flowers are perfect."

"May we now begin?" asked the vicar.

Emma's face grew hot. He'd been waiting? She should have known. After all, the man had baptized her.

The vicar recited the service efficiently, though it was unbearably difficult to pay attention. There she stood before God and her kin pledging eternal love for Ciar MacDougall, chieftain of Dunollie, the only man she had ever and would ever love from the depths of her soul. It was difficult to believe that merely two months ago she had been content with spinsterhood. Because of her blindness she had been afraid to venture anywhere outside of Glenmoriston.

So much had transpired since then, and now she was

embarking on a new adventure—willfully going to a home where she had never been.

But Emma could do anything with Ciar at her side.

Now she harbored no fear of learning to negotiate a new home. A place where she would be Lady Dunollie, wife of the most fearsome chieftain in the Highlands. And she could hardly wait to begin.

Together they recited their vows, and when the vicar called for the ring, Ciar took her hand and circled a stone in her palm. "This was worn by my mother and my grandmother, and by generations of Dunollie women. With this ring I thee wed."

Emma felt as if she were floating on a cloud as he slipped it onto her finger and kissed her hand.

"I now pronounce you man and wife," said the vicar.

Each moment growing more ethereal than the next, she smiled at her husband.

Husband?

Now she was definitely floating. "We're married?"

Ciar pulled her into his warm, soothing, and wonderful embrace, pressing his lips against her forehead. "Aye, lass. You will be mine for the rest of our lives."

The crowd around them faded into oblivion. "And you mine."

* * *

After they'd shared a glass of oak-aged sherry, Ciar was only too happy to usher his bride toward the waiting coach.

"Write to us as soon as you arrive at your new home!" Janet called.

Robert stopped his sister and pulled her into his arms. "Och, I'll miss you, lass."

"Ye ken I'll miss you as well."

He kissed her and released her, shifting his gaze to Ciar. "Bring her back to visit often."

Ciar took his friend's hand and gave it a sincere shake. "I will, but after the bairn is born, I hope you'll see fit to venture to Dunollie. I'll teach the lad how to sail."

Emma clapped a hand to her chest and gasped. "Who told you?"

Janet looked every bit as shocked, but she rested her hand on her tummy as she had been doing of late.

"Och, it did not take a seer to figure it out." He bowed and kissed her fingers. "God's speed, m'lady."

Turning his attention to Emma, he helped his wife into the waiting coach and scooted Albert off the velvet bench.

Emma took his place and patted her knee. The dog was all too happy to rest his head there and receive a pet. "Are you ready for a new adventure, laddie?"

Ciar smoothed his palm around her shoulders. "A new adventure. I like the sound of that."

The coach rocked as it started away. "Ye ken I trust you implicitly, but will you tell me where you're taking me?"

"Well." He kissed her lips, then nibbled along her jaw to the tune of her delightful giggles. "I wanted our first days together as man and wife to be unforgettable."

Her shoulders shimmed as he licked the blue vein running down her neck. "I'll never forget."

"Nay, because I've an armada of fourteen ships waiting out at the mouth of the River Ness."

She gasped. "Fourteen ships?"

"Aye, and we'll be sailing in luxury, staying in the captain's cabin of my new cutter."

"A tall ship?"

"Mm hmm." He kissed her rosy cheek. "We'll sail around

the southern point of Britain and up the west coast until we reach the Firth of Mull."

"I ken where that is—and we'll sail past Gylen Castle and the isle of Kerrera."

"Indeed, though we'll not stop until we're moored at the estuary beneath Dunollie."

"Is Betty sailing?"

"Aye, she'll be with us."

"And Albert."

The dog's tail wagged at the sound of his name.

Chuckling, he pulled her onto his lap. "Of course Albert."

Ciar supported her back with his left hand while he cupped her cheek, admiring the delicate lines of her lips. "I love you," he whispered right before he lowered his mouth to hers. Closing his eyes, he savored her taste. As he sealed their lips together, he seduced her with hot glides of his tongue while slowly inching up the hem of her yellow gown.

She stilled his wrist. "Ciar, no."

"No?" he asked, moving his mouth to the luscious tops of her breasts—tempting, creamy flesh that had beguiled him throughout the ceremony. Sliding his fingers past her garters, he found a gloriously silken thigh. "Mayhap just a wee sample of what's to come."

"But we're in a coach."

He slipped his hand just a wee bit higher, high enough to make her blood thrum. "Aye—enclosed inside where nary a soul can see us."

"No one?" she asked, a grin spreading across her lips.

He coaxed her legs open, sliding his hand up until he lightly brushed downy curls. "Only Albert."

Emma arched into him, a hint of her nipple showing from her scooped neckline. With a sweep of his tongue it slipped free of the silk and lace, and he teased it while his finger slid into the warm, wet folds beneath her skirts.

She placed her palm on his chest and moved it downward, until she touched the tip of his cock, hard and wedged beneath the soft curve of her hip.

He moved his finger along her parting, making her head drop back with a rapturous gasp. "Let me pleasure you, my love."

She lightly brushed her fingers, making his balls tighten. "Just me?"

"Not to worry," he whispered, moving his mouth up to her lobe. "My pleasure will come later."

"Mm. And I will see to it," she said, reclining her head and moving her hips with the gentle caressing of his finger. As her passion mounted, he slid inside and worked faster, using his thumb to tantalize her. And when her mewls grew louder he covered her lips with his, relentlessly stroking her, until he muffled the elated cries of her peak with his mouth.

Panting, she brushed her hand over his hair. "I love you, Ciar MacDougall."

"And I you," he said, as he slowly slid his hand away and straightened her skirts.

"We've hit the cobblestones of Inverness. It won't be long now before we arrive at the wharf."

Emma patted her hair. "I must look a fright. Have I smashed my flowers?"

He examined the lovely daisies and cornflowers inserted among the curling pile of red tresses and pulled out one with crushed petals and tossed it out the window. "I must say your coiffure withstood my attack quite well."

"I would refer to it as no more than a surprise."

He tugged up her bodice to ensure all returned to its proper place. "A pleasant one, I hope."

She nuzzled into his neck. "Delicious. Delightful. Dizzying."

As the coach rolled to a halt, Emma clasped his hand between hers. "I cannot believe I shall have two adventures in my lifetime."

"I believe the bounds on such things are without limits." He took her hand as the footman opened the door. "Let the rest of our lives be an endless adventure."

Chapter Thirty

*W*oooooooah!" Emma cried as she clung to the ropes of a gamming chair. She'd been on a swing before, but this one made her stomach fly to her throat as the crew winched her aboard Ciar's ship, the *Flying Ceilidh*.

Up, up she went while the sea slapped against the hull of the boat.

"You're doing well," Ciar called from the skiff below, which had ferried them out to where the ship moored.

"Swing the boom!" Livingstone hollered.

As the timbers creaked, Emma's trajectory suddenly shifted sideways. "There you are, my lady," said Ciar's man-at-arms, right before the chair abruptly stopped swinging.

Emma didn't realize he was talking to her until he took her hand. Goodness, she was now a real lady. "My heavens, that took my breath away."

"'Tis quite a ride, even for a seasoned sailor." He helped her down. "Give us a moment to send the winch down to Dunollie, and then we'll introduce you to the crew."

She smiled, turning her ear. Though the men on the deck were quiet, she felt their presence and their eyes upon her. A wave of trepidation washed over her as she wondered if they knew—or if they would fear her.

But then Albert's toenails tapped the deck. He barked, brushing her skirts and smacking her thigh with his tail.

She couldn't resist giving his head a pat. "Och, laddie, we're off on a new adventure."

The winch creaked and groaned much more loudly than it had with her. She turned, praying the ropes wouldn't snap and send her husband plummeting to the sea. But with a whoosh of air, Ciar hopped to the deck with a resounding bang.

"How did you weather the gamming chair, my love?" he asked.

"It was exhilarating, like nothing I've ever experienced before."

"'Tis quite a height."

"Then it is a good thing I cannot look down."

He chuckled and turned her shoulders, whispering into her ear. "The men have assembled to greet you."

"All bow," bellowed Livingstone. "Welcome His Lairdship's bride, Lady Dunollie!"

Emma clasped her hands and curtsied while those two words resounded in her ears. *Lady Dunollie*. Oh, how she loved them. "Thank you for your warm welcome."

Ciar grasped her elbow and walked her down the line of men, each one taking her hand and kissing it as he was introduced.

"And finally Cook—who prepares our meals both at sea and at the castle," said Ciar.

Emma gaped. "Truly? Who tends the hob when you're away from Dunollie?"

"Och, m'lady, this is a special occasion. Now that you are here, my orders are to be at your beck and call at all times."

"I will look forward to discussing menus with you."

"As will I." Cook kissed her hand. "And you'll find a meal fit for a king prepared and ready for you in His Lairdship's cabin."

"Our cabin," Ciar corrected.

"Would you like me to look after Albert until I'm needed, Your Ladyship?" asked Betty.

"Please," Ciar answered on Emma's behalf. "And you may have the evening off to enjoy the brisk Scottish air as we cruise down the eastern coast of our glorious isle."

"Thank you, m'laird."

Somehow, Emma didn't think Betty would have trouble occupying her time. Not among an entire crew of Dunollie men.

Ciar placed his hand in the small of her back. "Since dinner is served, allow me to show you aft."

"I'm famished," she whispered.

"So am I."

"Did you miss breaking your fast?"

"Aye—too nervous to eat."

"You?"

"I admit to being a wee bit anxious as well. 'Tis not every day a man marries."

He opened a door, and when she stepped inside, everything went quiet. There was no wind at her face, no rush from the sea. "'Tis so peaceful in here."

"We'll be underway soon and, God willing, the weather will be fair." Behind her, he slid his hands to her waist, pressing warm, succulent lips to her neck. "Then the *Flying Ceilidh* will rock ye like a bairn."

Emma turned, dancing a bit. "I think I'd rather be rocked by you, husband."

"Mm, I adore your vigor. Ye must ken I went to heaven when we said, 'I do.'" He took her hand and twirled her deeper into the cabin. "But first we need sustenance."

Emma breathed in the musky scent of roast lamb. "It smells delicious."

"I'm certain it will be." He helped her sit in a wooden chair with a padded seat and back—far more elegant than she would have expected. "I asked Cook to ensure you are pleased this night."

"You asked?"

"Hmm. I may have told him that his longstanding reputation hinged on this meal."

"Oh, my. 'Tis a wonder he spoke to me at all."

"He's a good man. He was one of my mother's favorites."

Emma reached out, finding a regal setting with a china plate, silverware, a serviette, and a wineglass. Beyond was a loaf of bread. "'Tis still warm."

"Cook misses nothing. But I requested no soup and no service. You see, wife, I wanted you all to myself with no interruptions." Ciar's chair scraped the floor as he sat. "Allow me."

She placed the serviette in her lap and folded her hands atop. "I want complete details of everything before us."

"As you may be aware, I'm slicing the bread." After the grating of the knife stopped, he put a piece on her side plate. "You'll find the butter on your right."

Perfect.

"And you guessed right with the lamb—'tis a succulent rack of lamb with a ring of peas and pearled onions in the middle, swimming in rosemary sauce."

Emma spread the butter and licked her lips. "Delicious."

Liquid sloshed in her glass.

"And the Burgundy is from the Dunollie private reserve."

"But from France." She sipped. "Oh, my. 'Tis like silk on my tongue."

"Only the best for you, *mo leannan*."

Together they ate their fill, topping off the meal with a wild strawberry–and-vanilla pudding. Having supervised the kitchens at Moriston Hall, Emma knew exactly how dear vanilla was.

Emma rubbed her stomach. "I am filled to the brim."

"Come here." Ciar tugged her fingers. "You're too far away from me."

"I was just thinking the same," she said, her heart skipping a wee beat as she slid across his lap.

He held a glass to her lips. "We'd best sample the port."

She sipped. "Mm."

"My thoughts exactly. But try this." He moved his lip to hers, and as she opened for him, a delightful yet powerful liquid filled her mouth.

Kissing her, he swirled his tongue around before she swallowed. "What was that?"

"A bit of whisky steeped with port. Did you like it?"

"Very much."

"But we mustn't drink too much—'tis as potent as a sleeping potion."

She took the glass from his fingertips and set it on the table, pushing it away. "I'm not yet ready to sleep."

"Nor am I."

Smoothing her hand from his chest to his brooch, she unfastened it. "Make love to me."

* * *

When Emma's sultry voice expressed the words he'd needed to hear for sennights, Ciar forced himself not to rip the wedding gown from her body and haul her to the bed. He'd dreamed of this moment for so long.

"I want this night to last forever," he whispered into her ear. "A memory to cherish throughout eternity."

"I will be with you forever." Emma stood and began pulling the pins from her hair.

Ciar circled beside her, making quick work of the task. "I also gave your lady's maid the evening off so that I could have you entirely to myself."

A delightfully sultry smile spread across her lips. "As you said, no interruptions."

When Her Ladyship's coppery tresses cascaded in waves around her, he gathered them over her shoulder and inched behind her. "Have I told you how stunning you looked today?"

"Aye."

He began untying her laces, savoring every moment. "I want to have a portrait of you painted wearing this gown so I will never forget."

"Oh." The corners of her mouth tightened. "If only..."

His stomach squeezed. He knew what she meant—she'd never be able to see it herself. "What would remind *you* most of today?"

She turned her ear to her shoulder and slid her fingers into his view. "I have the honor of wearing this exquisite ring. The stone is so smooth. It reminds me of a rose petal."

"You are such a treasure." As each lace eased, a little more of her scent ensnared him—fresh, floral, and womanly. Betty had bound the stays so tight, Ciar wondered how Emma had been able breathe without swooning all this time. When he unlaced the final constricting ribbon, she inhaled deeply. He ran his hands from her long neck out to her shoulders and urged both bodice and stays to drop, fluttering kisses along her nape.

As he stepped in, her skirts brushed the tip of his cock. Even through his kilt, he was exceedingly sensitive to touch. His eyes rolled back and he worked faster, unlacing the ties at her waist and sending the skirt to the floor. His impatience grew as he released not one but three petticoats.

When at last she wore nothing but her shift, he slid his hands down her narrow waist and pulled her hips against his. A luscious, soft bottom teased his throbbing cock as she rubbed against him. Rocking his hips forward, he bit his lip and pressed harder, until his thighs shuddered.

I haven't even made it to the bed and I'm ready to spill.

He eased away, and she turned, her eyes dark, her lips red and parted. In one motion, she unlaced the front tie of her shift and slipped it from her shoulders.

He was afraid to move; her beauty entranced him, stunned him. Good God, if his cock met the slightest friction, it would erupt. His tongue slid to the corner of his mouth as he ached to have his lips on her pert little breasts. He needed her. He needed her now.

Wearing only her hose and slippers, Emma said nothing but told him what she wanted by slowly swirling her finger around her nipple. Swallowing hard, Ciar knelt to untie her garters, putting him at eye level with her sex. His cock strained, demanding to be set free. He jerked the ribbons as fast as he could, removed her slippers and tugged down her stockings. Mouth completely dry, he brushed a finger around the triangular outline of the auburn locks that hid her treasure.

And then she opened for him, and he smelled the delicious scent of her desire. His tongue darted out and lapped her. Moaning, Emma thrust her hips forward as he swirled his tongue around her sensitive button. Gripping his hair, she rocked against him.

He slid a finger inside her slick, wet core.

"Don't stop," she growled, her voice hoarse, incredibly erotic.

Ciar took her cue. He slid his finger faster while his tongue relentlessly licked.

Emma's breathing sped until she gasped. Her body stiffened, and then her thighs convulsed. Crying out, she came undone in his mouth.

Clenching his gut against his urge to release his seed, he continued to lick until her breathing ebbed.

She tugged at his shirt. "Now you."

Chuckling, Ciar stood. "I'd hoped to last until we made it to the bed, but the journey is questionable now."

"How far is it?"

"About seven paces."

A wicked grin spread across her lips. "Oh, my."

"I can make it," he growled, scooping her into his arms and carrying her to the bed. Gently, he rested her atop the pillows.

"But you're still clothed," Emma objected.

"I'll remedy that faster than you can blink."

Ciar unfastened his belt, dropped his kilt, and tugged off his shirt. Then he climbed in beside her. "Now where were we?"

* * *

As she reclined on the bed, Emma's insides still quivered with pleasure. "Every night since you left Gylen, I've wished to lie with you again."

"And now you will forever." He pulled her into his arms and kissed her like a man starved. "I'm so very hungry for you."

She matched his fervor, trailing kisses along his throat. "A hunger no meal can assuage."

His voice rumbled with a deep chuckle as he rolled atop her. His tongue danced with hers, his hard body enticing her flesh. The thick column of his manhood jutted between her thighs, making the coil of hot desire fill her again. But this time she needed him inside her.

"I'm dangerously close to spilling my seed," he whispered.

"We have a lifetime ahead of us." She grasped his shaft and guided him toward her. "But I need all of you this time, my love."

He slowly slid inside, his breath ragged. He filled and stretched her, caressing the spot that would send her to the stars.

His tempo increased, and Emma gripped his buttocks to urge him faster.

"I. Cannot. Hold. Back!" His voice came out strained as he met her demands.

When she bucked against him, he thrust wildly. The masculine scent of cedar and spice drove her mad. His cock filled her. Every inch of her skin craved more until she froze at the pinnacle of ecstasy. In one earth-shattering burst, she exploded around him. "Ciar, oh Ciar, I love you, I love you!"

With a bellowing roar, he thrust deep and spilled within her. His body violently shook with his release as he panted into her hair.

When at last the tension ebbed from his muscles, he swept the damp locks from her forehead and kissed her. "You consume my every thought."

Emma used her fingers to see his face—his beauty, his kindness. Finding not a hint of worry or tightness at the corners of his mouth, she knew he was content. "Thank you for making my dreams come true."

Chapter Thirty-One

*S*tanding at the estuary below Dunollie Castle, Emma took in a breath of fresh Highland air. At last they had arrived at her new home. The past week of sailing had been as perfect as if she'd existed in the pages of a fairy tale.

She sighed and swayed in place while a wind blew her skirts against the back of her legs and made her bonnet strain against its ribbons. "Perhaps I should have brought my cane." Emma clutched her husband's arm. "After a sennight on the *Flying Ceilidh*, I still feel as if I'm rocking with the ship even though we're standing on dry ground."

Ciar patted her hand. "Not to worry; if you swoon, I shall sweep you into my arms."

She sniggered. "Be careful, my dearest. Being in your arms sounds rather enjoyable."

"Och, I ought to throw you over my shoulder."

"Is it a brute ye are now?"

His quiet yet deep and sensuous rumble made her insides flutter. "You bring out the beast in me." As he cleared his throat, Emma sensed his change from playful to officious. "The wagons are here to haul your things above." Ciar stood beside her, the wind making his kilt flap loudly. "It is quite a strenuous walk up a winding path to the keep from here. Would you rather I send for a pony?"

"Och, nay." Albert stepped beside her, his cold nose nuzzling her hand. "It will be good for us to stretch our legs."

"I think a pony is wise," mumbled Betty from the rear.

Emma turned her ear. "Mayhap next time, but today I want to walk at my husband's side."

As they started up the incline, leaves rustled overhead, but the trees helped to block the wind coming off the firth. "A forest?" she asked.

"Aye, they're turning gold and red."

"So soon?"

"No matter how long our summers, autumn always seems to come faster than I'd like."

Emma's breathing grew deeper. "My, it is a climb."

"We're not yet halfway. Would you care to stop for a wee bit?"

"Nay. I'd run if I could."

"Are you excited to see your new home?"

"Ever so." She was nervous as well but said nothing. No, no, she'd be mortified if anyone discovered the unease gripping her chest.

"I think you'll like it here," said Livingstone.

"I do as well." Emma turned her head toward the Dunollie man-at-arms. "But why do you say so?"

He sputtered. "Well, for starters, we're all kin, and there is no clan in Scotland who will protect you like the MacDougall."

She liked that, though her brother was most likely every bit as vigilant.

"And I love you like no other," Ciar whispered in her ear.

His warm breath tickled, making the nervousness fade a tad. Emma reached up and brushed a clump of drying leaves.

"They're coming!" called a youthful voice ahead.

"Who is that?" she asked.

"It sounds like Scottie, Cook's son."

"He didn't tell me he had a boy."

"I'm sure there are a great many things you'll learn in time."

As the incline gave way to level ground, the wind picked up, and applause roared.

"Welcome, m'lady!" said a woman.

Ciar leaned in. "The serving staff has assembled to greet you."

Emma's palms suddenly perspired inside her gloves. "Already?"

"They're eager to see the new Lady Dunollie."

Emma gulped as he led her forward. "I-I am so gloriously happy to be here."

"This is the housekeeper, Mrs. MacClarin."

"Pleased to meet you, m'lady," the woman said in the same voice that had called out the welcome.

Emma held out her hand and, after some mummering from the crowd, the housekeeper took it. "So very lovely to meet you as well. I look forward to coming to know you better."

"Mrs. MacClarin," said Ciar. "This is Betty, my wife's lady's maid. Please show her to Her Ladyship's chamber. I'm having her effects delivered there directly."

"Straightaway, m'laird," said the housekeeper.

"Excellent, and please do take Betty under your wing."

"Of course. Perhaps I ought to start by taking her on a tour of the servants' quarters?"

"Fine idea."

Ciar led Emma down the row of servants, each one offering their tidings, though something seemed off—tense, and she could have sworn she heard unpleasant whispers. Were they disappointed with her appearance? How much had Livingstone told them? Did they not know of her malady? Did they fear her?

Suddenly, she felt cold. Even though Ciar had hold of her hand, she felt alone, lost among a sea of people like she had been right after Kennan and Divana's wedding at Achnacarry.

At the end of the line, Livingstone gave Emma Albert's lead while her husband took her up the steps and inside the castle. "Are you all right?" he asked.

"I'm well, why?"

"Because you are squeezing my palm like you're trying to crack a walnut with your bare flesh."

She eased her grip. "Forgive me. I suppose I am nervous."

"'Tis natural." He pulled her farther inside. "This is the entry—a rather small vestibule—to the right is the library, to the left is a spiral staircase leading above stairs, and straight ahead is the great hall. Beyond it are the kitchens."

"How many floors?"

"Five." His lips pressed against the back of her gloved hand. "I was thinking of starting at the top of the tower and showing you our lands, but I think it would be more fitting if I asked where you would like to begin?"

Facing what suddenly struck her as an insurmountable task to learn the paces and layout of every floor, Emma bit her lip. "Lead on to the tower. I do not think I'll memorize five floors of rooms all at once."

He tugged her to the left. "No one expects you to do so."

Up and up they went with Albert walking beside her,

the endless winding stairs reminding her of the labyrinth at Achnacarry. At least she'd have Ciar to help her if she grew hungry in the middle of the night. "Will I be sleeping in my own chamber?"

He pulled her out through the door, the wind picking up the ribbons on her bonnet. "I'd rather assumed you'd sleep with me, unless you'd prefer—"

"Nay, nay." She shook her head. "I had visions of being lost and ending up in the wrong chamber."

He pulled her into his arms, plying her with a gentle kiss. "The only chamber I want you to stumble into is mine."

Oh, how his soothing voice could put her at ease. "I like that."

He pressed his hand into the small of her back and led her onward. "We are now atop the tower, the highest point for miles aside from the mountains to the west."

"Is that what you like most of all?"

"The seasons change on the foothills—the heather at the end of summer, the autumn colors, the brown and skeletal tree limbs of winter, and the verdant promise of spring. I like that as far as the eye can see, these are our lands, tilled by our kin."

"I hear cattle."

"You're correct. A herd of yearlings is grazing on the slopes yonder. Providing our winter isn't too harsh, they'll fetch a good price come next Samhain."

He continued around the turret, urging her to face the wind. "If I had to pick my favorite, I'd say this view is the best. Right now we are looking out across the Firth of Lorn, straight at the narrows of the sound of Kerrera."

"Kerrera? But we cannot see Gylen from here, can we?"

"You remember. Indeed, we can only see the isle's north

shore, but there is a view of the Isle of Mull and the Sound of Mull leading out to the North Sea."

"And we just sailed through those waters."

"Aye."

A gust of wind blew Emma's bonnet, and she threw up her hand to keep it in place. Goodness, the castle was so strange. Presently she didn't know north from south or east from west. And they'd had to walk up such an inordinately steep hill to reach the keep. "I do not smell the horses."

"That is because they are stabled down the slope."

"But I didn't notice them by the water, either."

"They're on the opposite side of the hill."

"Is Dunollie on a peak?"

"Of sorts. It sits atop a rocky outcropping, which gives us an advantage against attack."

"Attack?"

"Och, 'tis why no one has attempted to put the castle to fire and sword in over six hundred years. There are simply easier targets to raze."

"Like Gylen."

"Indeed. Mind you, it was less than seventy years ago when Cromwell laid siege to her."

Emma rubbed her outer arms. The perils of war were never far away.

"Beg your pardon, m'laird," said Livingstone from behind. "Roderick Chisholm has arrived with a message from the Earl of Mar."

Emma's stomach clenched as she moved her hand to her throat. The Jacobites were expecting Mar to raise the standard in favor of Prince James.

Please, no. Not now!

"His timing is impeccable," Ciar grumbled.

"I told him the same."

"Take him to my solar, and I'll meet you there forthwith."

"Straightaway."

As Livingstone's fading footsteps echoed from the stairwell, Ciar took Emma's hand between his palms. "I'll show you to your chamber."

"But the tour has only begun."

"Forgive me. I promise we'll resume just as soon as I've met with Chisholm."

Emma pulled on Albert's lead. "Very well."

She counted two flights of stairs before they exited into the corridor. "Are the servants' quarters on the top floor?"

"Some, though many stay in cottages down by the stables."

"Is there not enough room for them?"

Ciar cleared his throat. "Well, the nursery is on the fifth floor."

Nursery? Emma's throat constricted. Perhaps one day soon their children might occupy those rooms. *God save they have the gift of sight.*

Stopping, Ciar opened a door. "Here we are."

Emma cued Albert to walk on, but the dog only went a few paces and sat. She studied him. "I would have thought you'd want to explore every corner."

Ciar stepped behind her. "Your trunks have arrived, but Betty's not yet here."

"She's most likely with Mrs. MacClarin."

"Indeed. I'm sure she'll be here directly." Ciar took Emma's hand and led her deeper inside, turning left, right, moving forward, then seeming to walk in a circle. "In the interim, why not make yourself comfortable on the settee."

She brushed her fingers over the velvet upholstery. "Must you go?"

His lips whispered over her cheek. "The sooner I meet with Chisholm, the faster I will return."

Emma gave a nod while Ciar slipped out the door. As it closed, a shiver coursed through her.

Should she start counting steps and learning the layout of the chamber? But how could she with her trunks strewn about?

"What are we to do, Albert?"

The dog yowled and lay at her feet.

Dropping the lead, Emma tried to retrace her steps, but when she thought she'd reached the door, there was nothing. Where was the bed? Where was the window? Perhaps she ought to wait.

"Albert?"

The dog shook.

Starting toward the sound, something caught her foot. "Ack!" she screeched, flinging out her arms, grasping for anything to stop her fall. But down she went, tumbling facefirst to the floorboards.

Flat on her belly, Emma fumbled, completely disoriented. Her nose throbbed as she rolled to her side and sat. "Ow," she mumbled, drawing her hands to her nose. Hot, sticky blood oozed through her fingers.

"Albert!" she cried.

The dog's toenails tapped the floorboards as he hastened to her.

Emma groped for her kerchief. If only she'd had her cane or at least hadn't dropped his lead. She held the cloth to her nose and tipped back her head. "How could I have been so daft?"

And now her face must look a fright, her gown ruined.

A sob pealed from her throat. She'd been so excited to arrive at Dunollie Castle, and there she sat alone on the floor in a foreign chamber, bleeding profusely.

For the first time since her wedding day she missed

Moriston Hall. She didn't belong here. Aye, she'd heard the whispers from the servants. They had been shocked to see a blind woman. She'd felt their eyes upon her in the courtyard, judging her as if she were not worthy of Ciar's love.

Albert circled and lay down beside her, but Emma pushed him away and buried her face in her kerchief. "What am I doing here?"

* * *

In his solar, Ciar shook hands with Roderick Chisholm—son of the Chisholm, a stalwart Highland chief. "I'm told you have news from Mar?"

The young man was solidly built, of good Highland stock like his da. "I do. He's in London."

"Still?" Ciar had hoped the earl would be on his way to France.

"He's under Argyll's watchful eye. The duke and his allies have mobilized Britain's army and navy alike to ensure George makes the crossing from Hanover without incident. Their orders are to use whatever force is necessary to stop any insurrection."

"But what of our supporters in parliament?" Ciar asked. "Is there a chance of rescinding Anne's mindless succession legislation? Any chance of peace?"

"The prospect of war nears with each passing day. Mar broached the subject in the House of Lords and was met with the threat of immediate arrest for treason."

"Good God. Has the world gone completely mad?"

"It appears the entire kingdom has."

Ciar dropped into his chair at the head of the table. "It all began with Cromwell's wars. Ye ken the bastard murdered my grandfather and MacDougall clansmen at Gylen Castle—and for naught."

Roderick slid into the chair beside him. "Aye, and we've been left to pick up the pieces."

"What else does Mar say? Keep our armies at home and our mouths shut whilst the new king strangles us with taxes?"

"He cautions us to remain vigilant. See what George has to offer. Find out how he stands with Scotland."

"That sounds like Bobbin' John—never one to take up the sword when the sword needs to be wielded."

"Mayhap caution is best for the moment. The Jacobites can raise an army, but not one powerful enough to face Argyll when they've already organized their conscripts," said Chisholm. "Mar believes it is best to bide our time and, if need be, attack when the opportunity presents itself."

Ciar slammed his fist on the table. "But the Hanoverian usurper has not yet been crowned. If we act now we can instill fear in his heart."

"I agree with you, but there is one more *critical* item to be considered."

"And what is that?" Ciar asked.

"Thus far, we've received no word from the prince."

Ciar raked a hand through his hair. "What an unmitigated disaster. Someone must sail across the channel and confront him, bless it."

"We were hoping *you* would."

"Me?" *Good God, why do they always come crawling to me begging for favors?* "I've been home for all of two hours at the most. Moreover, my new bride is waiting in her chamber. I cannot possibly leave for the continent."

"But you are allies with more clans than anyone in the Highlands."

"So that is my due for being good-natured."

"We need you."

"My wife needs me—and ye ken she's no ordinary woman."

"True."

Ready to spit, Ciar gripped the chair's velvet armrests. "My vote is for you to go."

"I beg your pardon?" The man sat back. "But I am not yet a laird, sir."

"Why not sail across with your father?" Ciar asked, his mind drumming up a plan. "Chisholm is a respected name throughout the Highlands, just as is Dunollie. You must take a letter with you—one pledging our fealty and our arms and signed by the chieftains. James must know we will stand behind the true heir.

Ciar looked his ally in the eye. "Will you do it?"

"Aye."

Chisholm rapped his knuckles on the board. "I'm certain a pledge of support will encourage him to set sail for Scotland once again."

For the next two hours, Ciar made a list of the Highland clans and their numbers, estimating how many men each clan might bring to arms. Roderick left with the folded piece of parchment tucked inside his doublet, but the heavy weight of duty hung from Ciar's shoulders like an anvil. Was he the best man to visit James? Perhaps he was. Nonetheless, he could not commit to sailing across the channel mere hours after he'd brought Emma to the castle.

Damnation, Ciar might be a loyal vassal of the true succession, but clan and kin must always come before king and country. He had a new duty now.

Chapter Thirty-Two

*C*iar's heart flew to his throat when found Emma collapsed on the floor, lying in a pool of blood. "God, no!" he cried, dropping to his knees and gathering her into his arms while Albert stood and hovered. "What happened?"

She jolted, sobbing as she wiped a bloody kerchief across her brow. "No!" she bawled, struggling to catch her breath. "T-this cannot possibly work. They haaaate m-m-meeeee!"

"Easy, lass. Calm yourself." He rocked her as his blood turned icy. How had she transformed from happy bride to nearly hysterical in a few hours? "Who did this? I swear I'll slice my dirk across their cowardly throats!"

"No." She pounded her fists on his chest as she sniffed, tears streaming from her eyes. "You...you...do not under-staaaaaand."

Ciar sat cradling her for a moment while a tic twitched in his jaw. The last thing he wanted was for Emma's first experiences at Dunollie to be miserable. What the bloody hell had happened, and why had no one come? The sight of her unhappy, bleeding, and crying made a boiling rage pulse through his blood. He must act swiftly to ferret out the scoundrel who'd hurt her. But first he needed to see to her care.

He pressed his lips against her forehead. "Shhh, *mo leannan*." Tightening his arms, he rose and carried her to the bed.

After he fluffed the pillows and ensured her comfort, he hastened to the bowl, but there was no water in the ewer. "Where the blazes is Betty?"

"She's…" Emma patted her chest, trying to control her staccato breaths. "…with…the houskeeeeeeper." Albert jumped onto the bed, and she immediately wrapped her arms around him. Thank God the dog had been there to comfort her.

Ciar could have kicked himself. He'd suggested Mrs. MacClarin take the lady's maid under her wing because it seemed like a good time for it. Of course, he had no idea he'd be called away only moments after arriving.

Dashing to the door, he jerked it open. "Bring water at once!" His bellow made the timbers rattle. "Livingstone! Come up here with a pair of bloody useless footmen!"

When movement hastened on the floors below, he hurried back to Emma's side. Carefully, he removed her bonnet and inspected her forehead. "Can you tell me what happened?"

As Emma's tears began to ebb, she drew in a few deep breaths. "I wanted to see the layout of the chamber."

"Without your cane?"

"I had Albert, but I dropped the lead in frustration and tried to retrace my steps."

Ciar brushed away a lock of her hair. "And you fell?"

"Aye, flat on my face. Ended up with a bloody nose and feeling hopeless . . . and useless . . . and lost!"

He clenched his fist. Bless it, he never should have left her alone with so many obstacles carelessly tossed into the chamber. "But what was it you said about *them* hating you? Who are *they*?"

Emma shook her head and curled forward. "I-I heard the servants' whispers when we arrived. They fear me, just like Robert said everyone outside of our kin would do. I ken they think I'm a demon."

Sitting, he surrounded her with his arms, rubbing a hand up and down her spine. "Och, nay, lass. They haven't had a chance to come to know you is all. I tell ye true here and now, every servant in this castle will come to adore you as I do." He braced his hands on her shoulders and whispered in her ear. "You are the most astounding, selfless, and loveable woman I have ever met."

Behind him, the hinges of the door screeched, and Livingstone clambered inside. "Forgive me. I was down at the stables." As his gaze shifted to Emma, his eyes popped wide. "God's bones, what happened?"

"'Tis my fault. I left Her Ladyship without helping her grow accustomed to her new bedchamber." Ciar gestured to the trunks. "Worse, some idiots saw fit to carelessly strew her things about as if someone else would tidy the mess."

"I'll have that fixed straightaway," said Livingstone, ushering in a pair of footmen. "Shall we move these to the garderobe?"

"Please," Ciar replied, taking Emma's hand. "Might I suggest they take your harps to the lady's solar, or would you prefer them here?"

A flustered, hapless expression crossed her face. "I have no idea. They were in the music room at Moriston Hall."

"Perhaps we can turn your solar into a music room. It is yours for your own particular use."

"Very well. The solar should be fine at least for the time being."

"Livingstone, where is the ewer of water?"

"Here," said Betty from the corridor.

"'Tis about time you appeared," Ciar groused, hopping to his feet while the footmen picked up the first trunk. "Pour it into the bowl."

"Oh, my heavens, my lady!"

"I fell," said Emma, tapping her fingers over her face. "I suffered a bloody nose is all. Goodness, I must look a fright."

The maid quickly poured the water and doused a cloth. "I am so sorry I wasn't here. I thought His Lairdship—"

Ciar took the cloth from Betty's hand. "I'll tend my wife. You set to washing the floor and finding Her Ladyship a clean gown as well as her cane."

"Very well. Put that down, please," she said, stopping the footmen and then opening the trunk. "Here is her walking stick. I put it on top because I thought she might need it straightaway."

"Clearly she did." Ciar snatched the piece of hickory and set it across the foot of the bed.

Betty continued on with the footmen while he tapped Emma's arm. "I'm going to clean your face. Are you ready?"

Her half-cast eyes opened for the slightest of moments. "Is it awful?"

He cleaned one side. "There might be a bit of bruising, but once we cleanse the blood away, you'll be as bonny as ever."

She clapped her hands to her cheeks. "Bruising?"

"'Tisn't bad, lass, and bruises fade." He gently ran the

cloth under her nose. "You gave me a fright, though. When I first saw you I thought you'd been bludgeoned."

"I'm ever so clumsy." She forlornly shook her head. "Leave it to me to be bludgeoned by the floor."

"Nay, you are as graceful as a swan." Ciar swiped away the blood across her brow. "Mark me, I will have a word with the serving staff before this day ends. There is no excuse for the careless way your crates and portmanteaus were strewn about."

Emma gripped his wrist. "I ken they were afraid to touch my things for the fear of it."

"Balderdash." Ciar finished his work and rocked back. She'd most likely have two black eyes, but he'd ensure not a soul uttered a damned word about it. "They're MacDougalls, and if anyone speaks of superstition, I will personally escort them out the door."

Sighing, Emma did not appear convinced. "Mayhap we'll end up with no servants whatsoever."

"Nonsense." He softly chuckled to put her at ease. "You'll have Betty. I'll have Livingstone...and Cook thinks the world of you already."

Thank heavens Emma smiled, even if it wasn't quite as radiant as usual. "What else do we need?"

"Only our happiness." Breathing a sigh of relief, he tossed the cloth on the bedside table and moved his hand to her knee. "Are your legs still in working order?"

She flexed her feet. "Aye."

He swung her knees over the side of the mattress and took her hands. "Well then, there's an entire keep with which you must acquaint yourself."

She groaned. "'Tis all so overwhelming."

"Now that the footmen have moved your trunks where they belong, we shall start with this chamber, and I'm going to count every damned pace with you. I swear, my love, within a month you will be as familiar with Dunollie as you are with Moriston Hall."

"A month?" She cringed as he put the cane in her hand and pulled Albert off the bed. "I cannot possibly."

"Hmm. I for one would never bet against you. Look how you took to Achnacarry and then to Gylen. You needn't have a fear."

* * *

Emma sat in her solar, practicing her Celtic harp with Albert at her feet. She'd only been at Dunollie a day and had already memorized several chambers in the keep, including her very own solar. Ciar had gone to speak to the servants, which made her nervous, though focusing on the music helped to ease her discomfort.

She prayed he was right, and the people here would grow fond of her—or at least not fear her. As Ciar had patiently helped her count paces, she realized she could accomplish and endure anything with him at her side. She was Lady Dunollie now. She had broken into a fortress and freed an innocent man. She had hidden in the cellars of a ruined castle and learned exactly what it was to love. She had endured the stocks and faced the ire of her brother. And through it all her feelings for Ciar had never faltered.

With her husband beside her, she must hold her chin high—have the courage to show the clansmen and women that she was worthy of her station.

Emma stopped playing as Albert growled and leaned against her.

"Beg your pardon, m'lady," said a young man from the doorway. "I'm Bram, and this is Tavish."

She uprighted her harp. "Good morning, gentlemen. How may I help you?"

After a moment's hesitation, she heard a smack—not a hard one, but these two lads were obviously nervous. "Go on," said another, seemingly Tavish.

"We came to apologize for leaving your things askew," said Bram.

"Uh..." Tavish seemed to be a bit tongue-tied. "We didn't intend for you to fall."

"Aye, and cause those awful bruises—"

"Enough," Ciar boomed from behind the lads as if he might be ready to give them each a hiding.

Emma smiled. Had he been in the corridor since the boys stepped inside? And what was it about the bruises? Her husband had insisted the marks were scarcely noticeable, but by the tenderness of her nose and beneath her eyes, they were probably worse than he let on. "I thank you for your apology."

"Your music is bonny," said Bram.

"It surely is," Tavish agreed.

"Would you like to hear more of it?" asked Ciar in a much more civil tone.

The two lads agreed with resounding ayes, and Emma reached for the harp, readying her hands.

"Well then. I do believe 'tis time to celebrate our nuptials with Clan MacDougall." Ciar stepped so near, his spiciness swirled about her. "Let us feast on the morrow, and Her Ladyship will play for you."

"Oh, no." Emma shoved the harp back. "I couldn't possibly."

He placed his hand on her shoulder. "Hmm, just like your reluctance to perform at Achnacarry?"

Emma's chest tightened. "Please, not the morrow. I need time to settle in—a sennight, a fortnight?"

"Very well, if that is what you wish." He removed his hand. "Off to the wood heap with you lads."

"I'm sorry." After the door closed, she gripped his wrist. "I cannot perform with these awful bruises. I'd prefer to wait for them to fade."

He lightly pinched her chin and moved her head left then right. "Your bruises are nothing Betty cannot hide with a wee bit of powder. And mark me, the sooner you demonstrate your indisputable qualifications to be the lady of this house, the sooner you'll earn your due respect."

Emma plucked a high E. "I have a meeting this afternoon with Cook to review the menu. At that time I will discuss the feast. Mark me, we will plan a meal like no other."

"In a week," he said as if it were decided. "And I shall ensure the excitement builds among the clan. By the time the day comes, people will be champing at the bit to file into the hall."

She kissed his hand. Oh, how she loved this man. "See? With a wee bit of planning it will be marvelous."

Giving her a squeeze, he chuckled. "Ye ken you can charm the grumpiest troll in Christendom with your music. I vow, by the end of the evening every last one of them will fall in love with you."

* * *

It took no time at all for a sennight to pass, thank God. And though his wife had her reservations about playing, Ciar felt it was best to astound the clan with a demonstration of Emma's brilliance. He would have preferred it sooner, but he understood, and the bruising on her face had faded markedly. In truth, when they'd first arrived, he'd also heard the whispers and seen the stunned looks from the servants, and the most fitting time to show them the extent of his wife's charm was now.

The crowd grew quiet as he took his place on the dais. "What say you?" he asked. "Did Cook not prepare the most delicious feast you have ever enjoyed?"

"Aye!" they responded with raucous applause.

"Indeed, our bellies are full, which, in part, is due to Lady Dunollie's particular attention to this evening's menu."

Again came applause, though somewhat more reserved.

Ciar clasped his hands behind his back. "Let me share with you a wee morsel about Her Ladyship. I have known Emma since I was a lad. And I think I fell in love with her the first time we met. She was about seven years of age at the time, and full of happiness and laughter. In fact, I challenge each of you not to smile when you find yourself in her presence."

He paced a bit. "Born early, she was not given the gift of sight which most of us take for granted. But she sees so much more of the world than any of us can imagine." Ciar thrust his hand toward his wife, who waited along the east wall with Betty. "She taught me more about honeysuckle and flowers than I ever learned from my tutors. In a mere week, her keen mind has already conjured a detailed diagram of every chamber and every piece of furniture in this keep. And if it weren't for her courage, I might have swung from Fort William's gallows as an innocent man."

As gasps and murmurs resounded, Ciar held up his hands. "Without further ado, please join me in welcoming Lady Dunollie, my wife. And if you are not thoroughly enchanted by her music, then I say there is no hope for you."

He took his seat while Emma confidently climbed the stairs and situated herself with her Celtic harp. She'd chosen a series of Highland folk songs familiar to everyone. Ciar closed his eyes and thoroughly enjoyed the first two pieces, but on the third, he glanced over his shoulder.

No one moved. All eyes focused on her. Each face had a smile or an expression of utter awe. His heart soared. By God's grace, she would be happy here. And by the applause at the end of the performance, she had earned the admiration of young and old alike.

Ciar climbed the dais, pulled Emma into his arms, and kissed her. "You were astonishing, as always."

She patted her chest. "I hope they liked it," she said as the applause continued.

"They're standing for you. If that's not a fine display of appreciation, I do not know what is."

Cook met them on the dais with a plate in his hand. "As a surprise for Her Ladyship and to show our appreciation, I have made a trifle smothered with elderberry syrup. 'Tis my understanding elderberries are your favorite, m'laird."

Grinning, Emma drew her fingers over her lips. "I told him we are quite fond of elderberry jam."

Ciar threw his head back and laughed. "Indeed, I believe it is my favorite and will be forevermore."

After the dessert was served with glasses of port wine, Ciar took his wife to his chamber, where they had been sharing his enormous four-poster bed, and Albert welcomed them with excited wags of his tail.

Ciar gave the dog a scratch. "Did ye ken your lady is a musical genius?"

Emma scoffed. "I wouldn't say that."

Taking both of her hands, he pulled her around in a circle. "I believe you are. You captured my heart with your playing for certain."

"Oh, 'twas my harp that won your heart?"

"Nay, lass." He wrapped his arms around her and gazed

upon the bonniest face he'd ever seen. "Ye ken my heart was lost the first time I set eyes on you. It just took my stubborn head near fifteen years to realize it, is all."

Dipping his chin, he captured her bow-shaped lips, claiming them thoroughly and possessively.

As he nuzzled her neck, Emma swayed in his arms. "I must also admit I've loved you since the first day you visited Moriston Hall."

"Truly?"

"Aye, but unlike you, I realized it straightaway. Since that day no other has made my heart flutter the way it does whenever you are near."

Epilogue

Nine months later

"How can you be so bloody idle at a time like this?" Ciar paced in front of the hearth in his bedchamber while Livingstone had the gall to calmly sit at the table and nurse a dram of whisky.

The man-at-arms poured a second glass. "Come join me. Only the Lord kens how much longer this will last."

Another shriek of complete and utter agony came from Emma's adjoining chamber. Every time she cried out, Ciar wanted to kick in the door and grovel at her bedside while begging God to assail him with her pain.

At his wit's end, he marched across the floor and threw back a gulp of spirit. The amber liquid burned his gullet on the way down, though the rush spreading from his empty stomach did nothing to assuage his worry.

His eyes watered. "What if she doesn't survive?"

Livingstone looked to the ceiling's plaster relief. "If I ken anything about your wife, she's as strong as they come. She will weather childbirth as she has everything else."

"Push, m'lady!" shouted Betty.

Ciar hastened to the door and grabbed the latch.

"You'd best not go in there until you're summoned." Livingstone cleaned his thumbnail with a dagger. "There's nothing you can do."

"Blast!" Ciar cursed, dropping his hand.

"'Tis nearly over," cooed the midwife. "You'll be holding your bairn in your arms in no time."

"Argh!" Emma cried. "It. . . . eeeee. Hurts!"

Unable to withstand his wife's screaming for a moment longer, he pulled open the door.

"No!" Emma cried, hugging her knees.

"Out!" shouted Betty, thrusting her finger at the door.

"We'll fetch you soon," said the midwife. How she could remain calm was beyond him.

Grumbling, Ciar marched back to the table and threw back the rest of his dram to the sound of Betty shouting, "Push, push, push!" like a sergeant at arms belting orders.

Emma's screeches grated akin to iron spikes running down Ciar's back. "When will this torture be over?"

As soon as the words escaped his lips, everything grew eerily silent.

Ciar's breath stopped.

His heart stopped as well.

Ice shot through his blood . . .

Then came a smack and a shrill cry. A glorious, magical, blessed cry. He stood stunned until the door opened and the midwife appeared holding a bundle of swaddling. "You have a son, m'laird."

Tingles spread from the top of his head all the way down to his toes. "'Tis a lad?"

"Aye."

Hardly stopping to look at the bairn, Ciar raced into the lady's chamber, straight to Emma's side. Grasping her hands, he fell to his knees. "Please forgive me. Please, please, please. I love you and can never, ever put you through this again."

Emma smoothed her hand over his head. "There is nothing to forgive, my love."

"He can see, m'lady," said Betty, slowly moving a red ribbon in front of the babe's face. "He's tracking."

Ciar slowly pushed himself to his feet. "Truly?"

With a reassuring smile, the midwife set the bairn in his arms. "The bairn's eyes are not yet developed, but the maid is right. I'm certain he is not blind."

He froze where he stood while the warm bundle wriggled in his arms. The wee lad was so tiny; what if Ciar squeezed too tight or, God forbid, dropped the precious child? His child. His firstborn.

With his next blink, the babe's face turned bright red, followed by a hellacious wail. Every muscle in Ciar's body tensed as he held the infant at arm's length, thrusting it toward the midwife. "W-what's wrong with him?"

Chuckling, the woman urged him to draw the babe back into his chest. "Relax, m'laird. All he needs is a bit of affection."

He dumbly stared at the wailing lad. "Affection?"

"Aye, give him a wee bounce and use a soothing voice."

Ciar took in a deep breath and willed the tension away. "Is this how you greet your father, with a mighty MacDougall wail?" he asked as softly as a man of his size could, moving toward the bed. With his movement the crying stopped. "That's quite a bit better, son. You wouldn't want to appear unhappy the first time you meet your mother, now would ye?"

As Ciar leaned toward his wife, cradling his newborn son, Emma carefully swept her fingers across the lad's face. The radiance of her smile lit up the entire chamber. "I see you, little man. And you are perfect."

Author's Note

Hello and thank you for joining me for Ciar (pronounced *Key-ar*) and Emma's story! I had originally planned something different for the MacDougall laird, but after Emma's supporting role in *The Highland Renegade*, so many readers wrote in and asked for her happily ever after, I absolutely had to write it.

I initially developed Emma's character simply to add a new dynamic to *Renegade* and hadn't planned for her to have her own story. But some things must come about by popular vote! Let me tell you, it was very difficult to write a blind heroine, and I copiously studied Helen Keller's autobiography to help me work through it.

Ciar was born John (Ian Ciar) MacDougall, 22nd Chief of Dunollie. In truth, he married Mary, daughter of William MacDonald of Sleat. He did, however, sail fourteen ships to the Isle of Skye to bring her to Dunollie. Ciar was renowned for his bravery and swordsmanship, and his man-at-arms, Livingstone, remained a staunch ally throughout Dunollie's life.

Also of note, Gylen Castle on the Isle of Kerrera, built by Ciar's ancestors in 1582, was razed by Cromwell forces in 1647 in the Wars of the Three Kingdoms. A detachment of Covenanters, drawn from Colonel James Montgomery's Regiment of Foot, besieged the castle, eventually forcing the clansmen inside to surrender. The castle was then sacked and burned while Cromwell's men massacred the MacDougalls save John, a child who happened to be the heir and the man who became Ciar's grandfather. Unfortunately, Gylen does not have a labyrinth of cellars rebuilt as a hiding place, which would have been wise. After Queen Anne's death, fifty-three Catholics were passed over in the succession to bring a protestant king to the throne, causing outrage among the Jacobites and thus the ensuing risings of 1715 and 1745. After Anne's death, Ciar supported James Francis Edward Stuart and the fruitless attempts of the "Old Pretender" to claim the throne. Dunollie ended up spending twelve years in exile in Ireland before he was pardoned in 1727, at which time he returned to his ancestral home.

About the Author

Award-winning and Amazon All-Star author Amy Jarecki likes to grab life, latch on, and reach for the stars. She's married to a mountain-biking pharmacist and has put four kids through college. She studies karate, ballet, and yoga, and often you'll find her hiking Utah's Santa Clara Hills. Re-inventing herself a number of times, Amy sang and danced with the Follies, and was a ballet dancer, a plant manager, and an accountant for Arnott's Biscuits in Australia. After earning her MBA from Heroit-Watt University in Scotland, she dove into the world of Scottish historical romance and hasn't returned. Become a part of her world and learn more about Amy's books at amyjarecki.com.

Looking for more historical romances?
Fall in love with these sexy rogues
and darling ladies from Forever!

A DUKE BY ANY OTHER NAME
by Grace Burrowes

Lady Althea Wentworth has little patience for dukes, reclusive or otherwise, but she needs the Duke of Rothhaven's backing to gain entrance into Society. She's asked him nicely, she's called on him politely, all to no avail—until her prize hogs *just happen* to plunder his orchard. He longs for privacy. She's vowed to never endure another ball as a wallflower. Yet as the two grow closer, it soon becomes clear they might both be pretending to be something they're not.

THE TRUTH ABOUT DUKES
by Grace Burrowes

Lady Constance Wentworth never has a daring thought (that she admits aloud) and never comes close to courting scandal...as far as anybody knows. Robert Rothmere is a scandal poised to explode. Unless he wants to end up locked away in a madhouse (again) by his enemies, he needs to marry a perfectly proper, deadly dull duchess, immediately—but little does he know that the delightful lady he has in mind is hiding scandalous secrets of her own.

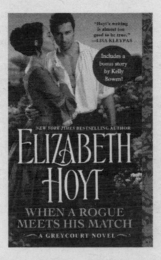

WHEN A ROGUE MEETS HIS MATCH
by Elizabeth Hoyt

After clawing his way up from the gutters as the Duke of Windemere's fixer, ambitious, sly Gideon Hawthorne is ready to work for himself—until Windemere tempts Gideon with an irresistible offer. Witty, vivacious Messalina Greycourt is appalled when her uncle demands she marry. But Gideon proposes his own devil's bargain: protection and freedom in exchange for a *true* marriage. Only as Messalina plots to escape their deal, her fierce, loyal husband unexpectedly arouses her affections. But Gideon's last task for Windemere may be more than Messalina can forgive...Includes a bonus story by Kelly Bowen!

"Irresistible."
—*Publishers Weekly*, Starred Review, on *The Viscount's Promise*

A GOOD DUKE IS HARD TO FIND
by Christina Britton

Next in line for a dukedom he doesn't want to inherit, Peter Ashford is on the Isle of Synne only to exact revenge on the man responsible for his mother's death. But when he meets the beautiful and kind Miss Lenora Hartley, he can't help but be drawn to her. Can Peter put aside his plans for vengeance for the woman who has come to mean everything to him?

ANY ROGUE WILL DO
by Bethany Bennett

For exactly one season, Lady Charlotte Wentworth played the biddable female the *ton* expected—and all it got her was society's mockery and derision. Now she's determined to take charge of her own future. So when an unwanted suitor tries to manipulate her into an engagement, she has a plan. He can't claim to be her fiancé if she's engaged to someone else. Even if it means asking for help from the last man she would ever marry.

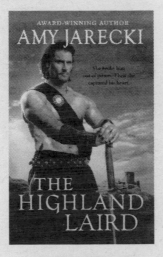

THE HIGHLAND LAIRD
by Amy Jarecki

Laird Ciar MacDougall is on a vital mission for Scotland when he witnesses a murder—and then is blamed for the death and thrown into a Redcoat prison to rot. He never thought he'd be broken out by a blind slip of a lass and her faithful hound. He soon learns that Emma Grant is just as fierce and loyal as any clansman. But now they're outlaws on the run. And as their enemies circle ever closer, he will have to choose between saving his country or the woman who's captured his heart.